Brushstrokes FROM THE HEART

Eric Misak

Cover design by Jennifer Stimson
Interior formatting by Jennifer Stimson
Published independently by Eric Misak

First Edition: October 2025

For more information, visit: ericmisakbooks.com.

ISBN:979-8-9997944-2-0 (hardcover)
ISBN:979-8-9997944-1-3 (pbk)
ISBN:979-8-9997944-0-6 (ebook)

CHAPTER 1

Encounter At The Shore

The sun was a vibrant orb hanging low in the sky, its golden rays spilling generously over the sandy beach, painting the world in shades of warmth and light. Waves danced rhythmically against the shore, creating a symphony of whispers and laughter, an endless serenade for those who chose to linger by the ocean. Among them was Christian, sprawled on a soft blanket, the scent of saltwater and coconut oil enveloping him like a comforting embrace. He was in his element, his canvas propped up on a wooden easel, a kaleidoscope of colors swirling in his mind as he prepared to bring yet another masterpiece to life.

Christian was not just any artist; he was a rising star in the art world, known for his spontaneous brush strokes that captured the essence of adventure and emotion. With tousled dark hair framing his chiseled features and a physique honed by years of surfing and outdoor exploration, he radiated effortless charm. Today, wearing a simple white tank top and board shorts, he looked every bit the part of a carefree beachgoer. Still, there was a fire behind his blue-green eyes, a restless energy burning, a flicker of something untamed that flared to life whenever inspiration took hold.

As he dipped his brush into a palette of vibrant colors, he could almost taste the salty air and feel the gentle breeze teasing his skin. He was working on a piece inspired by the ocean itself, blending turquoise and deep navy to reflect the seas. Each stroke was a dance, an expression of his unyielding passion for life and art. He loved the beach; it was a boundless horizon, a reminder that anything was possible, that the world stretched wide and waiting beyond the shore.

Just then, his concentration was broken by a distant sound, a melodic laugh that seemed to cut through the hum of the waves. Curiosity piqued, Christian looked up from his canvas, scanning the shoreline. That's when he saw her, a woman walking along the water's edge, her silhouette backlit by the sun. She was beautiful, her long hair cascading in gentle waves down her back, catching the light like spun gold. Her carefree spirit radiated as she playfully splashed her feet in the surf, leaving delicate footprints in the wet sand.

Kara, the woman in the distance, was taking a rare moment away from her responsibilities as the manager of a bustling doctor's office. Though she loved her job and thrived on the organization and structure it provided, there were times when the confines of her professional life felt suffocating. On this particular day, she had decided to escape to the beach, a sanctuary where the world slowed down, where she could breathe and simply be.

With each step, she felt the soft sand give way beneath her feet, the cool water kissing her ankles. Kara was a nurturing soul, someone who found joy in the little things, a bright shell, a playful breeze, and the sound of laughter. She loved snorkeling, often spending weekends exploring the colorful underwater world, but today, she just wanted to bask in the sun and let her thoughts drift like the clouds above.

As she strolled along the shore, Kara's gaze was drawn to a man immersed in his art. There was something enchanting about him. He was focused yet relaxed, his hands moving with confident grace as he coaxed life from the canvas. Intrigued, she decided to approach him, her heart fluttering with a mix of excitement and nervousness.

Kara called out, her voice bright and playful, cutting through the sound of the waves. "Hey there! What are you working on?"

Christian looked up, momentarily startled, but then his lips broke into a contagious smile. "Just trying to capture the essence of summer," he replied, his tone casual and lighthearted. "What about you? Enjoying a break from the daily grind?"

"Absolutely." Kara laughed, stepping closer. "I'm Kara, by the way. I manage a doctor's office, but I needed a little escape. This place is like a breath of fresh air."

"Nice to meet you, Kara. I'm Christian," he said, rising to his feet and offering a hand. The moment their palms touched, a spark of connection ignited, sending a rush of warmth through them both.

"So, what's your inspiration?" Kara asked, tilting her head slightly as she admired the colors swirling on the canvas. "It looks absolutely vibrant!"

"Thanks! I'm trying to capture the feeling of freedom that comes with being by the ocean," Christian explained, his eyes lighting up as he spoke. "There's something about the waves, the way they ebb and flow... It's like life, you know?"

Kara nodded, captivated by his passion. "I completely agree. The beach has a way of reminding us to let go and just be. It's where I come to recharge. I love snorkeling too—there's so much beauty beneath the surface."

"Really? That's awesome! You should join me sometime. I've been meaning to explore some new spots," he suggested, a playful glint in his eyes. "We could make a day of it—art and adventure!"

Kara felt her heart race at the thought. "That sounds like a lot of fun! I'd love that. But you'll have to promise not to let me drown," she teased, her tone light.

"Deal! I'll make sure you're well-equipped." Christian chuckled, his laughter blending seamlessly with the sounds of the beach. There was an undeniable chemistry between them, a connection that felt as natural as the ocean breeze.

As they talked, Kara found herself drawn to Christian's adventurous spirit. He spoke with such enthusiasm that his words painted vivid pictures of his travels and artistic endeavors. She shared her own stories, recounting her experiences at the doctor's office and her love for the beach, each anecdote punctuated by laughter and playful banter.

The sun began its slow descent, casting a warm glow over the horizon. Christian returned to his canvas, but this time, Kara sat cross-legged beside him, watching as he worked. As he painted, he would occasionally glance at her, captivated by the way her eyes sparkled with curiosity and joy.

"Do you want to try?" he asked suddenly, handing her a brush. "I could use an extra set of hands."

Kara hesitated, her brow furrowing slightly. "I'm not exactly an artist, you know."

"Neither am I, half the time," he replied with a grin. "Just have fun with it! No pressure."

With a playful roll of her eyes, Kara took the brush and dipped it into the paint. At first, her strokes were hesitant, but with Christian's encouragement, she began to lose herself in the process. They laughed and joked, their playful energy echoing against the backdrop of crashing waves, and for Kara, the world outside drifted away, leaving just the two of them in their little bubble of creativity and connection.

"See? You're a natural!" Christian exclaimed, beaming as he watched her add splashes of color to the canvas.

"I think you're just being nice," she replied, feigning modesty, but her cheeks flushed with pride.

As the sun dipped below the horizon, casting a golden hue across the water, Kara felt a warmth spreading through her, a sense of belonging that she hadn't felt in a long time. With Christian by her side, the beach transformed from a simple escape into a canvas of possibilities, each moment painted with laughter and the thrill of their newfound connection.

The light began to fade, but the spark between them only seemed to grow brighter as they shared stories, dreams, and laughter. In that moment, amidst the colors and the sounds of the ocean, something beautiful was beginning to unfold—a story that was just starting to be written, one brush stroke at a time.

CHAPTER 2

Whispers of Tomorrow

The last rays of sunlight hung like molten gold over the horizon, casting a warm glow on Christian and Kara as they packed up their things. The canvas, now a riot of colors, reflected the vibrant energy of their newfound connection. Kara felt a pang of reluctance in her heart as she rolled up the blanket, each movement a reminder that their magical evening was drawing to a close. The laughter, the playful exchanges, the spark that ignited between them—it was all too beautiful to let go.

"Do you think the beach will always feel this magical?" Kara asked, her voice tinged with a hint of nostalgia as she took one last look at the ocean before turning away.

"Absolutely," Christian replied, his tone light and confident. "The ocean has a way of holding onto moments like this. Just think of it as a canvas that's always changing, just like us."

With a playful smile, Kara shook her head, chuckling. "You and your metaphors. You're going to make me see the world as one big art project."

"Isn't that the goal?" he quipped, tossing the last of his paint supplies into his bag.

There was a playful glint in his eyes that made Kara's heart flutter. The connection they had felt so effortless, as if they had known each other for much longer than just a few hours.

As they strolled towards a nearby ice cream stand, the air filled with the sweet scent of vanilla and chocolate. The night was alive with the sounds of laughter and chatter from families enjoying the beach. Kara felt a sense of warmth envelop her, the kind that came from being surrounded by joyful energy.

"What's your favorite flavor?" Christian asked, glancing at her with a mischievous smile.

"Definitely mint chocolate chip. It's refreshing and sweet, kind of like a summer evening."

"Mint chocolate chip it is, then!" he declared, nodding with a grin. "I'll take a scoop of adventure in a cone, please."

As they stood in line, Kara couldn't help but steal glances at Christian. The way he interacted with the world around him—so effortlessly charismatic—filled her with a mix of admiration and intrigue. There was an authenticity about him that she found refreshing, a stark contrast to the structured world she inhabited at her job.

Once they had their ice cream, they found a small bench overlooking the beach, the gentle sound of the waves crashing against the shore serving as a backdrop to their conversation. Kara took a bite of her ice cream and closed her eyes for a moment, savoring the coolness and the burst of flavor.

"Okay, Kara, spill it," Christian said, leaning forward with an expectant look. "What's something most people don't know about you?"

Kara chuckled, her heart racing a little at the prospect of sharing something personal. "Well, I guess I could tell you that I've always wanted to travel the world. I've never really had the chance to, though. With work and everything, it's been tough to break away."

Christian nodded, his expression thoughtful. "Traveling is one of the best ways to expand your horizons, both literally and figuratively.

I often find inspiration for my art in the places I explore. What's stopping you from taking that leap?"

She hesitated, the weight of her responsibilities pressing against her. "I guess I'm just afraid. Afraid of the unknown, of leaving the comfort of my routine. What if I'm not good enough at it?"

Christian's eyes sparkled with understanding as he leaned back, allowing her words to sink in. "You know, fear is just a part of the process. I face it every time I pick up a brush. What if the painting doesn't turn out the way I envisioned? But that's the beauty of it—every stroke teaches you something new. Every adventure adds a layer to who you are."

His words resonated with Kara. She had always been the nurturing type, the one who put others' needs before her own. The thought of exploring the world, of stepping outside her comfort zone, felt exhilarating—and terrifying.

"What about you?" she asked, eager to shift the focus back to him. "What's your biggest fear when it comes to your art?"

Christian took a moment, his expression turning serious for the first time. "Honestly, it's the fear of not being seen. I pour so much of myself into my work, and sometimes, I wonder if it resonates with anyone. What if it's all just noise?"

Kara reached out, placing her hand over his in a gesture of comfort. "I think your work speaks volumes. It's full of life and energy. You have a gift, Christian."

The warmth of her touch sent a rush of energy through him, and Christian couldn't help but smile. "Thanks, Kara. That means a lot coming from you."

They continued to share stories, revealing their dreams, insecurities, and the little things that made them who they were. Each revelation deepened their connection, weaving an intricate tapestry of trust and understanding.

As they finished their ice cream, Christian looked out at the ocean, his expression thoughtful. "You know, there's an art retreat happening this weekend not far from here. It's all about creativity and exploration, and I was thinking... would you like to join me?"

Kara's heart raced at the suggestion. The thought of spending a weekend immersed in art and adventure with Christian was both exhilarating and nerve-wracking. "An art retreat? I've never been to one before. What if I'm not good enough?"

"Who says you have to be 'good enough'?" he countered, a playful glint in his eyes. "The whole point is to explore and create without judgment. Plus, I think your perspective could bring something unique to the group."

Kara bit her lip, caught in a whirlwind of excitement and apprehension. "I don't know, Christian. I have responsibilities at work. What if they need me?"

"Sometimes you have to take a leap, Kara," he said. "You deserve to do something just for you. I promise you won't regret it. We'll have fun, and who knows? This could be the beginning of something amazing."

His words hung in the air, tempting her to break free from her self-imposed limitations. The allure of adventure tugged at her heart, a whisper of freedom that she couldn't ignore.

Taking a deep breath, she felt the weight of her decision. "Okay... I'm in. Let's do it."

A grin broke across Christian's face, and he leaned forward, his excitement palpable. "Yes! I promise it'll be worth it. We'll create, we'll explore, and most importantly, we'll have an adventure."

As they walked back to their cars, Kara felt a sense of anticipation. This was more than just a weekend getaway; it was a chance to discover herself, to embrace the unknown, and to explore the connection she felt with Christian.

CHAPTER 3

A Canvas of Choices

The morning sun streamed through the window of Kara's small apartment, illuminating the space with a warm, golden hue. She lay in bed, eyes wide open, her mind racing with thoughts of the previous evening. Christian's laughter echoed in her ears, a melody that seemed to dance along with the gentle crashing of the waves. The connection they had forged felt like a burst of color on a blank canvas—vibrant, unexpected, and utterly captivating.

Kara swung her legs over the side of the bed, her heart fluttering with excitement. She had never been one to rush into things, but there was something about Christian that stirred a fire within her, an adventurous spirit that challenged her to step outside her comfort zone. The idea of the art retreat loomed large on her horizon, igniting a spark of possibility she hadn't felt in years.

After a quick shower and a few moments spent standing in front of the mirror, she dressed with care, choosing a light summer dress that billowed gently around her knees. It was a stark contrast to her usual business attire, but today felt different—today felt like the beginning of something new. She paired it with a simple necklace and slid on her comfortable sandals before heading out the door.

The drive to the doctor's office was uneventful, but Kara's mind was anything but calm. Thoughts of Christian flitted through her mind like butterflies, each one reminding her of his playful banter, the sparkle in his eyes, and the way he encouraged her to embrace her dreams. She parked her car and stepped into the bustling office, her heart racing at the thought of sharing her excitement with her best friend, Jodi.

The office was alive with the usual sounds of ringing phones and murmuring patients, and Kara greeted her coworkers with a bright smile as she made her way to her office. She settled into her chair, the familiar routine settling around her like a comforting blanket, but her heart still ached for the thrill of adventure.

As she organized her desk, Kara pulled out her phone and scrolled through her contacts until she found Jodi's name. She pressed call and waited, her heart racing with anticipation.

"Hey, Kara! What's up?" Jodi's voice was warm and inviting, as always.

"Jodi! You won't believe what happened last night!" Kara exclaimed. "I met someone—his name is Christian, and he's an artist! We spent the evening painting on the beach, and it was just... magical!"

"Whoa, slow down there, Miss Spontaneity!" Jodi laughed. "This sounds like the beginning of a romantic novel. Tell me everything!"

Kara couldn't help but grin. "I mean, it really felt like something special, you know? We connected over art, and he invited me to this art retreat this weekend. I'm really considering going!"

There was a brief silence on the other end of the line, and Kara could almost hear the gears turning in Jodi's head. "An art retreat? That sounds amazing, but Kara, are you sure you're ready for something like this? I mean, it's a big commitment."

"Commitment?" Kara echoed, a hint of confusion lacing her voice. "It's just a weekend! It's not like I'm signing my life away. I just want to explore and have a good time. Christian makes me feel alive!"

"Of course, but remember the last time you dove headfirst into something?" Jodi's tone shifted, becoming more serious. "You don't want to rush into things, especially when it comes to relationships. You need to be sure."

Kara frowned, her excitement faltering for a moment. "I get that, but this feels different. Christian is different. He encourages me to break out of my shell, to embrace my artistic side. I feel like I can be myself around him."

"Being yourself is important, absolutely," Jodi replied. "But just make sure you're not wearing rose-colored glasses. It's easy to get swept away in the moment, especially with someone as charming as he sounds."

"I know, I know." Kara sighed, her heart a mixture of hope and doubt. "But what if this is my chance? What if this is the adventure I've been waiting for?"

Jodi paused, and Kara could almost picture her friend's thoughtful expression. "Okay, hear me out. Why not try it? Attend the retreat and see how it feels, but keep your mind clear. Enjoy the moment without letting it consume you. You deserve to explore, Kara."

"Thanks, Jodi. I really appreciate your perspective," Kara said, her heart warming at her friend's support. "You always know how to ground me."

"That's what best friends are for! Just promise me you'll keep me updated, okay? I want to hear every detail."

Kara laughed, feeling a renewed sense of excitement. "I promise! I'll fill you in on all the artistic drama."

After a brief conversation about weekend plans and their usual shenanigans, Kara hung up the phone, her mind buzzing with thoughts of Christian and the retreat. She spent the rest of her morning in a daze, answering calls and managing schedules while her heart danced with anticipation.

When lunch rolled around, she found herself at her favorite café nearby, a quaint little spot with outdoor seating that overlooked a small park. The sun shone down warmly, and as she sat with her salad and iced tea, she couldn't help but think of Christian's infectious enthusiasm. She pulled out her sketchbook and began to doodle, letting her mind wander to the possibilities that awaited her at the retreat.

Kara sketched the ocean, waves crashing against the shore, interspersed with colors that mirrored the vibrant sunset from the night before. As she drew, she imagined herself standing on the beach beside Christian, paintbrush in hand, creating something beautiful together. The thought sent a thrill through her, and she found herself smiling at the idea of sharing that experience with someone who understood her passion.

After lunch, Kara returned to the office, her mind still buzzing with creativity and the thrill of the unknown. The afternoon passed in a blur, and as the clock ticked closer to quitting time, she felt a mixture of eagerness and nervousness for the weekend ahead.

When she finally clocked out and stepped into the warm evening air, she found herself hesitating for a moment. Should she call Christian? She checked her phone, seeing that she had received a message from him earlier that day, his words filled with excitement about the retreat.

"Hey Kara! Just wanted to check in and see if you're still on for the weekend. Can't wait to make art and memories together!"

Kara smiled, her heart racing as she typed a quick response. "Absolutely! Looking forward to it. Can we meet before? I'd love to discuss our plans!"

She hit send, her stomach fluttering with anticipation as she waited for his reply. The sun dipped lower in the sky, painting the world around her in hues of orange and pink, and she couldn't shake the feeling that this weekend was going to change everything.

Moments later, her phone chimed with a response. "Definitely! Let's meet tomorrow afternoon at the beach. I'll bring the supplies. Can't wait to see you!"

Kara's heart soared. Tomorrow would be the beginning of an adventure, a chance to explore not only her artistic side but also the connection she felt with Christian. As she drove home, the setting sun drenched the road in amber light, a quiet reminder that this was more than just a get-together. Jodi's words lingered in her mind, a gentle warning: don't lose yourself in the moment.

CHAPTER 4

Canvas of Possibilities

The morning light spilled across the sky, casting a brilliant blue hue that promised a perfect day at the beach. Kara stood in front of her closet, her heart racing with anticipation. Today was the day she would meet Christian at the beach for their art retreat, and she wanted everything to be just right. She selected a light, flowing blouse and a pair of comfortable shorts, tying her hair back in a loose bun that danced with the ocean breeze. As she applied a hint of sunscreen, she couldn't help but smile at the thought of spending the day with him.

After grabbing her art supplies—her sketchbook, a set of vibrant paints, and brushes—Kara slipped on her sandals and headed out the door. The drive to the beach was filled with an electric energy, the kind that made her feel alive and ready for whatever the day had in store. The salty air greeted her as she approached the shore, and the sound of the waves crashing against the sand sent a thrill coursing through her.

When she arrived, Christian was already there, setting up a small easel near the water's edge. The sun glinted off his tousled hair, and he looked every bit the artist she had imagined. Kara's heart raced at the sight of him, and she couldn't help but admire the way he moved with confidence, his athletic build accentuated by the casual tank top he wore.

"Hey there, sunshine!" Christian called out, his voice warm and inviting as he spotted her approaching. "You made it!"

"Wouldn't miss it for the world!" Kara replied, her heart fluttering as she approached. "This place is beautiful!"

Christian gestured to the expanse of the beach, where the ocean sparkled under the sunlight. "It's the perfect canvas, isn't it? Just wait until we start painting. I can already feel the creativity flowing!"

They set up their supplies side by side, the sand warm beneath their feet. As Kara unpacked her paints, she felt a surge of excitement at the prospect of sharing this experience with him. "So, what's your inspiration for today?" she asked, glancing at him as she arranged her colors.

"I'm thinking about capturing the waves," he said, his eyes sparkling with enthusiasm. "There's something so powerful about them, don't you think? They crash and retreat, but they always come back. It feels like a metaphor for life, you know?"

Kara nodded, intrigued by his perspective. "That's a beautiful thought. I was thinking about painting the horizon—how it meets the sea. It symbolizes endless possibilities, a reminder that there's so much out there waiting for us."

"Wow, I love that!" Christian exclaimed, his smile broadening. "You really have a way with words, Kara. I can see your passion shining through."

As they began to paint, the playful banter flowed easily between them. Kara felt a lightness in her heart, the kind that came from being with someone who truly understood her. They laughed about their artistic choices, teasing each other about color selections and brush techniques, their voices mingling with the sounds of the ocean.

"Is that turquoise I see? Bold choice!" Christian quipped, glancing at her canvas. "I didn't know you were such a risk-taker."

Kara chuckled, enjoying the playful challenge. "I think you underestimate my adventurous side. But you know, I'm still learning. It's easy to stick to what's safe, but I want to push my boundaries."

"Same here," Christian admitted, his tone shifting slightly as he grew more contemplative. "When I first started painting, I was terrified of sharing my work. I thought people would judge me, that they wouldn't understand my vision. But then I realized that art is about vulnerability. It's about expressing who you are, regardless of how others perceive it."

Kara paused, the sincerity in his voice resonating deeply with her. "That's so true. I often feel like I'm hiding behind my responsibilities, like I'm afraid to truly embrace my own creativity. It's comforting to hear that even someone as talented as you has faced those fears."

Christian glanced at her, his expression earnest. "We all have our struggles, Kara. It's part of being human. But the important thing is to keep pushing through, to keep creating. That's where the magic happens."

Their eyes locked for a moment, and Kara felt a warmth spreading through her, a connection that went beyond mere words. She smiled softly, feeling emboldened by his honesty. "You're right. I want to embrace that magic more in my life. It's just so easy to get caught up in the mundane."

"Then let's make today about embracing that magic," Christian suggested, a spark of mischief in his eyes. "Let's paint our fears and dreams onto our canvases. We can even create a little friendly competition—whoever captures the spirit of the beach best gets to pick dinner tonight!"

Kara laughed, the idea lighting a fire of excitement within her. "Alright, challenge accepted! But be prepared to lose because I'm determined to channel every ounce of creativity I have!"

As they painted, the sun climbed higher in the sky, casting a warm glow over the beach. Kara lost herself in the rhythm of the brush against the canvas, the sound of the waves providing a soothing backdrop. She felt alive, the colors blending under her touch, reflecting the emotions within her.

Time slipped away, and before long, they were both engrossed in their artwork, laughter and playful teasing punctuating the air. Christian's playful comments about her artistic choices continued to flow, and Kara found herself responding with equal wit, their connection deepening with each exchange.

"Okay, let's take a break," Christian finally suggested, wiping his brow with the back of his hand. "I need to step back and see how our masterpieces are coming along. Plus, I'm getting hungry."

"Good idea!" Kara agreed, stepping back from her easel to admire her work. The vibrant colors danced across the canvas, and she felt a sense of pride in what she had created. "Not too shabby, if I do say so myself!"

Christian chuckled, gesturing dramatically toward her painting. "I'd say you've captured the essence of the horizon beautifully. It's full of hope and potential, just like you."

Kara felt her cheeks flush at his compliment. "Thanks, Christian. That means a lot. I appreciate your encouragement."

He looked at her, his expression softening. "Honestly, Kara, you have this light about you. It's contagious. I'm glad I get to share this experience with you."

As the moment hung between them, Kara felt a shift in the air, a shared understanding that transcended their playful banter. It was a vulnerability that had been laid bare, drawing them closer in a way that felt both thrilling and terrifying.

"Do you ever feel like you're standing at the edge of something great, but you're just too afraid to jump?" Kara asked.

Christian nodded, his gaze unwavering. "Every day. But I've learned that sometimes you have to take that leap of faith. It's the only way to truly live."

Kara's heart raced at his words, the weight of their conversation grounding them both. She took a deep breath, feeling a shift within herself—a desire to embrace the unknown, to step out of her comfort zone. "I want that. I want to be brave enough to take risks."

At that moment, the playful banter melted away, leaving only the genuine connection between them. Christian leaned closer, his gaze intense yet tender. "Then let's promise each other to embrace that bravery, to support one another as we navigate this journey."

With a shared understanding, Kara nodded, her heart pounding. "I promise."

The air was charged with an unspoken tension, and as if drawn together by an invisible force, they leaned in closer. The world around them faded away, the sound of the waves becoming a distant whisper. In a heartbeat, their lips met in a tender kiss, igniting a spark that would mark the beginning of something undeniably beautiful between them.

CHAPTER 5

The Canvas of Connection

As the kiss lingered, Kara felt a rush of warmth and possibility washing over her like the gentle tide that lapped at her feet. It was a moment suspended in time, an electric pulse that ignited something deep within her. Breaking apart, they shared shy smiles, both surprised by the sudden shift in their connection. The world around them—vibrant and alive—seemed to fade into the background as they stood there, hearts racing, captivated by the newfound depth of their relationship.

"Wow," Christian said, his voice a mix of surprise and delight. "I didn't expect that, but I'm definitely not complaining."

Kara laughed softly, her cheeks flushing. "Neither did I. I mean, we were just painting, and then... well, that happened."

"Maybe it was the magic of the beach," he suggested, a playful glint in his eye. "Or perhaps it's your incredible artistry inspiring me."

"Or maybe it's just the universe conspiring to bring us together," Kara replied, her heart fluttering at the thought. "I mean, this day has been more than I could have imagined."

They both turned toward the ocean, letting the sounds of the waves fill the space between them. Kara tucked a loose strand of hair behind her ear, contemplating the shift in their dynamic. She had always been focused on her career, her responsibilities, and yet here she was, standing at the edge of something exhilarating and terrifying.

"Can I be honest with you?" Christian's tone shifted slightly, becoming more sincere. "I've always been someone who's been afraid to let people in. I guess I've built this wall around myself because I didn't want to get hurt."

Kara turned to him, intrigued by the vulnerability in his voice. "I can relate to that. We often hide behind our own fears, don't we? I've had my own battles with vulnerability."

"What do you mean?" Christian asked, genuinely curious.

Kara took a deep breath, her heart racing as she prepared to share a piece of herself she rarely revealed. "When I was younger, I was always the responsible one. I took care of everyone around me—my family, my friends. I was good at it, but somewhere along the way, I lost a part of myself. I had dreams of traveling, of painting, of exploring the world, but I buried them under the weight of my responsibilities."

Christian listened intently, his expression softening as he absorbed her words. "That sounds tough. It's like you've been living for others instead of yourself."

"Exactly," Kara agreed. "It took me a long time to realize I was missing out on my own life. I've started to embrace my passions again, but it's scary, you know? It's like standing at the edge of a cliff, ready to leap but afraid of the fall."

Christian nodded, understanding flickering in his eyes. "I get it. I think we all have those cliffs in our lives. For me, it's the fear of failure. I've always had this pressure to succeed, to create something amazing. But what if it's not enough? What if people don't see the value in my art?"

Kara reached out, placing a reassuring hand on his arm. "But the beauty of art is that it's subjective. What matters most is that it reflects who you are. You have a gift, Christian, and sharing it is what makes it valuable."

He smiled at her encouragement, the warmth of her touch grounding him. "Thank you, Kara. I really appreciate that. It's refreshing to talk about this stuff. I feel like I can really be myself with you."

"And I feel the same way," she admitted, her heart swelling with gratitude for this connection they were forging. "I didn't expect to open up like this today, but it feels... right."

As they stood there, the sun began to dip lower in the sky, casting a golden hue over the beach. Kara felt a sense of peace settling over her, as if the universe was affirming their bond. "So, what do we do now?" she asked, a playful smile tugging at her lips.

"Now?" Christian mused, a mischievous grin spreading across his face. "Now we continue to create our masterpieces, but with a little more honesty and heart. Let's paint our fears and hopes and really embrace what we want our lives to look like."

Kara's eyes sparkled with excitement. "I love that idea! Let's make our canvases not just about the beach, but about us—our stories and dreams."

They returned to their easels, the playful banter resuming as they splashed colors onto the canvas, each stroke becoming a reflection of their shared experiences. Kara found herself lost in the rhythm of painting, her brush gliding over the surface as she infused her emotions into every hue. The vibrant colors she chose began to represent her journey—layers of hope, freedom, and the courage to embrace her dreams.

Christian, meanwhile, poured his heart into capturing the essence of the waves crashing against the shore. He painted with abandon, allowing his brush to dance across the canvas as he translated his insecurities into powerful strokes, depicting the struggle between fear and courage. The intensity of his colors mirrored the tumultuous emotions he felt inside, and for the first time, he felt liberated.

"Look at this!" Christian exclaimed, stepping back to admire his work. "It's like the waves are alive, pulling me in. I can feel the energy!"

Kara glanced over, her heart swelling with pride for him. "It's incredible, Christian! You've captured the spirit of the ocean perfectly. It looks like it could leap off the canvas."

"Thanks! And yours is turning into something beautiful too," he said, nodding toward her painting. "It's as if I can sense the horizon reaching out, full of promise."

Kara beamed, feeling a surge of encouragement from his words. "It's all about pushing ourselves, isn't it? I'm realizing that our fears don't have to hold us back. They can actually fuel our creativity."

"Exactly! And it's easier to face those fears when you have someone beside you," Christian replied, meeting her gaze with a depth of understanding that made her heart flutter.

As the sun began to set, casting a warm orange glow over the ocean, Kara and Christian found themselves stepping back to admire their work. The canvases stood side by side—a beautiful representation of their individual journeys and the connection they were forging.

"Shall we take a break and grab some dinner?" Christian suggested, glancing at the horizon. "I'm starving, and I think we've earned it after this artistic endeavor."

"Absolutely! I have a feeling I might win this little competition," Kara teased, her eyes sparkling with mischief. "But I'm happy to share my victory meal with you."

"Confident, are we?" he shot back, laughing. "We'll see about that! But regardless of who wins, I'm just glad we're in this together."

As they gathered their supplies, a sense of contentment washed over Kara. The day had evolved into something deeper than she had anticipated, and she could feel the promise of a beautiful partnership beginning to take shape. There was a magic in this connection, one that transcended the canvas and painted a picture of hope and possibility for their future.

With laughter and teasing, they made their way toward the beachside café, the sound of waves crashing behind them, carrying with it the whispers of their dreams, fears, and the untold stories waiting to unfold.

CHAPTER 6

Storms and Secrets

Kara and Christian arrived at the beachside café, the salty breeze swirling around them as they stepped inside. The café was warm and inviting, with whimsical decorations that echoed the vibrant colors of the beach outside. Strings of fairy lights hung overhead, casting a soft glow that mingled with the scent of fresh seafood and the promise of adventure in the air. Kara felt a flutter of anticipation as they settled at a cozy table by the window, the rhythmic sound of waves providing a soothing soundtrack.

"So, what are you in the mood for?" Christian asked, scanning the menu with an eager expression. His eyes sparkled with mischief, and Kara couldn't help but smile back.

"I think it's a seafood kind of night," she replied playfully. "How about we share a few dishes? That way, we can taste everything!"

"Sharing? I like where your head's at." Christian grinned, his enthusiasm infectious. "I'll order the catch of the day, and you can't go wrong with the coconut shrimp. Deal?"

"Deal," Kara agreed, her heart warming at his spontaneity. "And maybe we can get some of their famous key lime pie for dessert? I heard it's amazing."

"Now you're speaking my language." He laughed, signaling to the waiter with a wave. As they placed their order, Kara couldn't shake off the giddiness that bubbled within her, a thrilling mix of excitement and nervousness.

Once the waiter left, the conversation effortlessly flowed between them as they shared stories of their lives. They talked about their favorite beach spots, with Kara reminiscing about childhood summers spent snorkeling in crystal-clear waters and Christian sharing tales of surfing escapades that had him riding waves in far-flung corners of the world.

"Honestly, I think the ocean has a way of calling to us," Kara mused, her eyes brightening. "There's something about the water that feels like home. It's where I can breathe, where I can be free."

Christian nodded and leaned in closer. "I completely get that. It's where I find my inspiration. Every wave tells a story, and it's like I'm tapping into something bigger than myself when I'm out there."

Their laughter mingled with the sounds of clinking cutlery and soft chatter around them, creating an embrace of warmth and intimacy. As their food arrived, the conversation took a deeper turn. They began discussing their dreams—those vibrant aspirations that danced just out of reach.

"What about you, Kara?" Christian asked, his expression earnest as he leaned forward. "What's your biggest dream? The one that sets your heart racing?"

Kara paused, considering the question. "Well, I've always wanted to open an art therapy program for children. I believe that creativity can heal, and I want to help kids express themselves through art. They deserve a safe space to explore their feelings."

"Wow, that's incredible," Christian said, admiration shining in his eyes. "You're such a nurturing soul. I can see how passionate you are about it. It's inspiring."

Kara felt a rush of warmth at his words. "Thank you. I just... I want to make a difference, you know? Sometimes it feels like I'm stuck in my day-to-day routine, but art has always been my escape."

"I can relate to that," he replied, a thoughtful look crossing his face. "For me, I want to create a body of work that resonates with people on a deeper level. I want my art to evoke emotions and provoke thought. But sometimes I wonder if it's enough."

"Enough?" Kara echoed, raising an eyebrow. "What do you mean?"

Christian took a sip of his drink, gathering his thoughts. "I guess I feel this pressure to succeed—to be recognized as a 'great' artist. My last relationship put a lot of that into perspective. It ended because my partner felt I was too focused on my art and not enough on us. It made me question whether I'm chasing a dream or running away from something."

Kara felt a thread of connection weaving between them, the vulnerability in his voice deepening the bond they were forming. "That sounds really tough, Christian. It's hard to juggle personal aspirations with relationships. People often don't understand the sacrifices we make for our passions."

His gaze met hers, a flicker of understanding passing between them. "Exactly. I poured my heart into my work, thinking that it would bring fulfillment. But I lost sight of what truly mattered. I don't want to repeat that mistake."

The café suddenly dimmed as the lights flickered overhead, an ominous rumble of thunder rolling in from the horizon. Kara glanced outside, watching dark clouds gather above the ocean like an approaching tempest. "Looks like we might be in for a storm," she said, trying to keep the mood light.

"Perfect timing for a cozy dinner," Christian replied with a grin. "I've always found storms to be oddly comforting."

Moments later, the power went out, plunging the café into darkness, save for the flicker of candles that had been lit on each table. The soft glow illuminated Christian's face, casting shadows that danced with the flickering flames. Kara felt her heart race, both from the thrill of the unexpected and the intimacy of the moment.

"Looks like we're having a candlelit dinner after all," Christian said, his tone playful as he leaned back in his chair, a mischievous glint in his eye. "What's next? A game of charades?"

"Actually, I was thinking more along the lines of some deep, philosophical debates," Kara replied. "What do you think is the meaning of life?"

"Wow, going right for the jugular, huh?" Christian laughed, his eyes sparkling in the candlelight. "I think the meaning of life is about experiences—living fully, embracing adventure, and seeking connection with others."

"Interesting perspective," Kara mused, leaning in closer, the warmth of the candle flickering between them. "But what happens when those connections become complicated? When your dreams clash with someone else's?"

Christian's expression turned serious, and he regarded her thoughtfully. "I think it's about finding balance. Compromise isn't always easy, but if both people are willing to grow together, then it can be beautiful."

As the rain began to pour outside, the rhythmic patter against the windows created a soothing backdrop. Kara felt a magnetic pull toward Christian, the space between them narrowing as they engaged in these deeper conversations.

"Have you ever thought about what your life would look like if you could do anything without fear of consequences?" she asked, her curiosity piqued.

"Absolutely," he replied, his eyes glimmering with excitement. "I would travel the world, live in different cultures, and paint everything I saw. But I'd also want to share those experiences with someone special. I realize now that having someone to share the journey with makes it all the more meaningful."

Kara felt her heart swell at his words, a warmth spreading through her. In that moment, the distance between them felt electric, the connection palpable. "I think I'd want that too," she confessed. "Someone who understands my passion and encourages me to chase my dreams."

"You deserve that, Kara," Christian said softly, his gaze intense as it locked onto hers. "You're so passionate about life and helping others. It's inspiring, and I can't help but admire that."

As they continued to talk, sharing stories and laughter, the world outside faded away. The storm raged on, but inside the cozy café, it was just the two of them—two souls connecting over dreams, fears, and the essence of who they were.

With each shared story, the magnetic pull between them intensified, creating a space filled with possibility. Kara felt as if they were on the brink of something profound, a moment that could change everything. In the midst of the storm, there was a sense of calm, a feeling that perhaps they were exactly where they were meant to be.

CHAPTER 7

Beneath the Candlelight

The rain lashed against the windows with a ferocity that seemed to echo the tumult of emotions swirling within Kara. The storm outside had transformed the café into a sanctuary, where the flickering candlelight cast warm shadows on their faces. Kara glanced across the table at Christian, whose eyes sparkled with a mix of mischief and sincerity. The intimacy of the moment felt like a haven, wrapping them in a world where nothing else mattered—just the two of them, their hopes, their fears, and the uncharted territory of their budding connection.

"Alright, let's switch gears a bit," Christian said, leaning in with a conspiratorial grin. "How about a game? We can take turns sharing our biggest regrets. It's like a trust fall, but with words."

Kara raised an eyebrow, intrigued and slightly nervous. "Regrets? That sounds heavy. Are we really ready for that?"

"Why not?" he challenged. "We're already talking about dreams and fears. Regrets are just part of the journey, right? I promise to go first so you can see how it's done."

"Okay, you're on," she replied, feeling the thrill of vulnerability creeping in. "Let's hear it."

Christian took a deep breath, his expression shifting to one of seriousness. "Alright, here goes. My biggest regret is probably not taking more risks in my relationships. I always chased after my art, thinking that it would bring me happiness. But I missed out on some incredible connections because I was too focused on my work. It's like I was running a race, but I forgot to look around and appreciate the people cheering me on."

Kara felt a pang of empathy for him. "That's really profound, Christian. It's easy to get so caught up in our passions that we forget to nurture the people around us."

"Exactly." He nodded, keeping his gaze steady on hers. "So, your turn. What's your biggest regret?"

Kara hesitated, her heart racing. "I think mine would be not pursuing my art more seriously. I've always loved it—painting, drawing, even crafting—but I never allowed myself to explore that side of me fully. Instead, I've been stuck in this safe, predictable routine. I love my work at the doctor's office, but sometimes I wonder if I'm playing it too safe and missing out on my true passion."

Christian's expression softened, and he leaned closer, the candlelight flickering between them like a heartbeat. "You should never feel like you have to choose one over the other. There's beauty in both worlds. But if art is what sets your soul on fire, then why not find a way to incorporate it into your life?"

Her heart swelled at his encouragement. "You're right. I guess I've just been so afraid of failing that I convinced myself it wasn't worth it. But talking to you makes me feel like maybe I can take that leap."

"Then let's take the leap together," he said, his voice earnest. "What's stopping you?"

The question hung in the air, and Kara felt a rush of warmth at the thought of sharing her dreams with someone who genuinely understood. "I suppose I worry about what others will think. Family expectations weigh heavily on me. They've always seen me as the responsible one, the one who plays it safe. I fear disappointing them if I choose a path that's less conventional."

"Family can be tough," Christian replied, his tone soothing. "But at the end of the day, you have to live for yourself. When I started my art career, I faced skepticism too. But I realized that my happiness is my own responsibility. The people who truly care about you will understand your choices."

The rain continued to pour, creating a rhythmic backdrop that made the moment feel even more intimate. Kara felt the tension in her chest begin to ease, as if Christian's words were a gentle balm.

"You make it sound so easy," she said, a smile creeping onto her face. "I wish I had your confidence."

"Confidence is overrated." He chuckled, waving his hand dismissively. "It's all about embracing the fear and doing it anyway. Besides, you have this incredible spirit. I can see it in the way you light up when you talk about art. Don't let anyone dim that light."

"Thank you, Christian. That means a lot," she said, her heart fluttering. "It's refreshing to talk to someone who gets it, who doesn't just see me as a manager or a responsible adult."

"Exactly! You're so much more than that. You're a creative soul, and you deserve to explore that side of you," he encouraged, his eyes locking onto hers with an intensity that made her pulse quicken.

The air between them thickened with unspoken possibilities. Kara felt a spark of connection that transcended their earlier conversations. As if sensing the shift, Christian leaned back slightly, breaking the spell but still maintaining that captivating gaze.

"Okay, my turn again," Christian said, his playful demeanor returning. "Let's keep this going. What's something you wish you had done differently in your last relationship?"

Kara bit her lip, considering the question. "I think I wished I had communicated better. There were times when I buried my feelings instead of being honest, thinking I was protecting him. But in the end, it only led to misunderstandings and resentment."

"Communication is key," Christian agreed, his expression thoughtful. "I learned that the hard way too. I used to think I could just keep everything bottled up, but it only pushed people away."

Kara nodded, feeling the weight of their shared revelations. "It's so easy to let fear dictate our actions, isn't it? Fear of rejection, fear of vulnerability. But in reality, we're all just trying to connect."

"Exactly," Christian said softly, the intensity in his gaze returning. "And when you find someone who understands you—who you can be completely open with—it's worth taking that leap."

Just then, the power flickered back on, filling the café with a bright light that momentarily blinded them. The ambiance shifted, and the spell they had woven began to fray. Kara blinked, momentarily disoriented by the sudden brightness. She glanced at Christian, whose expression mirrored her own—confusion and a twinge of disappointment at the interruption.

"Wow, that was sudden," she said, laughing lightly to mask the shift in atmosphere.

"Yeah, talk about a buzzkill," Christian replied, a teasing smile creeping onto his face. "But hey, at least we have the lights back. Candles are great, but I prefer to see what I'm eating."

Kara chuckled, but the moment felt different now. The vulnerability they had shared lingered in the air, but the energy had shifted, reminding her of the reality waiting outside their little bubble. She reached for her phone, and her heart sank as she saw a message from her mother flash across the screen—a reminder of a family obligation that she had known was coming but had hoped would somehow disappear.

"Ugh, I can't believe it," she muttered, her heart racing. "I completely forgot about dinner with my family tonight. It's been planned for weeks, and I can't just bail on them."

Christian's expression changed, concern etched on his face. "Is everything okay?"

"Yeah, it's just... my family has this expectation that I'll always be there for every gathering. They don't really understand my need for independence, for pursuing my passions," she explained, feeling torn. "I was really looking forward to spending more time with you tonight. This was... nice."

"Hey, I get it. Family obligations are important. But what do you want to do?" Christian asked, leaning back in his chair, his eyes searching hers. "If this is something you really want to pursue, then maybe it's worth having that conversation with them."

Kara felt the weight of his words settle heavily in her heart. She could either uphold family expectations or embrace the spark that was igniting between her and Christian. The choice felt monumental, like standing at a crossroads where one path led back to the familiar and the other beckoned her toward the unknown.

"I want to go to the art retreat this weekend, and I want to see where this connection with you leads," she finally admitted. "But I don't want to disappoint my family either."

"Then maybe talk to them. It's possible to be there for them without losing yourself in the process," he suggested. "You deserve to pursue what makes you happy, and they might surprise you with their understanding."

Kara could feel the tension in her chest ease as she considered his words. "You're right. I need to find a way to express my desires while still honoring my family. It's just... hard."

"I believe in you," Christian said, his tone gentle yet firm. "You have the strength to stand up for what you want, and I'll be here cheering you on."

With those words, a sense of clarity washed over her. The storm outside may have been raging, but inside her heart, a new resolve was taking shape. The connection with Christian had opened her eyes to the possibility of balancing her aspirations with her responsibilities.

As they finished their meal, the lively chatter of other patrons filled the café, but Kara and Christian remained in their own world. The conversation flowed easily, the bond between them strengthening with every shared laugh and glance. She knew that whatever decision she made, she wouldn't be making it alone. Christian's presence felt like a safe harbor amidst the storm—a reminder that sometimes, the choices that challenge us are the ones that lead to the most growth.

CHAPTER 8

A Palette of Choices

Kara stood in front of her bathroom mirror, the dim light casting a soft glow on her reflection. She meticulously brushed her hair, the rhythmic strokes offering a moment of calm amidst the storm brewing in her mind. Tonight was no ordinary dinner; it was a family gathering infused with expectations that wrapped around her like a heavy cloak. As she carefully applied her makeup, she felt the weight of Christian's words from their earlier conversation echoing in her thoughts, urging her to embrace her true self.

"Just be honest, Kara," she whispered to herself, a hint of determination creeping into her voice. "You can do this."

She couldn't shake the nervous energy coursing through her veins. The idea of discussing her hopes and dreams with her family felt like standing at the edge of a cliff, ready to leap into the unknown. What if they didn't understand? What if disappointment clouded their faces? Yet, the thought of continuing to suppress her passion for art gnawed at her, a persistent reminder of the dreams she had tucked away for far too long.

As she slipped into a comfortable yet elegant dress, she caught a glimpse of her phone lighting up on the counter. It was a message from Christian, a playful note that read, "Hey, beautiful! Just wanted to remind you that you're amazing and to go for it tonight. I'll be thinking about you! Can't wait for our adventure this weekend."

Her heart fluttered at the sight of his words. They instilled a sense of courage within her, a reminder that she was not alone in this journey. With a deep breath, she replied, "Thanks, Christian. Your support means the world to me. I'll let you know how it goes!"

As she finished getting ready, Kara replayed their earlier conversation in her mind. Christian's belief in her, his encouragement to embrace her artistic side, had ignited a fire within her that had long been dormant. She realized that it was time to stop living for others and start creating a life that resonated with her own desires.

Stepping out of her apartment, Kara took a moment to inhale the salty air. The ocean was nearby, its rhythmic waves calling to her like an old friend. If only she could take that leap into the sea of her dreams, where both art and her heart could swim freely. She chuckled softly at the thought—her playful side emerging. "Soon enough," she promised herself, envisioning a future where she could balance her responsibilities with the freedom to create.

Arriving at her parents' house, the familiar warmth enveloped her as she walked through the door. The lively chatter of her family greeted her, making her heart swell with affection. Her mom, always the cheerful host, was busy setting the table, layering each dish with care and nostalgia. Kara felt a pang of love for her mother, grateful for the countless family dinners that had shaped her childhood.

"Kara, darling! You're here!" her mother exclaimed, turning with a radiant smile. "You look lovely! How was your day?"

"Thanks, Mom! It was good, just the usual work stuff," Kara replied, forcing a smile despite the whirlwind of emotions beneath the surface.

"Wonderful! Dinner will be ready soon. We made your favorite—lasagna!" her mom said, her eyes sparkling with joy. "And your father is excited to hear about your day too."

Kara nodded, her heart warm but heavy. The familiar routine of family dinners had always provided comfort, yet tonight felt different. She could almost hear her dreams whispering in the back of her mind, urging her to share her aspirations with the people she loved most.

As they gathered around the table, the conversation flowed effortlessly. Kara's dad filled the room with laughter, recounting amusing stories from his work. Her brother chimed in with his usual banter, and her sister shared updates about her latest adventures. Kara felt herself being swept along in the current of their camaraderie, but she couldn't shake the feeling that she was sitting on a precipice, ready to leap into uncharted waters.

"So, Kara, what's new with you?" her father asked, turning toward her with genuine curiosity. "Anything exciting happening?"

The question hung in the air like a ripe fruit, ready to be plucked. Kara's heart raced as she searched for the right words. "Well, actually..." she started, the courage Christian had instilled in her surging to the surface. "I've been thinking a lot about my art lately."

Her family paused, the casual chatter fading as they turned their attention to her, their expressions shifting from casual interest to something more focused. "Art?" her mother echoed, a hint of nostalgia threading through her tone. "You used to love painting and drawing as a child. Have you thought about pursuing it again?"

"Yes, I have," Kara said. "I've realized that I want to explore that side of me more seriously. There's an art retreat this weekend that I want to attend. It feels like the right step for me."

Her father's eyebrows raised in surprise, and she could see the gears turning in his mind. "That sounds interesting, but what about your job? You have responsibilities, Kara. We've always counted on you to be the stable one in the family."

Kara felt a pang of frustration but quickly tempered it with understanding. Her father had always been her biggest supporter, but his words reflected the weight of family expectations that she had felt her entire life. "I know, Dad. But I've been feeling unfulfilled, and I want to find a way to balance my work and my passion. I believe I can do both."

Her mother's expression shifted from surprise to concern. "But Kara, art is such a risky path. What if it doesn't lead to anything? You have a secure job, and we've always encouraged you to play it safe. We just want what's best for you."

Kara's heart raced at the tension rising at the table. "I appreciate that you want what's best for me, but I also need to find my own happiness. I don't want to look back years from now and regret not pursuing something that brings me joy."

The room fell silent, her family processing her words. Kara could feel the weight of their expectations pressing down on her, but she summoned every ounce of courage Christian had inspired in her. "I want to create art, to explore that side of myself, even if it means taking risks. I'm ready to embrace that."

Her brother shifted uncomfortably in his seat, and her sister looked between their parents and Kara, sensing the tension. "It's not like you're quitting your job or anything, right?" he asked, trying to lighten the mood. "You can always come back to it if you want."

"Exactly!" Kara replied, feeling the heat of the moment. "I'm not abandoning my responsibilities. I just want to make room for my dreams, too."

Her father sighed, his expression softening as he leaned back in his chair. "I just want you to be happy, Kara. I know how hard you work, and I admire your dedication. But I worry about the uncertainty of pursuing art professionally."

"I understand that, Dad. But sometimes, uncertainty can lead to the most beautiful adventures. I want to live my life with passion, not just follow a predetermined path," she asserted.

The conversation ignited a passionate debate, each family member voicing their concerns and support. Kara felt a mix of anxiety and exhilaration as she stood her ground. It was a whirlwind of emotions, but amidst the chaos, she sensed a shift—a growing understanding that her family might not completely agree with her choices, but they loved her enough to listen.

Meanwhile, as the dinner continued, Christian was at home, planning their weekend getaway to the art retreat. He envisioned a space where Kara could unleash her creativity, surrounded by nature and like-minded souls. He imagined her laughter mingling with the sound of paintbrushes on canvas, the joy illuminating her face as she embraced her passion.

"Just wait until she sees this place," he murmured to himself.

He could picture them exploring the retreat together, sharing ideas, and inspiring each other. The thought made him smile, and he felt a sense of pride in supporting Kara's journey.

Back at the dinner table, as the debate began to settle, Kara's heart raced with a mixture of relief and anticipation. She could feel the love of her family surrounding her, even in their disagreement. It was a moment of growth, of pushing boundaries, and she felt empowered by the conversation they had shared.

"Thank you for hearing me out," Kara finally said, her voice breaking the silence that had settled over the table. "I know this is a lot to take in, but I genuinely believe that pursuing my art is part of who I am. I hope you can support me on this journey."

Her father reached across the table, placing his hand on hers. "We love you, Kara. We just want you to be happy. We may not fully understand this decision, but we'll support you in finding your path."

Her mother nodded, her eyes glistening with unshed tears. "Yes, dear. Just remember that we're always here for you, no matter what you choose."

Kara squeezed her father's hand, feeling an overwhelming sense of gratitude. "Thank you. That means more than you know."

As they finished dinner, Kara felt lighter, as if the burdens of expectation had been lifted, even if just a little. The conversation had been challenging, but it was also transformative—a step toward embracing her true self.

Later that night, as Kara lay in bed, she replayed the events of the evening in her mind. With Christian's encouragement and her family's love, she felt emboldened to chase her dreams. The art retreat awaited her, a blank canvas ready to be filled with the vibrant colors of her life. She closed her eyes, envisioning the possibilities that lay ahead, her heart racing with anticipation for the adventure that awaited her and Christian.

CHAPTER 9

Colors of Courage

The first rays of sunlight filtered through the curtains, casting a warm glow across Kara's room. She stirred awake, the events of the previous evening dancing in her mind like a vibrant tapestry woven with emotions. The discussion with her family had been intense, but it had also ignited a fire deep within her—a fire that whispered to her to embrace her dreams, to dive headfirst into the world of art where her heart longed to wander.

Sitting up in bed, Kara took a moment to breathe in the crisp morning air through her open window. The salty tang of the nearby ocean mingled with the scent of fresh coffee wafting in from the kitchen, creating a perfect blend that invigorated her spirit. Today was the day she had been anticipating, the day she would meet Christian at the art retreat. A flutter of excitement raced through her as she imagined the possibilities that awaited her.

With renewed determination, Kara hopped out of bed and began her morning routine. As she washed her face, she couldn't help but smile at her reflection. "You got this, Kara," she said. "Today is about you and your art."

After a quick breakfast, Kara grabbed her bag filled with art supplies, a sketchbook, and a few carefully chosen pieces from her collection. Each item was a symbol of her journey, a reminder of the passions she had tucked away for too long. With one last glance around her cozy apartment, she stepped into the world, ready to embrace the unknown.

The drive to the retreat was filled with a mix of anticipation and nervous energy. The winding roads led her through lush landscapes dotted with wildflowers that painted the scenery in bursts of color. Kara turned up the music, letting the rhythm fuel her excitement. She envisioned the workshops, the creative expressions, and, most importantly, the moments she would share with Christian.

As she arrived at the retreat, her heart raced at the sight before her. Nestled between tall trees and overlooking a serene lake, the rustic cabins and outdoor spaces seemed to beckon her. The air felt alive, charged with creativity and inspiration. Kara parked her car and stepped out, inhaling the invigorating scent of pine and earth.

"Wow," she whispered, letting the beauty of the surroundings wash over her.

The retreat was everything she had imagined and more. She took a moment to appreciate the peace that enveloped her. It was as if the universe was conspiring to support her decision to follow her dreams.

As she made her way toward the main gathering area, Kara's eyes scanned the crowd of participants. Her heart skipped a beat when she spotted Christian standing by a picturesque easel, his handsome features illuminated by the morning sun. He looked effortlessly cool, wearing a casual white T-shirt and faded jeans, his athletic build and excitement radiating a magnetic energy.

"Hey, beautiful!" Christian called out, his voice sounding light.

He waved, and Kara felt her face warm at his words. The way he effortlessly complimented her made her feel seen, cherished, and alive.

"Christian!" she replied, an infectious smile spreading across her face as she approached him. "I can't believe we're finally here!"

"Neither can I! This place is incredible," he said, gesturing to the vibrant surroundings. "You're going to love it here. I can already tell you're going to create something amazing."

Kara's heart fluttered at his enthusiasm. "I hope so! I've been so excited to explore my artistic side."

As they walked toward the main workshop area, their hands brushed against each other, sending sparks of electricity through her. The connection between them felt almost tangible, a thread woven from shared dreams and budding affection. They entered a large, airy space filled with canvases, paint, and eager participants ready to unleash their creativity.

The first workshop began, led by a charismatic artist who encouraged everyone to embrace their unique styles. Kara listened intently, her heart racing as she picked up a brush for the first time. The canvas stood before her like a blank page, waiting to be filled with her thoughts and emotions. She dipped the brush into vibrant colors, feeling the texture of the paint glide across the canvas.

"Let it flow, Kara!" Christian called from across the room, his encouraging words resonating with her.

His presence felt like a safety net, allowing her to explore without fear. She glanced over at him, and their eyes met, a silent understanding passing between them.

As the workshop continued, Kara lost herself in the act of creation. Each stroke of her brush felt liberating, and with every layer of color, she began to unveil more of herself. Laughter echoed around the room as participants shared their work, each piece a reflection of the artist's spirit.

During a break, Kara and Christian stepped outside to catch their breath. The sun bathed them in warmth, and the gentle sound of the lake lapping against the shore was a soothing backdrop.

"This is amazing," Kara said. "I can't believe how freeing it feels to just create without any pressure."

Christian nodded, his eyes sparkling with enthusiasm. "Exactly! That's what it's all about. Just letting your imagination run wild. You have so much potential, Kara."

A moment of vulnerability washed over her, and Kara hesitated before speaking. "But what if I fail? What if I'm not good enough? I've always been so focused on being practical, on what's expected of me. What if I can't live up to my own dreams?"

Christian's expression shifted to one of deep understanding. He stepped closer, his voice soft yet resolute. "Kara, everyone feels that way at some point. But you have to remember that failure is just a stepping stone to growth. It's part of the journey. What matters is that you're trying, that you're following your passion. And no matter what happens, I'll be by your side."

Her heart swelled at his words, the reassurance wrapping around her like a warm embrace. Kara felt a surge of gratitude, realizing how much his support meant to her. "Thank you, Christian. That really means a lot."

Their eyes locked for a moment, the world around them fading away as the intensity of their connection deepened. Kara could feel the magnetic pull between them, a spark that ignited something she had never anticipated. It was thrilling and terrifying all at once.

As they returned to the workshop, Kara felt invigorated, ready to pour her heart onto the canvas. With each stroke, she embraced her fears and doubts, transforming them into vibrant shades of hope and possibility. She lost track of time, completely immersed in the process of creation.

By the end of the day, as the sun dipped below the horizon, Kara stood back to admire her work. The canvas before her was a reflection of her journey—bold, colorful, and full of emotion. It was a testament to her courage and her willingness to embrace the unknown.

"Kara, this is incredible!" Christian exclaimed, standing beside her, his admiration evident in his voice. "You really captured something special here."

Kara felt a rush of pride at his words. "Thank you! I couldn't have done it without your encouragement."

As they packed up their supplies, the atmosphere buzzed with excitement and camaraderie. Kara and Christian exchanged playful banter, their laughter blending with the sounds of the retreat. The bond they were forging felt like a beautiful dance, one that had only just begun.

That evening, as they gathered around a bonfire with the other participants, Kara felt a sense of belonging like never before. The flickering flames illuminated their faces, and stories were shared, laughter echoed, and dreams floated into the night sky.

Sitting beside Christian, Kara felt a warmth that surged through her, igniting a spark of passion and connection. They shared glances, their unspoken words hanging in the air, a promise of what was to come. The night felt alive with possibility, and Kara couldn't help but envision a future where art and love intertwined seamlessly.

As the stars twinkled above, Kara knew that this retreat was just the beginning. She was ready to embrace her dreams, to step boldly into the vibrant world of creativity, and to explore the depths of her heart alongside Christian. In that moment, surrounded by laughter and light, Kara felt the colors of courage infusing her spirit, ready to paint the canvas of her life with bold strokes of passion and love.

CHAPTER 10

The Canvas of Collaboration

As dawn broke, the first light of day spilled into Kara's cabin, casting a gentle glow that danced across the walls. She stretched lazily, feeling the warmth of the sun seep into her skin. Today was the day she had been eagerly anticipating—a collaborative workshop where she would partner with Christian to create a joint piece of art. The thought sent a thrill of excitement racing through her veins, and she could hardly contain her enthusiasm as she hopped out of bed.

After a quick shower, Kara dressed in her favorite comfortable yet stylish outfit—light denim shorts paired with a flowy white blouse that fluttered with each movement. She caught a glimpse of herself in the mirror, her dark hair cascading over her shoulders, framing her face. "You're ready for this, Kara," she whispered, her heart racing with a mixture of anticipation and nerves.

As she made her way to the common area, the aroma of freshly brewed coffee wrapped around her like a warm embrace. Participants were already gathering, their voices merging into a lively hum of excitement. Kara grabbed a cup of coffee, letting the rich flavor awaken her senses, and scanned the room for Christian.

He was easy to spot, his athletic build leaning against a wall, chatting with a few participants. The way he animatedly gestured with his hands made her smile. He was a natural, effortlessly drawing people in with his charm. As their eyes met, a spark ignited, and Kara felt her heart flutter.

"Good morning, sunshine!" he called out as she approached. "Ready to create something epic today?"

"Absolutely!" Kara replied. "I can't wait to see what we come up with together."

As they settled down at a large table strewn with canvases, brushes, and an array of vibrant paints, Kara felt a wave of inspiration wash over her. The atmosphere buzzed with creativity, and she couldn't help but feel grateful for the opportunity to collaborate with someone as talented as Christian.

"Alright, let's brainstorm!" Christian said, leaning closer, his energy radiating as he spoke. "What do you want to express today?"

Kara took a moment to gather her thoughts. She had always loved the beach—the way the waves danced, the colors of the sunset, the feeling of freedom that swept over her when she was near the ocean. "How about we create something that captures the essence of the ocean? The movement, the colors, the feeling of being alive in that space?"

Christian's eyes lit up. "I love that! We can do something abstract, like a wave crashing or a sunset reflecting on the water. Let's blend our styles—your nurturing touch with my adventurous flair!"

The excitement bubbled between them as they tossed around ideas, sketching out a rough composition. Kara felt a surge of confidence as they worked together, their visions intertwining into something beautiful. But as they began to paint, a shadow of doubt crept into her mind.

What if she overshadowed Christian? What if her style clashed with his? Kara bit her lip, hesitating as she dipped her brush into a swirl of blue paint. She watched as Christian effortlessly laid down bold strokes of orange and yellow on the canvas, his daring approach electrifying the piece.

"Kara, come on! Don't hold back," he encouraged, catching her gaze. "We're in this together. Your touch is what will make this special."

"Right," she replied, but the nagging self-doubt lingered. "I just... I want to make sure I'm not overpowering what you're doing."

Christian paused, a thoughtful expression crossing his face. "You know, I get it. Sometimes I worry about being too much myself. Like, what if my style is too loud? What if people don't understand my art?"

His admission caught Kara off guard. "You feel that way? But you're so talented, Christian! Your work speaks for itself."

"Thanks, but that doesn't mean I don't have my moments of insecurity," he confessed, his voice sincere. "I think we all do, even in our creative pursuits. It's part of being an artist."

Kara felt a rush of empathy for him, realizing that vulnerability was something they both shared. "I guess it's easy to forget that everyone has their struggles," she said softly. "Even the most successful artists."

"Exactly. And that's why collaboration is so powerful," Christian replied, a smile creeping back onto his face. "We can lift each other up, help each other shine."

The conversation shifted something within Kara. With a newfound sense of camaraderie, she picked up her brush, feeling the weight of her doubts lift. "Let's do this, then. Let's create something that represents both of us."

They painted side by side, laughter, and playful banter punctuating their work. Kara let herself be swept away by the joy of the moment, the colors merging on the canvas like their dreams intertwining. Each stroke felt liberating, a dance of creativity that allowed them to express their deepest selves.

As the day progressed, they began to uncover the beauty of their collaboration. The canvas transformed into a vibrant representation of the ocean—a swirling abyss of blues, greens, and sunlit yellows that seemed to pulse with life. Kara added delicate touches, capturing the gentle ebb and flow of the waves, while Christian's bold strokes created a sense of adventure and excitement.

"Look at this!" Christian exclaimed, stepping back to admire their work. "It's amazing how well our styles complement each other. You bring such depth to the piece."

Kara beamed at his praise, her heart swelling with pride. "And you bring so much energy! I never imagined we could create something this beautiful together."

As they neared completion, the atmosphere shifted. The light-heartedness of their banter gave way to a deeper connection, a recognition of their shared journey and the fears they had both faced. They stood side by side, eyes locked on the canvas, each feeling a sense of accomplishment that transcended mere artistic expression.

Kara stated, "This piece is more than just art. It's a reflection of us—our fears, our strengths, our willingness to embrace vulnerability."

Christian nodded, his gaze softening. "Exactly. It's a reminder that we don't have to face our doubts alone. We can lean on each other, and that makes all the difference."

With their hearts laid bare, Kara and Christian finished the final touches, each stroke a testament to their growing connection. As they stepped back to admire their creation, Kara felt a rush of gratitude for the journey they had embarked upon together. The canvas before them was not just a piece of art; it was a celebration of their collaboration, a symbol of the bond they had formed.

When the workshop came to an end, participants gathered to showcase their works. As Kara and Christian stood together, their hearts swelled with pride as they unveiled their joint piece to the group. The vibrant colors and dynamic forms elicited gasps of admiration, and they beamed at each other, knowing they had created something truly special.

"This is incredible!" one participant exclaimed. "You two make a fantastic team!"

As applause erupted around them, Kara felt a warmth envelop her, a sense of belonging that resonated deep within her soul. She had stepped into her dreams, faced her fears, and discovered a connection with Christian that was both exhilarating and grounding.

As the sun dipped below the horizon, painting the sky with hues of orange and pink, Kara knew that this experience was just the beginning of a beautiful journey. Together, she and Christian had created not just a piece of art but a bond that would continue to evolve—a canvas waiting to be filled with the colors of their shared dreams and aspirations.

CHAPTER 11

Waves of Change

The sun had just dipped below the horizon, casting a warm glow over Kara's small town as she drove home from the workshop. The vibrant colors they had splashed onto the canvas together filled her mind, mixing with the laughter and joy she had shared with Christian. Each brushstroke felt like a celebration of their newfound connection, and Kara couldn't wait to call Jodi and share every detail of the day.

As she pulled into her driveway, she could already envision Jodi's enthusiastic reaction. "You and Christian, huh? Tell me everything!" Jodi would say, her eyes sparkling with mischief. Kara chuckled to herself, imagining how her friend would tease her about the undeniable chemistry that had blossomed between them.

She stepped into her cozy home, the comforting scent of vanilla candles filling the air. Dropping her bag by the door, Kara grabbed her phone and dialed Jodi's number, her heart racing with anticipation.

"Hey, Kara! What's up?" Jodi answered.

"Jodi! You won't believe the day I've had!" Kara exclaimed, her excitement spilling over. "Christian and I created this amazing piece of art together. It's like we were in sync the entire time!"

"Oh, I can't wait to hear about it! Did you two hit it off?" Jodi prodded, her playful tone evident.

Kara felt her cheeks flush at the thought. "We did! It was incredible. We shared our fears, our dreams, and the art just flowed. It felt like—"

Just then, her phone buzzed, interrupting her call with Jodi as she glanced at the screen and saw her mom's name. She suddenly told Jodi she needed to take the call.

A shiver of unease washed over her as she answered, "Mom? Everything okay?"

"Kara, sweetheart," her mom's voice came through, tinged with worry. "Your father has fallen ill. He's been taken to the hospital."

The words hit Kara hard, as if a wave had crashed over her, knocking the breath out of her lungs. "What do you mean, ill? What happened?" she asked, her heart pounding.

"He started feeling unwell this morning, and when it didn't get better, we decided to take him in," her mom explained. "The doctors are doing all they can. I just thought you should know."

Kara's vision blurred as panic gripped her. "I'll be right there," she said.

She hung up and gathered her things, her mind racing. Memories of her father flooded her thoughts—the laughter they shared during beach days, the way he taught her to ride a bike, the long talks they had about life and dreams. They were so precious, and the thought of losing him felt unbearable.

As she drove to the hospital, Kara fought to keep her emotions in check. The road blurred by, her thoughts consumed with worry. What if this were serious? What if she didn't have more time with him? She recalled every moment they'd spent together—the fishing trips, the beach vacations, the simple evenings watching old movies. Each memory was a treasure, and she clung to them like lifelines.

Upon arriving at the hospital, she rushed through the familiar halls, her heart racing faster with each step. The waiting room was a cacophony of anxious families and hushed conversations, yet all she could focus on was her destination. She spotted her mom sitting in a corner, her face pale and drawn.

"Mom!" Kara rushed over, her heart aching at the sight of her mother's worried expression.

"Kara, I'm so glad you're here," her mom said. "The doctors are still assessing him. It's... It's hard to say right now."

As they waited, Kara's mind raced. "What do you think is wrong? Did he have any symptoms before this?" she pressed, needing to understand.

Her mom sighed, her eyes filling with tears. "He said he felt a bit dizzy this morning and thought it was just a cold. I didn't think it would lead to this." The pain in her mother's voice made Kara's heart ache. They both knew how strong and vibrant her dad was. He was the anchor of their family, always the one with the jokes and the hugs.

The hours dragged on, and Kara felt the weight of uncertainty hanging over them like a dark storm cloud. When a doctor finally approached, Kara's heart raced with hope.

"Ms. Kara? Mrs. Carter?" he said, his face serious but compassionate.

"Yes, how is he?" Kara asked.

"We're doing everything we can. Your father is stable for now, but we need to run more tests to determine the cause of his symptoms," the doctor explained. "He's in good hands, but I can't give you a clear answer yet."

"Stable?" Kara whispered, trying to cling to the glimmer of hope in his words. "What does that mean? Can we see him?"

"Of course, just a moment," he replied, gesturing for them to follow him.

As they entered her dad's hospital room, Kara's heart sank. He looked so small and vulnerable lying there, connected to machines that beeped softly. She rushed to his side, taking his hand in hers.

"Dad," she whispered. "It's me."

His eyes fluttered open, and though he looked pale, his smile was still warm. "Hey there, kiddo," he said, his voice raspy but filled with love. "What are you doing here?"

"I came as soon as I heard. Mom told me you weren't feeling well," Kara said, fighting back tears. "I was so worried."

"Don't worry about me," he said gently, squeezing her hand. "I'll be fine. Just need some rest."

A lump formed in Kara's throat as she looked at her dad, feeling an overwhelming rush of emotions. How could she not worry? He had always been her rock, her guiding star. "I love you, Dad," she said.

"I love you too, sweetheart," he replied, a soft smile gracing his lips. "You're my brave girl."

As the conversation continued, Kara tried to stay strong, but in the back of her mind, the fear loomed large. She wanted to talk to him about everything—the memories they shared, the dreams she had for the future, and how much he meant to her. But she couldn't shake the feeling that time was slipping away.

When her mom stepped outside for a moment, Kara felt a rush of frustration. "Why didn't you tell me it was this serious?" she whispered, her emotions spilling over. "You should've called me earlier!"

"I didn't want to worry you, Kara," her mom replied defensively, her eyes shining with tears. "I thought it was just a minor issue. I thought—"

"Thought what? That we could just brush it off? This is Dad we're talking about! He's always been there for us. We need to be there for him now!" Kara's voice rose, frustration boiling over as the weight of the situation pressed down on her.

"Yelling at me won't change anything," her mom said. "I'm scared, too. We need to stay calm for him."

Kara took a deep breath, feeling the tension in the air. "I know. I just... I can't bear the thought of losing him," she said softly, her anger fading into despair. They stood there, the weight of uncertainty hanging over them, both afraid to confront the reality of what might happen.

The air felt heavy with unspoken fears as they returned to her dad's room. Kara took his hand again, feeling the warmth of his skin. "You're going to get better, right?" she asked.

"Of course I am," he replied, his voice steady despite the situation. "You know me—I'm not going anywhere. I've still got a lot of fishing stories to tell you."

Kara smiled through her tears, clinging to the hope in his words. She couldn't imagine a world without him. As they sat together, sharing stories and laughter, she realized this was what mattered most—making every moment count, embracing vulnerability, and cherishing the love that connected them.

CHAPTER 12

Colors of Hope

The fluorescent lights of the hospital flickered overhead, casting a sterile glow across the room where Kara sat, her hand still clasped tightly around her father's. The rhythmic beeping of the machines punctuated the silence, each sound a poignant reminder of life's fragility. Outside the window, the world continued on, blissfully unaware of the turmoil within these walls. Kara's heart felt heavy as she glanced at her father, his face pale against the stark white of the hospital sheets.

"Do you remember the summer we went camping at Lake Pine?" Kara's mother asked. She perched on the edge of the bed, brushing a stray hair from her husband's forehead. "You caught that enormous trout, and we cooked it over the fire. It was the best meal we ever had, wasn't it?"

Kara smiled through her worry. "Dad, you were so proud of that catch. You kept showing it off to everyone at the camp."

Her father's eyes fluttered open, a hint of color returning to his cheeks as he replied, "I still have the picture somewhere. You two were so impressed. It was an all-time great catch."

As they reminisced, the memories poured forth like a cascading waterfall. They spoke of beach days filled with laughter, sandcastle competitions, and the time they had gotten lost on a hiking trail only to discover a hidden waterfall. Each story was a thread woven into the fabric of their family, a reminder of the love that had always bound them together.

Suddenly, the door creaked open, and a nurse walked in, her smile warm and reassuring. "Good morning, everyone. I just wanted to let you know that we're preparing your husband for surgery shortly. We need to identify the cause of his symptoms."

Kara felt her heart drop. "Tests? What kind?" she asked, her voice tinged with anxiety.

"Just exploratory to see what's going on with his heart, I understand it's a stressful time, but the doctors are doing everything they can to get to the bottom of this," the nurse replied, her tone professional yet empathetic.

Her mother nodded, but Kara felt a wave of helplessness wash over her. "What if it's something serious?" she whispered, her voice barely audible.

The nurse placed a comforting hand on Kara's shoulder. "It's understandable to feel this way, but worrying won't change anything. You need to focus on being here for him."

As she left the room, Kara's mind raced. She felt a churning mix of fear and frustration. Sitting idly by while her father battled something unknown felt unbearable. The thought of losing him was a weight she couldn't bear.

"I need to do something," Kara said suddenly, her voice firm. "I can't just sit here and wait."

Her mother looked at her, concern etched on her face. "What do you mean?"

"I want to create something—a mural, maybe," Kara said, her thoughts forming a plan. "To honor Dad's love for art and all our shared adventures. It could bring some light and color to this place."

Her mother hesitated, glancing at her husband, who had drifted back to sleep. "Kara, I don't know if that's such a good idea. This is a hospital; it's not exactly the right setting for art."

"Why not?" Kara countered, her passion ignited. "Hospitals are filled with people who are scared and worried. What if we could bring a little joy, a little color, to this sterile environment? Something to lift everyone's spirits?"

After a moment of contemplation, her mother nodded slowly. "If that's what you want to do, I'll support you. Just promise me you'll be careful."

"I promise," Kara said, her heart racing with excitement.

With newfound determination, Kara left her father's room and made her way to the hospital administration office. Her mind buzzed with ideas as she requested permission to create the mural. To her surprise, the administrator was receptive to the idea, recognizing the potential for art to uplift patients and families alike.

"Just fill out some paperwork, and we can discuss logistics. I think it's a wonderful initiative," the administrator said, her enthusiasm making Kara's heart soar.

Once the plans were approved, Kara felt a surge of energy. She called Christian, knowing he would be the perfect partner for this project. "Hey, Christian! I need your help with something important," she said, her voice filled with urgency.

"Anything for you, Kara. What's up?" he replied, his tone casual yet attentive.

"I want to create a mural at the hospital where Dad is. Something colorful and hopeful. Can you come help me?"

"Of course! I'd love to. I'll grab some supplies and head over," Christian said, his excitement palpable even through the phone.

Within hours, Christian arrived at the hospital, a large canvas-covered van parked outside. He jumped out, his athletic frame full of energy as he waved to Kara. "Let's make this place pop!"

Together, they gathered supplies—paints, brushes, and vibrant fabrics. Kara felt a sense of purpose as they moved through the hospital, gathering support from other families and patients. They shared the plan, inviting anyone who wanted to contribute to join them.

"Art is for everyone!" Christian proclaimed, his enthusiasm infectious.

Slowly, people began to gather, drawn in by the idea of creating something beautiful. Children, parents, and even some hospital staff joined in, each person adding their unique touch to the mural. Kara watched in awe as the sterile walls transformed before her eyes, becoming a vibrant tapestry of colors and images that represented hope, resilience, and the shared experiences of the families in the hospital.

As they painted, Kara felt lighter, the worries about her father momentarily fading into the background. They painted scenes of fishing trips, beach days, and starry nights—each brushstroke a celebration of life and love. Christian's laughter filled the air, and Kara found herself smiling as they worked side by side, creating something that would honor her father's spirit.

Hours passed, and the mural began to take shape. It was a breathtaking collage of memories, a visual representation of the bond they shared as a family. Kara felt a sense of pride in what they were creating together, knowing her father would love it.

Finally, as they stepped back to admire their work, Kara felt a surge of hope. "It's beautiful," she whispered, her heart swelling with emotion.

Just then, her phone buzzed, and she glanced down to see a message from her mother. "The surgery went well. They're about to bring Dad to recovery."

Kara's heart raced with relief and joy. "He's going to be okay," she said, tears of happiness streaming down her cheeks.

With Christian by her side, she couldn't help but feel that this mural was more than just paint on a wall; it was a symbol of love and resilience, a testament to the strength of family. They had transformed a place of fear into one of hope, and as she closed her eyes for a moment, Kara envisioned her father standing before the mural, a smile on his face, proud of the legacy they had created together.

CHAPTER 13

The Tapestry of Connection

The vibrant colors of the mural seemed to dance in the bright lighting of the hospital corridor, each brushstroke a testament to the creativity and love that had been poured into it. Kara stood back, her heart swelling with pride as she admired the collective work of so many hands. Christian stood beside her, his eyes sparkling with excitement.

"Can you believe we pulled this off?" he said, clapping his hands together, his voice brimming with energy. "This place is practically glowing now!"

Kara laughed, her joy bubbling over. "I never thought we'd have so many people join us! I mean, look at it! It's more than I could have ever imagined." She gestured to the mural, which showcased scenes of family adventures—hiking, camping, beach days, and even a whimsical underwater world filled with fish and coral, a nod to her love for snorkeling.

"I think we've created something that can make a difference for people here," Christian said, his tone sincere. "Art has that power, you know? It can lift spirits, spark memories, and bring people together."

Just then, Kara's mother appeared at the end of the hallway, her face radiant and full of relief. "Kara! Christian!" she called, rushing towards them. "The surgery went wonderfully! Your father is awake in recovery!"

Kara felt a rush of emotions—relief, joy, and an overwhelming sense of gratitude. She dashed toward her mother, enveloping her in a warm embrace. "Oh, Mom! I'm so glad to hear that! How is he?"

"Groggy but doing well," her mother replied, pulling back with tears of happiness glimmering in her eyes. "He's asking for you."

"Let's go see him!" Kara said, her heart racing with anticipation. She turned to Christian, who flashed a reassuring smile.

"Let's do it. I'll carry the paintbrushes if you need me to," he said, winking at her.

Together, they made their way to the recovery room, Kara's heart pounding with hope. The sterile smell of antiseptic mixed with the scent of fresh paint from the mural as they approached her father's room. Kara could hear the soft beeping of monitors, a comforting rhythm that reminded her of the fragility of life, but she felt a new strength within her.

As they entered, Kara's father lay there, his eyes fluttering open, a hint of confusion still lingering in them. "Kara?" he whispered, his voice hoarse yet warm.

"Dad!" Kara rushed to his side, grasping his hand tightly. "I'm here! You did it; you're going to be okay!"

He smiled weakly, his eyes scanning the room until they landed on the colorful mural that adorned the wall. Kara followed his gaze, her heart racing as she wondered what he would think.

The sight of the mural brought a tear to his eye, and he blinked in amazement. "You did this?" he asked, his voice thick with emotion.

"We all did!" Kara exclaimed. "Christian and I started it, but so many people joined in. It's a celebration of all our family adventures!"

He let out a soft chuckle, a sound that filled Kara with warmth. "It's beautiful, just like you."

"Dad, you're going to make me cry," she said, wiping a tear from her cheek. "I just wanted to bring some brightness to this place, especially for you."

Her father shifted slightly, his expression serious yet tender. "You know, Kara, art has always been a part of our family. It tells our story and captures our memories. Your mother and I used to take you to that little art fair by the beach every summer. Remember the time you painted that horrible seagull?"

Kara laughed, the warmth of nostalgia flooding over her. "I thought it was a masterpiece! Until you pointed out that it looked more like a chicken than a seagull."

"Exactly! But you were so proud of it. It reminded us of how important it is to express ourselves, no matter how messy it may seem," he said, a proud smile spreading across his face.

"Dad, that's why I wanted to create this mural. I wanted to honor that spirit, to remind everyone here that art can heal, even in the darkest times." Kara glanced at Christian, who nodded in agreement, his eyes shining with admiration.

"Art is a reflection of our experiences," her father continued, his voice steady. "It connects us, strengthens our bonds, and reminds us of who we are. You've done an incredible job, Kara. The mural is a testament to that."

"Thanks, Dad," she said, feeling a rush of warmth. "I couldn't have done it without Christian and everyone else who helped."

"Speaking of which," Christian interjected, leaning against the wall casually, "I think we should have a little celebration once you're feeling up to it.

Her father nodded, a spark igniting in his eyes. "That sounds wonderful! I'd love to have a family get-together for dinner after I get out of the hospital."

Kara felt a wave of excitement wash over her. "It'll be a great way to celebrate your recovery and the community we've built here," she said, her heart light.

Just then, her mother stepped forward, her smile radiant. "I think that's an excellent idea."

"Absolutely!" Kara said, her mind racing with plans for the celebration.

As her father reminisced about the past, he remembered a masterpiece that Kara had created as a child.

"Don't forget about the seagull!" her father said, chuckling through his grogginess. "I want to see that masterpiece again!"

Kara laughed, her heart full. "I promise to hang it right next to the mural, Dad. You'll be the judge."

As they continued to talk and share stories, a deep connection began to form among them. It was as if the mural had become a thread weaving all their lives together, reminding them of the love that had always existed, even in the midst of uncertainty.

"Kara," her father said, his voice softening, "never underestimate the power of art, especially in times like these. It can be a bridge between our hearts, a way to communicate emotions that sometimes feel too big to express."

"I know, Dad," Kara replied, her voice steady. "That's exactly why I wanted to do this. I wanted everyone to feel connected, to see that we're not alone in our struggles."

Her father smiled, his eyes glistening with pride. "You've done that and more. You've created a tapestry of love, hope, and resilience. I can't wait to see how this journey unfolds for you."

Kara felt a warmth radiate from her father's words, a sense of reassurance that everything would be okay. As they continued to share stories and laughter, she realized that this moment, this connection, was the true essence of family. It was a reminder that love and creativity could indeed heal even the deepest wounds, stitching together the fabric of their lives in a way that would last forever.

CHAPTER 14

Colors of Healing

A week had passed, and the sun streamed through the large windows of the hospital, illuminating the bright mural that had become a beacon of hope. The vibrant colors danced against the sterile walls, showcasing the love and creativity that had poured into it. Kara stood before it, her heart swelling with pride and purpose. Today marked a new chapter, one that would unite patients and families in the spirit of healing through art.

"Are you ready for this?" Christian asked, his voice playful and filled with energy as he adjusted the easels in the room. His athletic build moved gracefully, and the excitement in his eyes reflected the potential of what they were about to undertake.

Kara took a deep breath, a mix of anticipation and nerves stirring within her. "Absolutely! I just hope everyone is as excited as we are."

"I think they will be," Christian replied, flashing his charming smile. "Art has a way of bringing people together. Just look at our mural! It's already made a difference for your dad, right?"

"You're right," Kara said, her mind drifting back to the warmth in her father's eyes when he first saw the mural. "And I can't wait to see how it touches others too."

As they prepared for the art therapy workshop, Kara's mother bustled around the room, arranging supplies and making sure everything was in order. Her cheerful demeanor radiated warmth, and she frequently glanced at Kara with a knowing smile. "This is such a wonderful idea, dear. Bringing the community together through creativity is truly a gift."

"Thanks, Mom," Kara replied, her heart full. "I just want to create a space where people can express themselves freely."

"Speaking of expression, have you seen Jodi?" Christian asked, glancing toward the entrance. "I thought she was coming to help."

Just then, Jodi appeared, her presence as vibrant as the mural itself. Dressed in a flowing sundress adorned with colorful patterns, she exuded an aura of freedom and adventure. "Sorry I'm late! I had to pick up some extra supplies," she announced, holding up a bag filled with paintbrushes and canvas boards.

"Perfect timing!" Kara exclaimed, rushing over to give her friend a warm hug. "We're just getting started. Are you ready to inspire some creativity?"

"Always!" Jodi said, her eyes sparkling with mischief. "Let's make this a day to remember!"

With everyone in place, Kara gathered the small group of patients and their families who had signed up for the workshop. The room was filled with a mix of nervous energy and excited chatter as people exchanged hopeful glances. Kara felt a surge of adrenaline; she was about to embark on something meaningful.

"Welcome, everyone! I'm Kara, and this is Christian and Jodi," she began, her businesslike tone softening into a more inviting melody. "Today, we're going to explore the healing power of art. We want you to express yourselves, share your stories, and connect with one another."

Christian stepped forward, his charismatic demeanor lighting up the room. "And don't worry; this isn't about being perfect. It's about having fun and letting your creativity flow! So, let's get started with some games to break the ice!"

Kara smiled as she watched Christian effortlessly engage the participants, leading them in a fun, lighthearted game that involved passing around a paintbrush while sharing their names and favorite colors. Laughter erupted, melting away the initial tension in the air.

Once the ice was broken, Kara gathered everyone around a large canvas set up in the center of the room. "Now, let's create something beautiful together, inspired by the mural! Each of you can add your own touch, whether it's a handprint, a drawing, or even a word that resonates with you."

As participants approached the canvas, Kara noticed her father sitting in the corner, a warm smile on his face. He had recovered well enough to join the workshop, determined to share his own journey of healing. Kara felt a swell of gratitude; he was the embodiment of resilience, and she knew that his stories could inspire others.

"Dad, do you want to share your story?" Kara called out.

He nodded, shifting slightly in his seat. "I'd be happy to," he replied, his voice steady yet filled with emotion. "I know what it's like to feel lost and uncertain. After my surgery, I found myself reflecting on all the times art has played a role in my life. It allowed me to express feelings that I couldn't put into words. I remember painting with Kara when she was little. Those moments were some of the best times we shared."

Kara's heart warmed at the memory, the picture of her father sitting beside her, surrounded by splatters of paint and laughter.

"Art helped me heal, not just physically but emotionally too," her father continued, looking around the room. "I encourage all of you to embrace this opportunity. Don't be afraid to let your feelings out. Whether it's joy, sorrow, or hope, paint it! Let's create something that reflects our collective journeys."

The room fell silent for a moment, each person absorbing his words. Then, a young girl with bright eyes stepped forward, a paintbrush trembling slightly in her hand.

"Can I start?" she asked, her voice soft yet brave.

"Of course!" Kara encouraged, stepping aside to give her space.

The girl approached the canvas, dipping her brush into a vibrant shade of blue. As she began to paint, Kara felt a wave of inspiration wash over the group. One by one, participants started to add their own colors, their individual stories unfolding across the canvas.

Christian moved around the room, checking in on each table where families were painting, joining in laughter, and sharing anecdotes. He pulled out a box of glitter, suggesting they add some sparkle to their masterpieces, and soon the air was filled with excitement and creativity.

Jodi floated around, engaging with the children. Her witty remarks and playful banter inspired their imaginations. "What if we painted a dragon that breathes rainbows?" she suggested, and the children squealed with delight, eagerly picking up their brushes.

As Kara observed the scene before her, she felt a profound sense of connection among everyone. It was more than just a workshop; it was a celebration of vulnerability and shared experiences. Each stroke of paint on the canvas was a testament to their stories—stories of struggle, healing, love, and resilience.

Kara wandered back to where her father sat, admiring his expression as he watched the interactions. "Dad, I'm so glad you're here," she said softly.

"Me too, Kara. This is beautiful," he replied. "You've created a safe space for everyone where they can express themselves without judgment. That's truly special."

Just then, a boy named Ethan, who had been quietly observing, approached Kara with wide eyes. "Can I paint a big sun?" he asked, his voice filled with determination.

"Of course, Ethan! The sun can represent hope," Kara replied, guiding him to the canvas. "How about you paint it right here?" She pointed to a blank space that needed some brightness.

As Ethan took his place, Kara watched him carefully paint the sun, his concentration evident. The bright yellows and oranges began to take form, and Kara felt a swell of emotion. Each participant contributed a piece of themselves to this collaborative artwork, weaving their stories into a tapestry of healing.

Hours passed, and soon the canvas transformed into a vibrant explosion of colors, each stroke representing a shared moment and a connection made. As they painted, laughter and conversation flowed freely, unexpected friendships blossoming among participants, creating a sense of community that filled the room with warmth.

When the workshop finally came to a close, Kara gathered everyone for a final moment. "Thank you all for sharing your stories and creativity today. This canvas is now a symbol of our journey together—a testament to the healing power of art."

Christian stepped forward, his eyes sparkling. "And remember, even when life gets tough, you can always pick up a brush and create something beautiful."

As Kara looked around the room, she saw smiles, laughter, and a sense of belonging that had emerged from the workshop. The colors of healing had united them, and she knew that this would be a day they would all remember—a day where creativity had woven their hearts together in a way that would last long after the paint had dried.

CHAPTER 15

Whispers of Love

The next evening, Kara, Christian, and Jodi got together to discuss their idea of creating another art therapy session for the community. The clinking of glasses and the gentle hum of laughter filled the air at the cozy local restaurant where Kara, Christian, and Jodi had gathered. The walls were adorned with vibrant artwork, each piece a testament to the creativity that thrived in their small community. Kara felt a surge of excitement as she settled into her seat, ready to dive deep into planning their next event.

"Okay, team," Kara said, her tone professional yet infused with warmth. "Let's come up with a theme that captures the essence of what we want to achieve in our next workshop."

Christian leaned back in his chair, his athletic build relaxed yet attentive. His eyes sparkled with enthusiasm as he flipped through a notebook filled with sketches and ideas. "How about something adventurous? Like 'Art from the Heart' or 'Creative Journeys'?"

Jodi, her mischievous nature shining through, chimed in with a grin. "Or we could go for something more daring, like 'Art

Unleashed!' Think about it: we could encourage everyone to break free from their comfort zones."

Kara chuckled, appreciating Jodi's spirited approach. "That's definitely a fun idea, but I want to focus on something deeper this time. I want to create a space where people feel safe to express their vulnerabilities."

Just then, Kara's phone buzzed, drawing her attention. She picked it up and smiled when she saw it was a message from Ethan's mother. After the last workshop, she'd exchanged a few words with the woman, who seemed genuinely grateful for the experience they had created. With a sense of anticipation, Kara opened the message.

As she read the heartfelt words, her heart swelled. Ethan's mother expressed how the workshop had helped her son open up about his fears, something he had struggled with for a long time. The letter was filled with gratitude, acknowledging that the creative outlet had allowed Ethan to express his emotions in a way he hadn't been able to before.

"Wow," Kara said softly. "This is incredible. Ethan's mother wrote me a letter about how much the workshop impacted him. He's starting to talk about his feelings more openly."

Christian leaned forward, intrigued. "That's amazing! It sounds like what we're doing really matters."

"Yes!" Kara exclaimed, her passion igniting. "This is exactly why we need to keep going. I think we should base our next session around this idea of courage—the courage to express oneself, the courage to confront fears. How about we call it Voices of Courage?"

"Perfect!" Jodi said, her eyes brightening. "It gives everyone a chance to share their stories and feelings. We can even invite participants to create pieces that represent their own courage."

Christian nodded in agreement, his expression thoughtful. "And we could incorporate a segment where everyone shares their stories. It could be incredibly powerful and inspiring."

As Kara jotted down the ideas, the trio brainstormed various activities for the workshop, melding their unique perspectives into a cohesive plan. They envisioned a space where participants could explore not just visual art but also storytelling, possibly through poetry or spoken word. Their enthusiasm was palpable, and Kara felt a sense of camaraderie blooming among them.

The evening rolled on, filled with laughter, creative sparks, and the occasional debate over what materials to use. Each suggestion was met with excitement, and Kara couldn't help but feel grateful for the partnership they were forging.

As they wrapped up their planning, Christian leaned back in his chair, a playful glint in his eye. "So, what do you think, Kara? Are we ready to take on the world with Voices of Courage?"

Kara smiled, her heart fluttering at the sight of his confidence. "I think we are! But it's going to take a lot of work, and we'll need to rally the community's support."

Jodi chimed in, "We should reach out to local businesses for sponsorship or even donations of art supplies. This workshop needs to be as accessible as possible."

"Great idea!" Kara agreed, her mind racing with possibilities. "We'll create a flyer to promote it and start spreading the word. I can reach out to my contacts at the doctor's office for any families who might be interested."

As the night drew to a close, they exchanged ideas on how to make the event truly special. The conversation flowed seamlessly, punctuated by laughter and camaraderie. Kara felt a warmth blooming in her chest—a connection not only to her friends but also to the purpose they were working towards.

After leaving the restaurant, Kara and Christian walked side by side through the moonlit streets, the cool night air filled with the scent of blooming jasmine. Kara loved these moments with

Christian—the way the world seemed to fade away, leaving only the two of them and the electric energy that sparked between them.

"So, what's next for us?" Christian asked, a hint of mischief in his voice. "Do you think we'll make this a monthly thing?"

"I hope so," Kara replied, her heart racing. "I want to keep building on what we've started. It feels like we're creating something meaningful."

They paused at a crosswalk, and Christian turned to face her, his expression softening. "You know, I've enjoyed every moment we've spent together planning these workshops. It's more than just art for me; it's about the connections we're building."

Kara felt her cheeks flush at his words, the sincerity in his gaze sending butterflies fluttering in her stomach. "I feel the same way. It's so rewarding to see how our ideas can make a difference."

As the light turned green, they continued walking, the conversation flowing effortlessly. They shared stories about their childhoods, their dreams, and their fears, each revelation deepening their bond. Kara found herself drawn to Christian's adventurous spirit while he seemed captivated by her nurturing heart.

When they finally arrived at Kara's apartment, the atmosphere shifted. The lighthearted banter gave way to a deeper silence charged with unspoken feelings. Kara's heart raced as she unlocked the door, letting them into the cozy space that felt like a sanctuary.

"Want to grab a drink?" she offered, trying to maintain her composure.

"Nah, I think I'd rather just talk," Christian replied, his voice low and intimate.

They settled on the couch, the soft glow of the lamp casting a warm light over them. Kara could feel the tension between them, a magnetic pull that was growing stronger by the second. They began discussing their relationship, the connection they had formed, and how it intertwined with their shared passion for helping others.

"I didn't expect to find someone like you, Kara," Christian confessed, his gaze steady. "You bring out a side of me I didn't know existed."

Kara's heart swelled at his words. "I feel the same way. You challenge me and inspire me, and I love that we're on this journey together."

Their eyes locked, and time seemed to stand still. Kara felt a rush of emotions—excitement, fear, and an overwhelming sense of belonging. Christian leaned closer, his breath warm against her skin, and she could no longer resist the pull.

Before she knew it, their lips met in a soft, tentative kiss that quickly deepened, igniting a fire within them both. Kara melted into him, her hands finding their way to his hair as the world around them faded away.

The kiss spoke volumes—of connection, of passion, and of the journey they were embarking on together. The evening unfolded into a whirlwind of shared breaths, tender touches, and whispered confessions as they lost themselves in the magic of the moment.

In the heat of their embrace, Kara felt a sense of freedom and courage, as if the very act of loving Christian was an art form in itself. Their bodies moved together, a dance of exploration and intimacy that filled the space between them with warmth and light.

As the night wore on, they discovered not only the beauty of their connection but also the depths of their desires. Each moment felt like a brushstroke on a canvas, painting a picture of love, trust, and shared dreams that would linger long after the night had passed. As they said their goodbyes with one last passionate kiss, Kara did not want the evening to end, but she knew she had to go to work in the morning.

CHAPTER 16

Ripples of Courage

The sun peeked through the curtains of Kara's apartment, casting gentle rays across the room and spilling warmth onto her face. She awoke to the soft chirping of birds outside, a sweet serenade that accompanied the fluttering of her heart from the night before. The memories of the kiss with Christian played on repeat in her mind, each replay sparking a new thrill of excitement. Kara sat up, running her fingers through her hair, and let out a content sigh.

As she prepared for work, her mind danced between thoughts of her job at the doctor's office and the upcoming Voices of Courage workshop. She felt a surge of purpose coursing through her veins, eager to bring the idea to life. Kara loved her work, but there was something exhilarating about the prospect of helping others express their vulnerabilities through art. It filled her with a sense of fulfillment that was hard to replicate.

After a quick shower and a healthy breakfast, Kara slipped on her favorite blouse—a soft, ocean-blue color that complemented her warm skin tone. She took a moment to admire herself in the mirror, a smile creeping onto her lips. "Today is going to be a good day," she murmured to herself, feeling the weight of anticipation mixed with joy.

The drive to work was serene, the morning sun casting a golden hue over the bustling streets. Kara turned up the radio and sang along to her favorite tunes, her spirits buoyed by the memories of the previous night. As she parked her car and walked into the doctor's office, she took a deep breath, ready to tackle the day ahead.

The office was buzzing with the usual activity as she greeted the staff and settled into her role. Kara loved the dynamic energy of the place, where she could help people navigate their health journeys. As she organized files and prepared for the day's appointments, her phone buzzed on her desk, interrupting her thoughts.

It was an unfamiliar number, but something urged her to answer. "Hello?" she said, her voice warm and inviting.

"Hi, is this Kara?" a hesitant voice replied. It was Ethan's mother, and Kara instantly recognized the concern woven into her tone.

"Yes, it is! How can I help you?" Kara asked, her heart tightening at the thought of Ethan.

"I hope I'm not bothering you. I wanted to talk about Ethan. He's been struggling more with anxiety lately. He mentioned he's feeling overwhelmed, and I'm worried about him. I thought maybe you could help us find a way for him to express what he's feeling."

Kara's heart ached at the mention of Ethan's struggles. She remembered how much he had blossomed during their last workshop, and the thought of him feeling lost sent ripples of concern through her. "Of course! I'm so sorry to hear that. I think incorporating a segment on mental health awareness into our workshop could be incredibly beneficial—not just for Ethan but for everyone. It could create a safe space for participants to share their experiences."

"That sounds wonderful! I think it would help him to know he's not alone," Ethan's mother replied.

Kara felt a sense of determination wash over her. "I'll reach out to my friends, Christian and Jodi, and we'll brainstorm some ideas. I'm sure we can create something meaningful that resonates with everyone."

"Thank you so much, Kara. I appreciate your support. It means a lot," Ethan's mother said with genuine gratitude before they exchanged goodbyes.

As Kara hung up, her mind raced with possibilities. The idea of integrating mental health awareness into Voices of Courage felt like the missing piece of the puzzle. It would not only provide a platform for art but also address the emotional struggles that so many faced. She quickly texted Christian and Jodi to share the news.

"Hey, guys! Just got off the phone with Ethan's mom. We need to incorporate a segment on mental health awareness into Voices of Courage. Let's meet up later to brainstorm ideas! I think it could help!"

In a matter of moments, responses flooded in.

Christian replied immediately: "Absolutely! I'm all in. Let's make this workshop unforgettable!"

Jodi's message followed suit: "Love that idea! Can't wait to brainstorm!"

Feeling invigorated, Kara dove back into her work, her heart light and energized. Each patient who walked through the door felt like an opportunity to make a difference, and she greeted them with renewed enthusiasm. The clock ticked by, but her thoughts frequently drifted to the workshop and the impact it could have on the community.

Later that afternoon, Kara's mind was still buzzing with ideas when she received a call from Christian. "Hey, Kara! Just finished my workout. Are we still on for brainstorming later?"

Kara replied, "Yes! I'm so excited to share the concept with you."

"Great! How about we meet at that little café down the street? I could use a caffeine boost."

"Perfect! I'll see you there in a bit," Kara said before hanging up, her heart fluttering at the thought of seeing him again.

As she arrived at the café, Kara spotted Christian sitting at a table outside, his athletic frame relaxed yet alert as he scanned the menu.

The warm afternoon sun illuminated his features, making him look even more handsome. Kara felt a rush of warmth spread through her as she approached him.

"Hey there!" she greeted, taking a seat across from him.

"Hey! You look radiant today," Christian said, his voice light and teasing. "Must be the glow from last night, huh?"

Kara felt her cheeks flush at his playful comment. "I think it's the excitement about our workshop! I just spoke with Ethan's mother, and we're going to integrate a mental health awareness segment. I think it's going to be amazing."

"Wow, that's awesome! It makes perfect sense given how important it is to talk about emotions and mental health," Christian replied, leaning forward with genuine interest. "What do you have in mind?"

"Well, I thought we could create a space for participants to share their stories about anxiety or fear—maybe have them express it through art, poetry, or even spoken word," Kara suggested, her passion evident in her voice. "We can also invite a local mental health professional to speak briefly about the importance of expressing emotions and seeking help."

"Brilliant!" Christian exclaimed, his eyes lighting up. "That could really resonate with people and encourage them to open up. We could even have some art supplies available for those who want to create something during that segment."

"Yes! And we could provide resources for local mental health services so people know where to turn for help," Kara added, feeling the excitement building between them.

Just then, Jodi arrived, her vibrant energy instantly filling the space. "Hey, team! What's the buzz?" she asked, her smile infectious.

Kara and Christian exchanged glances, their enthusiasm mirroring each other. "We were just brainstorming ideas for integrating mental health awareness into Voices of Courage," Kara explained.

"Perfect! I love it! This is going to take the workshop to another level," Jodi said, her eyes sparkling. "Let's make a list of activities we can include and think about how we can market this to the community."

The three friends spent the afternoon brainstorming, their ideas flowing freely as they crafted a vision for the workshop. They discussed potential art activities that would encourage self-expression, such as creating courage-themed paintings or crafting personal affirmations. They even toyed with the idea of having a Courage Wall where participants could display their work, a visual testament to the power of vulnerability.

As they worked, Kara found herself stealing glances at Christian, captivated by his passion and enthusiasm. The way he engaged with their ideas only deepened her feelings, and she felt warmth spread through her every time their eyes met.

Finally, as the sun began to dip below the horizon, casting a warm glow around them, Jodi clapped her hands together. "Okay, I think we've got a solid plan! Let's take it to the next level and make sure we promote it well. I'll talk to a few businesses about sponsorships and supplies."

"I can handle the flyer," Kara offered, her mind already racing with design ideas. "And I'll reach out to the mental health professional I know."

Christian chuckled, his joyful demeanor shining through. "And I'll be your muscle for setting up the event and making sure we have everything we need. Teamwork makes the dream work, right?"

"Absolutely!" Kara replied, her heart swelling with gratitude for the partnership they had formed.

As they packed up to leave, Kara felt a sense of accomplishment wash over her. They had not only crafted a meaningful workshop plan, but they had also solidified their friendship and connection in the process. The air was filled with possibility, and she couldn't wait to see how Voices of Courage would unfold.

But as they stepped outside, the evening air was crisp, and Kara found herself reflecting on her growing feelings for Christian. The way he understood her passion, supported her ideas, and shared in the excitement of their work only deepened the bond they were forming.

Little did she know, Christian was grappling with similar thoughts. As he walked beside her, he couldn't shake the feeling that their connection had evolved into something deeper. The workshop was more than just a project; it was a canvas for their emotions, their dreams, and the courage they were both learning to embrace.

As they parted ways that evening, Kara felt a sense of anticipation building within her—a mix of excitement for the workshop and the growing bond with Christian that she couldn't ignore. Each ripple of courage they created would not only touch the lives of others but also illuminate the path for their own journey together.

CHAPTER 17

The Canvas of Courage

Kara sat at her kitchen table, a cascade of papers strewn before her, each representing a vibrant idea for the upcoming Voices of Courage workshop. She sipped her coffee, the warmth of the mug grounding her as she flipped through her notes. Her mind was alive with possibilities: art projects, discussions on mental health, and ways to create a sense of community among participants. The thrill of it all sent a rush of excitement through her veins.

As she brainstormed, her laptop chimed, signaling a new email. She clicked it open, and her heart raced as she scanned the message from the local art gallery.

"Dear Kara,

We are excited to offer you the opportunity to host the Voices of Courage workshop at our gallery! We believe your vision aligns perfectly with our mission to promote community engagement through art. Please let us know a suitable time to discuss the details.

Looking forward to collaborating with you!

Best,

Samantha"

Kara felt as if she had just been gifted a golden ticket. The art gallery was a beautiful and inspiring space, and the idea of hosting the workshop there filled her with glee. She could already envision the walls adorned with artwork created by participants, each piece a testament to their courage and creativity.

With a wide grin, she quickly typed a reply, confirming her interest and suggesting a meeting for the following week. As she hit send, a wave of exhilaration washed over her. This was the breakthrough she had hoped for, and it felt like the universe was aligning in support of her vision.

Just then, her phone buzzed with a text from Jodi, brightening her already buoyant mood.

"Hey, superstar! How's the workshop planning going? Need a cheerleader?"

Kara chuckled and replied, "You just might be needed! I have some exciting news to share!"

Moments later, Jodi arrived, her energy filling the room. "Alright, spill it!" she said, plopping down in a chair across from Kara, her eyes sparkling with curiosity.

"The gallery wants to host our workshop!" Kara exclaimed, unable to contain her excitement. "Can you believe it? We're going to be in a real art space!"

Jodi clapped her hands together, her laughter ringing out. "That's amazing! I always knew you had a talent for bringing people together. This is going to elevate the workshop to a whole new level!"

After chatting about the details, Kara felt a surge of inspiration and purpose. She was eager to dive into the planning, but part of her heart lingered on the thought of Christian. She couldn't wait to tell him about the gallery's offer, envisioning his reaction and the way his eyes would light up with enthusiasm.

Meanwhile, across town, Christian sat on his apartment balcony, staring at a half-finished canvas. The sun was setting, casting a warm glow that mingled with the colors on his palette. But despite the beauty surrounding him, he felt a heavy weight pressing down on his chest. He had always been open with his emotions in his art, but when it came to expressing those feelings verbally, especially to Kara, he faltered.

"Ugh, why is this so hard?" he muttered to himself, running a hand through his tousled hair.

He had been wrestling with his feelings for Kara since their kiss, grappling with the fear of vulnerability and the risk of rejection.

He picked up his phone, contemplating reaching out to Jodi. She had always been the one to encourage him to express himself, and perhaps she could help him articulate his feelings toward Kara. After a moment's hesitation, he sent her a message.

"Hey, can we meet up? I could use some advice on something... kind of personal."

Jodi's response was immediate. "Of course! I'll swing by in an hour. Can't wait to hear what's brewing in that artist's mind of yours!"

As Christian waited, he paced the room, his thoughts swirling. He envisioned Kara's bright smile, the way her laughter lit up a room, and the undeniable connection they shared. But how could he possibly tell her that he loved her? What if it changed everything?

When Jodi arrived, she didn't waste any time. "Alright, spill it! What's going on? You seem a bit... intense."

Christian sighed, running a hand through his hair again. "It's about Kara. I really like her, Jodi. Like, I think I'm falling for her, but I'm scared to say anything. What if it ruins our friendship or the workshop?"

Jodi leaned forward, her expression serious but encouraging. "Christian, feelings are natural, and keeping them bottled up isn't going to help anyone. You've already taken a huge step by recognizing what you feel. What's holding you back?"

"I'm just not great with words, you know? I can paint my emotions, but when it comes to talking about them, I freeze up," Christian admitted, his frustration evident.

"Maybe you don't need to get it perfect," Jodi suggested, a knowing smile tugging at her lips. "Just be honest. Tell her how you feel and where you see this going. Kara is nurturing and understanding; she'll appreciate your honesty."

Christian nodded slowly, her words resonating. "You're right. Maybe I just need to embrace the uncertainty. I just— I want to make sure she knows how much she means to me."

"Exactly! And remember, the workshop is about courage. You're embodying that by being vulnerable. Just take that leap," Jodi encouraged, her tone light but firm.

Feeling slightly more confident, Christian decided he would tell Kara how he felt, but he wanted to wait for the right moment. They had a late-night brainstorming session planned for that evening to finalize the details for the workshop, and he thought it could be the perfect time to share his feelings.

As the evening approached, Kara prepared her workspace, a cozy corner of her apartment filled with art supplies, sketches, and ideas swirling on paper. The excitement of the gallery hosting their workshop fueled her energy, and she couldn't wait to share the news with Christian.

When Christian arrived, he looked slightly nervous but equally eager. They settled into their creative flow, bouncing ideas off each other and building upon each other's suggestions.

As the hours passed, laughter filled the room, and the atmosphere grew warm with camaraderie. But beneath the surface, both of them were battling their emotions, the weight of their unspoken feelings hanging in the air.

In a moment of spontaneity, Kara reached for a brush and began painting a large canvas that would serve as a backdrop for the workshop. "What do you think about this? A vibrant representation of courage?" she asked, her eyes alight with passion.

Christian watched her, mesmerized by her creativity. "It's beautiful, Kara. You have a way of capturing emotions. It's inspiring."

"Thanks! I want everyone to feel that same inspiration during the workshop," she said. "It's about showing our vulnerabilities and celebrating our strengths."

Christian felt a surge of courage. "You know, I've been thinking a lot about vulnerability lately," he said, his voice steady. "It's scary, but I think it's essential. Especially when it comes to feelings."

Kara paused, her gaze steady on him. "I agree. It's not easy to open up, but it's necessary for growth."

He took a deep breath, feeling a rush of adrenaline. "Kara, I... I need to tell you something important."

Her attention sharpened, and she set down her brush, her heart racing. "What is it, Christian?"

"I care about you, more than just as a friend. I think I'm falling in love with you," he confessed, his voice steady but laced with vulnerability. "I want to explore where this can go, but I'm scared of what that means for us."

Time seemed to stand still as Kara processed his words. A wave of warmth spread through her, igniting the very feelings she had been grappling with as well. The excitement, the fear, the hope—all mingled into a beautiful, chaotic sensation.

"I... I love you too, Christian," she said softly, her voice barely above a whisper but filled with a passion that mirrored his. "I've been feeling the same way, but I didn't know how to say it."

Their eyes locked, a deep understanding passing between them. The weight of their unspoken feelings had lifted, leaving only the beauty of their connection. In that moment, the world around them faded away, and all that existed was the shared courage between them.

As they embraced, the warmth of their feelings enveloped them, signaling a new chapter not just for their relationship but for the workshop they were creating together. They were ready to explore their vulnerabilities, both personally and professionally, with the same passion that drove their creative spirits.

The canvas of courage was no longer just a backdrop for their workshop; it was a reflection of their journey together, a testament to their love and the beauty of vulnerability that would inspire others to embrace their own stories.

CHAPTER 18

The Canvas of Ideas

Kara and Christian stood side by side in her cozy apartment, the late afternoon sun filtering through the sheer curtains, casting a warm glow over their workspace. The air was filled with the scent of fresh paint and the sound of soft music playing in the background. It felt like a dream come true as they began to plan the Voices of Courage workshop together, their hearts still fluttering from the confession they had shared just hours before.

Kara looked at Christian, her eyes sparkling with excitement. "So, where do we start? We have so many ideas swirling around, and I can't wait to see them come to life!"

Christian grinned, his spontaneous nature igniting a spark of energy in the room. "How about we brainstorm the main themes first? I think we should focus on what courage really means to each participant. It's such a personal journey, you know?"

"Absolutely," Kara agreed, her tone passionate. "Courage manifests in so many ways—overcoming fears, speaking out, embracing vulnerability. We should create art projects that reflect those themes.

Maybe we could have a mural that everyone contributes to? It could symbolize our collective strength!"

Christian nodded enthusiastically, already imagining the vibrant colors and unique expressions that would come together on the wall. "That would be incredible! A living testament to everyone's stories. I can almost see it now—each brushstroke telling a different tale."

As they continued to brainstorm, ideas flowed like the paint on their palettes. They envisioned interactive workshops, discussions on mental health, and sessions where participants could share their own experiences. With each suggestion, their connection deepened, the excitement of creating something meaningful infusing the air around them.

But as the evening wore on, the energy began to shift. Kara brought up the logistics of the workshop. "We need to be mindful of the community expectations as well. The gallery has a reputation to uphold, and we want to ensure that our projects resonate with them."

Christian's brow furrowed slightly. "I get that, but it's important that we stay true to our vision. If we focus too much on what others expect, we might lose the essence of what we're trying to achieve. It's about courage, right? We should embrace the rawness of that."

Kara felt the tension building. "I agree, Christian, but we also have to consider the audience. If we want to create a safe space, we need to find a balance between our artistic vision and the expectations of the community."

Christian crossed his arms, contemplating her words. He appreciated Kara's nurturing approach, but his adventurous spirit was itching to break free. "I just think we shouldn't dilute our message to fit a mold. What if we create something that challenges the status quo? Art is meant to provoke thought and inspire change."

Kara sighed, feeling the weight of their disagreement. "I understand where you're coming from, but we have to be strategic. We want to inspire people, not alienate them. There's a way to do both, but we need to work together on this."

The conversation took a pause, and an uncomfortable silence settled between them. Despite their chemistry and newfound romance, the pressure of collaboration was palpable. They were navigating uncharted territory—not just as partners in a workshop but also as partners in a relationship.

Just then, the doorbell rang, breaking the tension. Jodi stepped into the room, her vibrant energy lighting up the space. "Hey, lovebirds! What's cooking in here?" she exclaimed, oblivious to the charged atmosphere.

Kara offered a smile, grateful for the interruption. "We were just brainstorming ideas for the workshop, but we hit a bit of a snag."

Jodi raised an eyebrow, her academic nature quick to pick up on the underlying tension. "Ah, I see. Creative differences? That's completely normal. Why don't you tell me what you're both thinking? Maybe I can help."

Christian spoke first, his tone light but earnest. "I want to push the boundaries and create art that challenges people to think differently. I believe in the power of raw expression."

Kara quickly added, "And I want to make sure we create a safe and welcoming environment for everyone. It's important that we balance our artistic freedom with community expectations."

Jodi nodded, her expression thoughtful. "Both are valid points, and it's great that you're both passionate. The key is to find common ground. How about each of you listing your top three priorities for the workshop? Then we can compare notes and see where they overlap."

Reluctantly, Kara and Christian pulled out their notebooks, the tension in the air slowly dissipating as they focused on the task. Jodi observed with a knowing smile, appreciating the dynamic between her two friends.

After a few moments, they shared their lists. Kara emphasized community engagement, emotional expression, and creating a safe space. Christian prioritized artistic freedom, pushing the envelope, and challenging societal norms.

Jodi leaned back in her chair, a spark of inspiration lighting her eyes. "Look at this! You both care deeply about the impact of the workshop, just from different angles. What if you merge your ideas? You could have a segment dedicated to bold, avant-garde art that challenges perceptions and another that focuses on emotional storytelling and participation. That way, you're both contributing to the workshop's vision!"

Kara and Christian exchanged glances, the idea resonating with them both. "That could work," Kara said slowly, her tone warming. "We could have different stations or sessions that cater to both artistic styles."

"Exactly!" Jodi encouraged, her voice enthusiastic. "And you can promote it as an exploration of courage. Not just in creating art but in engaging with topics that might be tough for some. It's all about embracing the full spectrum of human experience!"

Christian felt a rush of excitement. "I love that! It allows for creativity and vulnerability in one space. We can inspire participants to step out of their comfort zones while still connecting with their emotions."

Kara's expression softened, and she nodded in agreement. "This could be a powerful experience for everyone involved. Let's make it happen!"

As they dove back into planning, the atmosphere shifted to one of collaboration and shared vision. With Jodi's encouragement, Kara and Christian began to blend their ideas seamlessly, their creativity flowing freely. The disagreement had transformed into a catalyst for growth, allowing them to explore new possibilities together.

As the night deepened, they finalized details for the workshop, laughter and playful banter replacing any lingering tension. Kara felt a sense of relief wash over her; they were not just partners in the workshop but also in life, navigating challenges together and learning to balance their artistic visions with their personal feelings.

When Jodi finally left, Kara and Christian found themselves alone once more. The warmth of the evening lingered in the air, and as they reflected on their progress, their eyes locked, the connection between them stronger than ever.

"Thank you for being open to my ideas," Christian said softly, his tone sincere. "I know we may not always see things the same way, but I really value your perspective."

Kara smiled, her heart swelling with affection. "And I appreciate your adventurous spirit, Christian. It pushes me to think outside the box. I think we're creating something beautiful together."

With that, they leaned in closer, sharing a tender kiss that solidified their commitment to each other and their shared mission. In that moment, they knew they could face any challenge that came their way, both in their relationship and in the workshop they were creating.

CHAPTER 19

A Heartfelt Dinner

The soft glow of the setting sun poured through the kitchen window, bathing the room in a golden hue. Kara stood at the stove, stirring a pot of her father's favorite vegetable soup. The aroma filled the air, a comforting blend of fresh herbs and simmering vegetables that felt like a warm embrace. She could hear the faint sound of her dad's laughter coming from the living room, where he was settling into his favorite armchair, a cozy blanket draped over his legs.

After a busy week spent planning the Voices of Courage workshop, Kara felt a sense of responsibility to check in on her dad. He had just returned from the hospital, and she wanted to ensure he was recovering well. The workshop was just a few days away, but family always came first. As she ladled the soup into bowls, her heart swelled with gratitude for the moments they shared.

"Dinner's ready!" she called out, wiping her hands on a kitchen towel.

Her father shuffled into the dining room, his face lighting up with a smile that warmed Kara's heart. "That smells amazing, Kara!

Just like when you were a little girl, trying to impress me with your cooking skills."

Kara chuckled, her cheeks flushing with nostalgia. "I remember burning the toast more often than not, Dad. But you always pretended it was the best breakfast ever."

"Of course, how could I resist those big puppy-dog eyes?" he replied with a wink, taking a seat at the table.

As they sat down to eat, Kara couldn't help but admire the way her father seemed to radiate warmth, even after everything he had been through. He looked healthier, his cheeks slightly flushed, and his eyes sparkled with life. They shared stories about their day, laughter punctuating the air as they reminisced about old family adventures.

"How's the workshop planning coming along?" her father asked, taking a spoonful of soup and savoring the flavors.

Kara's face lit up at the mention of the workshop. "It's going really well! Christian and I have been working hard to create something special. We've planned a variety of activities that focus on different aspects of courage—art, storytelling, and even some interactive sessions. I think it's going to be transformative for everyone involved."

Her father nodded, his expression a mix of pride and curiosity. "You've always had a knack for bringing people together, Kara. I'm sure it will be a success. And Christian—he's a good guy, isn't he?"

Kara felt a warmth spread through her at her father's approval. "He is. He's spontaneous, adventurous, and he challenges me in ways I never expected. It's exciting and a little scary, but I love it."

Her father leaned back in his chair, a thoughtful expression crossing his face. "You know, when I first met Christian, I could see the spark he brought into your life. You seem happier, more alive. Just make sure you're both on the same page. Relationships take work, and communication is key."

Kara nodded, a hint of seriousness creeping into her tone. "I know, Dad. We've had our ups and downs, especially with planning the workshop. But I think we're learning to navigate those differences. I just hope we can keep that balance."

As they continued to eat, the conversation shifted to lighter topics—shared memories of family vacations, Kara's childhood mishaps, and even her father's latest gardening endeavors. With each laugh, the room felt more vibrant, the bond between them strengthening.

But as dessert approached, Kara's mother entered the room, her cheerful demeanor brightening the atmosphere. "What's this I smell? Is that my favorite chocolate cake?" she exclaimed, glancing at the table.

Kara grinned, knowing her mother's sweet tooth well. "Just a little something I whipped up. I thought it would be a nice treat after dinner."

Her mother clapped her hands in delight, taking a seat and joining in the conversation. "I can't believe how quickly time flies. It feels like just yesterday I was worrying about you going off to college, and now you're planning workshops and dating a wonderful young man."

Kara's heart skipped a beat at the mention of Christian, and she felt her mother's gaze turn curious. "Speaking of young men, have you two talked about your future?" her mother asked, a teasing lilt in her voice.

Kara's fork paused mid-air, her cheeks flushing. "Mom, we're just focusing on the workshop right now. It's a big project, and we want to do it right."

Her mother raised an eyebrow, a knowing smile playing on her lips. "I understand, but it's never too early to discuss the future. I just want to make sure you're happy, Kara. And if Christian is the one, well..."

Kara felt a wave of panic wash over her. "Mom, we're still figuring things out! I mean, it's not like we're talking about marriage yet!"

Her father chuckled softly, clearly enjoying the playful banter between the two women. "Take it easy on her, dear. Relationships are a journey, not a race."

Kara took a deep breath, trying to regain her composure. "I just want to enjoy what we have right now. Christian and I are still learning about each other, and I don't want to rush into anything. There's so much to explore!"

Her mother nodded, her expression softening. "I understand, sweetheart. Just remember that communication is vital. If you ever feel ready to discuss your future with Christian, I'll be here to listen."

Kara smiled, appreciating her mother's support. "Thanks, Mom. I promise I'll keep you in the loop."

As dessert was served, the atmosphere shifted back to warmth and laughter. They shared stories and memories, the evening flowing seamlessly. Kara cherished these moments, the feeling of love and connection enveloping her like a warm blanket.

After dinner, they moved to the living room, where her father settled back into his armchair with a contented sigh. Kara curled up beside him, resting her head on his shoulder.

"Dad, I'm really glad you're feeling better," she said softly, her voice laced with affection.

"Me too, Kara. You have no idea how much your support means to me. It's a reminder of the strength we have as a family," he replied, his voice steady and reassuring.

As they sat together, Kara felt a sense of clarity wash over her. The love she shared with her father and the joy of creating something meaningful with Christian intertwined beautifully in her heart. She knew that whatever the future held, she was ready to embrace it with courage and an open heart.

CHAPTER 20

Unexpected Colors of Courage

The morning sun peeked through the curtains, casting a soft glow across Kara's room. She stirred awake, the warmth of the blanket nestling her in comfort. As she stretched, she felt a sense of anticipation bubble up inside her.

As she reached for her phone, she noticed a new message notification. It was from Christian. Her heart raced as she opened it, a smile spreading across her face.

"Good morning, sunshine! Surprise! I've planned a little adventure for us today. We're going to the art exhibit at the downtown gallery. It's all about stories of courage, and I know you're going to love it. Can't wait to see you!"

Kara's excitement was quickly mixed with a hint of trepidation. An art exhibit? She loved art, but what if it stirred up more emotions than she was prepared to face? She felt the weight of her thoughts about the future, especially regarding her relationship with Christian, hovering like a cloud in the back of her mind.

After a quick shower and getting dressed, she made her way down-stairs, where the smell of coffee wafted through the air. Her father was already at the kitchen table, flipping through the newspaper.

"Good morning, Dad!" Kara greeted, pouring herself a cup of coffee.

"Morning, Kara! You look bright and cheerful today. What's got you smiling?" he asked, looking up with a twinkle in his eye.

Kara hesitated for a moment, then decided to share Christian's surprise. "Christian has planned a surprise outing for us to an art exhibit this morning. It's supposed to showcase stories of courage."

Her father raised his eyebrows, a proud smile lighting up his face. "That sounds fantastic! You know, I've always believed that art has a unique way of expressing our innermost thoughts and feelings. It's wonderful that you're going."

"Yeah, but I'm also a bit nervous," Kara admitted, stirring her coffee. "I love art, but I can't shake off this feeling about the future. The exhibit might bring up some emotions I'm not entirely ready to face."

Her father leaned back in his chair, a thoughtful expression crossing his face. "Kara, sometimes spontaneity can lead to the most beautiful moments. You and Christian have a special connection, and embracing the unknown can be a part of that. Besides, it's all about sharing the experience together. Just be open to whatever comes."

Kara nodded, feeling a surge of gratitude for her dad's wisdom. "You're right, as always. I'll try to embrace it. Thanks, Dad."

After finishing her coffee, she quickly gathered her things and headed out the door. The drive to the gallery was filled with thoughts of Christian—the way his laughter brightened her day, how he made her feel alive, and the uncertainty of what lay ahead. The workshop was just around the corner, and she couldn't help but wonder how it would affect their relationship.

Arriving at the gallery, she spotted Christian waiting for her out-side, his handsome features illuminated by the sunlight. He wore a casual yet stylish outfit that highlighted his athletic build, his eyes twinkling with enthusiasm.

"Hey there, beautiful!" he exclaimed, pulling her into a warm embrace. "Ready for an adventure?"

"Absolutely! Your message got me all excited," she replied, her heart fluttering as they walked hand in hand toward the entrance.

The gallery was vibrant and alive with color and energy. As they stepped inside, Kara felt an immediate sense of awe wash over her. The walls were adorned with stunning pieces of art, each depicting various aspects of courage—overcoming fears, embracing vulnerability, and the strength found in connection.

Christian led her through the gallery, playfully pointing out different pieces and sharing his interpretations. They laughed and engaged with the art, their connection deepening with each shared moment. Kara felt a sense of joy enveloping her as she watched Christian express himself so freely.

As they wandered deeper into the exhibit, they stumbled upon a piece that made Kara's heart skip a beat. It was a striking painting of a couple standing on a cliff overlooking an expansive sea. The waves crashed against the rocks below, symbolizing the tumultuous journey of love and commitment. Beneath the artwork was a message: "Courage is not the absence of fear, but the triumph over it."

Kara felt a shiver run down her spine as she stared at the painting. It resonated with her fears about their future—the uncertainties, the pressure of expectations, and the question of where their relationship was headed. She couldn't help but wonder if she was ready for the leap that love often demanded.

"Wow, this one is powerful," Christian said, standing beside her. "What do you think it's trying to convey?"

Kara took a deep breath, her heart racing. "I think it speaks to the challenges we face in relationships. It's not just about the good times; it's about overcoming fears and uncertainties together."

Christian nodded, his expression turning serious. "That's a really insightful interpretation, Kara. Relationships do require courage, don't they?"

His words hung in the air, and Kara felt a weight settle in her stomach. This was the moment she had been avoiding—the moment she had to confront her feelings. She looked at Christian, his eyes searching hers for her thoughts.

"Yeah, they do," she replied slowly, her voice steady despite the turmoil inside her. "Sometimes I wonder if we're both ready for what that means. I mean, what does the future hold for us?"

Christian's brow furrowed slightly, and Kara could see the gears turning in his mind. "Are you saying you're unsure about us? About what we're building together?"

She felt her heart race, the vulnerability of the moment washing over her. "I guess I'm just afraid of what comes next. I care about you so much, Christian, but the idea of taking that next step—what if it doesn't work out? What if we're not on the same page?"

Christian reached for her hand, his grip reassuring. "Kara, I understand. It's natural to have those fears. I feel them too. But we can't let fear dictate our choices. We have to communicate and be honest with each other, no matter how difficult it may be."

Kara nodded, appreciating his openness. "You're right. I just want to make sure we're both on the same path and that we're ready for whatever that may look like."

He stepped closer, looking deeply into her eyes. "I'm willing to explore that path with you, even if it's uncertain. How about we take it one step at a time? We can learn and grow together, and I'll always be here to support you."

His words brought a wave of relief, and Kara felt her heart swell with gratitude. "Thank you, Christian. I really appreciate that. I think I needed to hear it."

As they stood in front of the painting, Kara felt a sense of clarity wash over her. The fears that had once felt overwhelming began to dissipate, replaced by the possibility of navigating their journey together.

Later that evening, after the exhibit had ended, they returned to Kara's home. The atmosphere was filled with a sense of warmth and connection as they settled on the couch, sharing a bottle of wine and reflecting on their day.

"I'm really glad we went to the exhibit," she said softly, leaning into Christian's side. "It opened my eyes to a lot of things."

"Me too," he replied, brushing a strand of hair away from her face. "I love that we can have these conversations. It makes me feel closer to you."

Kara felt a rush of emotion as she looked into his eyes. "You mean so much to me, Christian. I want us to keep exploring and growing together."

As the night wore on, they shared stories, laughter, and dreams for the future. The conversation flowed easily, and the tension that had once lingered between them began to fade.

Eventually, their playful banter turned into something deeper, a magnetic pull that drew them closer together. Kara felt a spark of passion ignite between them, the connection they shared intensifying.

With a gentle kiss, they began to explore the depths of their feelings for each other, surrendering to the warmth and love that enveloped them. The night became a canvas of emotions, where courage and vulnerability intertwined in a beautiful dance.

It was a night filled with love, laughter, and the promise of a shared future—one that they would navigate together, step by step.

CHAPTER 21

Letters of Courage

The soft rays of morning sunlight filtered through Kara's curtains, casting a warm glow across her bedroom. Kara stirred awake, feeling the lingering warmth of the previous night's shared laughter and connection with Christian. Her heart fluttered in anticipation as she recalled their deep conversation about courage and the future. Just as she reached for her phone to check the time, something caught her eye—a small envelope slipped beneath her door.

Curiosity piqued, Kara swung her legs over the side of the bed and padded over to retrieve it. The envelope was simple, made of crisp white paper, and bore her name scrawled in Christian's familiar handwriting. A flutter of excitement coursed through her veins as she settled back on her bed to open it.

Inside, she found a handwritten letter that seemed to pulse with Christian's energy. As she began to read, his words enveloped her like a warm embrace:

"Hey Kara,

I hope you're still basking in the glow of our incredible day at the gallery. I just wanted to take a moment to express my thoughts after our conversation. It's not always easy to open up about what we feel, but I truly believe that we're on the right path. You have a beautiful way of articulating your emotions, and it inspires me to be more open about mine.

I know we both have fears about the future, but I want you to know that those fears don't scare me. They remind me of how much I care about you and how much I want to explore this adventure together. I believe in us, Kara. I believe in the courage we have to face whatever comes our way.

Let's continue to talk, share, and write down our thoughts. I think it'll help us navigate this journey together.

Can't wait to see you again!

With all my heart,

Christian"

Kara felt her heart swell as she read his words, the sincerity and warmth radiating off the page. It was as if he had captured her fears and hopes and wrapped them in a beautiful bow of encouragement. The notion of exchanging letters intrigued her; it felt intimate, like a sacred space where they could express their innermost thoughts without the immediate pressures of face-to-face conversations.

Taking a deep breath, Kara grabbed a fresh piece of stationery and began to write back. She poured her heart onto the page, expressing her hopes for their relationship, her insecurities about the future, and how much his words had meant to her. After sealing the letter, she slipped it under his door, feeling a rush of vulnerability mixed with excitement.

Over the next few days, their correspondence blossomed into a beautiful ritual. Each morning, Kara would wake to find a letter from Christian waiting for her, filled with his thoughts on their relationship, his dreams, and the adventures he yearned to share. Each letter deepened their bond, weaving a tapestry of trust and understanding that was both exhilarating and terrifying.

Yet, despite the warmth of his words, Kara couldn't shake her insecurities. She found herself questioning whether she was enough for him, whether she could meet the growing expectations of their relationship. As she sat at her desk, contemplating her latest response to Christian, her thoughts spiraled.

What if he wanted more than she was ready to give? What if he envisioned a future that didn't align with her own?

Kara sighed, shaking her head as she pushed the thoughts aside. She picked up her pen and wrote, reminding herself that vulnerability was a strength, not a weakness. She had to be honest about her feelings, even if it meant exposing her fears.

The day of the Voices of Courage workshop arrived, and Kara was filled with a mix of excitement and nerves. The atmosphere buzzed with anticipation as she and Christian arrived at the venue. The walls were adorned with inspiring quotes and artwork that echoed the theme of courage, evoking a sense of empowerment.

"Are you ready for this?" Christian asked, his eyes sparkling with enthusiasm.

He looked effortlessly handsome, and Kara felt a familiar warmth spread through her at the sight of him.

"Ready as I'll ever be," she replied, trying to match his lighthearted energy.

Inside, though, she felt the weight of her insecurities creeping back in. The workshop promised to be an opportunity for growth, but it also meant confronting the very fears she had been grappling with.

As they participated in various activities and discussions, Kara began to feel a shift within herself. The stories shared by others resonated deeply, and she felt a sense of solidarity with those around her. It became clear that the journey of courage was not a solitary path; it was one traveled together, supported by shared experiences.

During a break in the workshop, Kara and Christian found a quiet corner to reflect on what they had learned. "What did you think?" he asked, his brow furrowed in curiosity.

"It was powerful," Kara replied. "Hearing everyone's stories made me realize that we're all navigating our own challenges. It's comforting to know we're not alone."

Christian nodded, his expression serious. "That's the beauty of this, isn't it? We can draw strength from each other and those around us. I hope you know that I'm always here for you, Kara."

She met his gaze, feeling the sincerity in his words. "I appreciate that, Christian. I want to be brave, but sometimes it feels so daunting."

"Bravery doesn't mean you have to have it all figured out," he said, reaching for her hand. "It means being willing to take that next step, no matter how small. I'm right here with you."

As the workshop continued, Kara felt a renewed sense of resolve. Each activity encouraged her to dig deeper and confront the fears that had held her back. By the end of the day, she felt lighter, empowered by the connections she had made and the insights she had gained.

After the workshop, as they drove home, Christian turned to her with a spark of spontaneity in his eyes. "How about we take a week-end getaway? Just the two of us. We can explore somewhere new, away from everything, and really dive into our relationship."

Kara's heart raced at the suggestion. A getaway sounded wonder-ful, yet the prospect of being away with Christian felt overwhelming. She hesitated, her mind racing with thoughts of what it would mean for them.

"Christian, that sounds amazing, but—" she began, her voice faltering.

"But?" he prompted gently.

"It's just... I have so many thoughts and fears about where we're headed. I don't want to rush into anything or make decisions based on excitement alone."

His expression softened, understanding her hesitation. "I get that. But maybe this trip could be a chance for us to confront those fears together. We can talk things through, explore what we want, and see where we stand without the usual distractions."

Kara bit her lip, contemplating his words. The idea of taking a step back, away from their daily routines, resonated with her. It could be a chance to evaluate their relationship and face the uncertainties head-on.

"Okay," she said slowly, her heart beginning to race with a mix of excitement and trepidation. "Let's do it."

As they made plans for their weekend escape, Kara felt the weight of her fears transform into a spark of courage. She realized that confronting the unknown, especially with Christian by her side, was a step toward growth. With every letter exchanged, every workshop attended, and every conversation shared, she was learning to embrace the courage that lay within her.

With a newfound determination, Kara was ready to explore not just the destination ahead but the journey that lay before them. The weekend getaway promised to be more than just an escape—it would be an opportunity to define their path together.

CHAPTER 22

Tides of Change

The ocean breeze danced through Kara's hair as she and Christian arrived in the quaint coastal town of Seabrook. The sun hung low in the sky, casting a golden hue over the charming streets lined with artisanal shops, vibrant art galleries, and inviting cafés. The salty air was filled with the promise of adventure, and Kara felt a rush of excitement that mingled with a hint of nervousness.

"Can you believe how beautiful it is here?" Christian exclaimed, his eyes sparkling with enthusiasm as he admired the colorful facades of the buildings.

He was in his element, his adventurous spirit igniting at the sight of the ocean waves crashing against the rocky shore. Kara couldn't help but smile at his infectious energy.

"It's stunning," she agreed, taking a moment to breathe in the salty air. "I can't wait to explore."

They strolled hand in hand down the cobblestone streets, pausing occasionally to admire the artwork displayed in the windows of local galleries. Each piece seemed to tell a story, capturing the essence of the ocean and the town's vibrant culture. Kara felt a sense of calm wash over her as they wandered, the worries that had nagged at her fading away with each step.

"Let's stop for coffee at that cute little café!" Christian pointed to a charming spot adorned with potted flowers, its outdoor seating shaded by colorful umbrellas.

The café had a cozy, welcoming atmosphere that felt like the perfect place to unwind and share their thoughts.

As they settled into their seats, Kara looked around, absorbing the ambiance. The smell of freshly brewed coffee mingled with the scent of pastries, creating a warm and inviting space. She felt her heart flutter with anticipation, eager to learn more about Christian's hopes and dreams, just as he had encouraged her to share hers.

"So, what are you most excited about this weekend?" Christian asked, leaning forward with genuine interest.

Kara took a sip of her latte, feeling the warmth spread through her. "Honestly, I'm excited to have some time away from our usual routines. It feels like we're on the brink of something new, and I want to explore what that means for us."

Christian's expression softened, and he nodded thoughtfully. "I feel that too. It's like a blank canvas, right? We can paint whatever picture we want."

"Exactly," she said, feeling a surge of courage. "But I also have my fears. I think about what happens after this weekend. Are we just living in the moment, or are we building something real?"

His gaze held hers, a mix of understanding and determination. "I think both are important. We have to enjoy the journey, but I want to build something lasting with you too. That's why I suggested this trip—to see what we can create together."

Kara's heart raced as she absorbed his words. She had been so focused on her insecurities that she hadn't fully realized how much Christian valued their relationship. "I want that too," she admitted, her voice slightly trembling. "But what if we want different things?"

Before Christian could respond, a cheerful voice interrupted them. "Hey there! I'm Ava, your barista for the day! What can I get for you?"

Kara and Christian exchanged amused glances, momentarily distracted by Ava's vivacity. They ordered their drinks and settled back into their conversation, but Kara's mind was still swirling with thoughts of the future.

After finishing their coffee, they decided to explore the nearby art galleries. Each space revealed the creativity of local artists, showcasing everything from vibrant paintings to intricate sculptures. Kara found herself captivated by a piece that depicted the ocean's waves crashing against the shore, a swirl of blues and greens dancing on the canvas.

"What do you think?" Christian asked, standing next to her.

"It's beautiful," Kara replied, her eyes fixed on the artwork. "It feels alive, like the waves are in motion."

Christian chuckled softly. "You have such a way of seeing things. It's inspiring."

They continued to wander through the galleries, with Kara feeling more at ease as she shared her thoughts on each piece. The connection between them deepened with every conversation, and Kara felt a growing sense of certainty about their relationship.

As they stepped out of the last gallery, Christian stopped abruptly, his expression shifting to one of excitement. "I have an idea! Why don't we take a pottery class? There's a studio just down the road, and I think it could be a fun way for us to express ourselves."

Kara raised an eyebrow, intrigued by the spontaneity of his suggestion. "Pottery? Really? That sounds... messy."

"Messy is good! It's all part of the experience," he said, grinning mischievously. "Plus, we can create something together. What do you say?"

With her heart racing at the thought of molding clay side by side, Kara nodded enthusiastically. "Okay, let's do it!"

The pottery studio was a cozy space filled with the earthy scent of clay. As they entered, Kara felt a wave of excitement wash over her. The instructor welcomed them warmly, and soon, they were seated at a table with their own lumps of clay.

"Alright, let's get our hands dirty!" Christian declared, rolling up his sleeves.

Kara laughed, the sound bubbling up with genuine joy. "This is going to be interesting."

As they began to mold the clay, Kara quickly found herself lost in the process. She shaped the clay into a small bowl, her fingers brushing against the cool material. Christian, meanwhile, attempted to create a quirky figure that resembled a cartoon character.

"What is that supposed to be?" Kara teased, glancing at his creation, which was more of a lopsided blob than a recognizable figure.

"It's a work of art!" he retorted playfully, his eyes twinkling with mischief. "Every masterpiece starts somewhere."

They laughed together, the atmosphere light and filled with a sense of freedom. With each pass of their hands over the clay, Kara felt herself opening up, sharing pieces of her heart that she had kept hidden.

"I've always been a bit of a perfectionist," she admitted, focusing on her bowl. "I worry that I won't be good enough, whether it's at work or in relationships."

Christian paused, his expression turning serious. "Kara, you are more than enough. You don't have to be perfect. It's about the journey, the fun along the way. Just like this pottery. Look at how unique each piece is."

She glanced at the bowl she was shaping, realizing he was right. "You're right. It's about the experience, not just the result."

As they continued to mold the clay, their conversation flowed into deeper waters. Christian shared his own insecurities—how he often felt the pressure of being a successful artist and the fear of not living up to expectations.

"I sometimes wonder if I'm just a flash in the pan, you know?" he confessed, his voice quieter now. "What if I can't keep creating? What if I lose that spark?"

Kara felt a rush of empathy, her heart aching for him. "You have such a gift, Christian. Your passion is contagious. I can't see you ever losing that spark."

His gaze met hers, a mixture of gratitude and vulnerability shining through. "Thank you, Kara. That means a lot."

But just as the moment felt like it was crystallizing into something beautiful, Christian's expression shifted, clouds darkening his features. "There's something else I need to tell you," he said, his voice low. "It's about my past."

Kara's heart started to race. The lightness of their earlier conversation faded, replaced by an unsettling tension. Her throat tightened, but she forced herself to ask. "What do you mean?"

Christian shifted, rubbing the back of his neck as if trying to ease a tension that ran far deeper than muscle. His gaze flickered to the floor, unwilling to meet hers. "Before I found success, I struggled a lot. I wasn't...a good person back then. I made choices I can't undo. I hurt people—some intentionally, some because I was reckless." He exhaled sharply, shaking his head. "I don't know if that version of me is truly gone."

The revelation hung in the air, thick and suffocating. Kara felt her stomach twist as uncertainty crept in. She had seen glimpses of his vulnerability before, but this—this was different. The past had claws, and she wasn't sure if it was trying to pull him back or if he was still holding on to it himself.

She swallowed hard. "Do you regret it?"

Christian looked up, and for the first time, his eyes met hers—raw, pleading, haunted. "Every day."

What did this mean for them? Would his past define their future?

CHAPTER 23

Beneath the Surface

The weight of Christian's revelation lingered in the air like the scent of saltwater after a storm. Kara's heart raced as she searched his eyes, trying to decipher the emotions swirling behind them. The carefree laughter they had shared moments earlier felt like a distant memory, overshadowed by the gravity of the confessions that had just unfolded.

"Christian," she began, her voice steady but soft, "I appreciate you sharing that with me. It takes a lot of courage to open up about the past, especially when it carries such weight."

He nodded, his brows furrowing slightly. "I just... I didn't want to hide anything from you. I don't want my past to define me, but I also don't want to keep secrets from someone I care about."

Kara felt her chest tighten. The vulnerability in his voice resonated deeply within her. She had always prided herself on being open and honest, yet here she was, grappling with her own fears. The truth was, she, too, had struggles lurking beneath the surface—insecurities that often threatened to drown her in self-doubt.

Taking a deep breath, Kara decided to confront her own shadows. "You know, I can relate to feeling like you're not enough. I've had my own battles with self-doubt," she admitted, meeting his gaze with determination. "Sometimes, I feel like I'm constantly trying to meet everyone's expectations—my boss, my parents, even my friends. It's exhausting."

Christian's expression softened, and he leaned in closer, encouraging her to continue. "What do you mean? How does that affect you?"

She hesitated for a moment, recalling the times she had felt overwhelmed by the pressures of her life. "I love my job at the doctor's office, but there are days when I feel like I'm just not doing enough. My parents have always had high hopes for me, and while I appreciate their support, it sometimes feels like a weight I can't carry. I worry that if I don't achieve what they expect, I'll disappoint them."

"That's a heavy burden to bear," he said quietly, his eyes reflecting understanding. "Have you talked to them about how you feel?"

Kara shook her head, a slight frown forming on her lips. "Not really. I guess I'm afraid they wouldn't understand. They want me to be successful, and I want that too. But what if my definition of success is different from theirs?"

Christian reached out, his fingers brushing against hers in a gentle acknowledgment of her struggle. "You have to define success for yourself, Kara. It's your life, after all. Just like art, it shouldn't be about fitting into someone else's mold. It's about what brings you joy."

His words struck a chord deep within her. She had always admired Christian's adventurous spirit, his ability to embrace life without the constraints of others' expectations. "You make it sound so simple," she said with a faint smile, though the weight of her fears still lingered.

"Maybe it is simple in theory, but hard in practice," he replied, his tone serious but gentle. "I've had to learn that true freedom comes from within. I spent years running from my past—trying to escape the mistakes I made and the people I hurt. But I realized that the only way to truly move forward was to confront those shadows. It wasn't easy, but it was necessary."

Kara watched him intently, trying to grasp the depth of his journey. "How did you do it? How do you forgive yourself for the things you've done?"

He paused, his eyes drifting to the pottery they had been working on, the unfinished pieces still sitting on the table, remnants of their earlier carefree laughter. "I had to accept that I was human—that I would make mistakes. I learned that forgiveness isn't just about absolving the guilt; it's about acknowledging the pain and choosing to move on. I started by making amends where I could, and then I focused on being better. It's a process, and some days are harder than others."

Kara felt a swell of admiration for him. "That's incredibly brave, Christian. It's not easy to face your past. I think a part of me has been avoiding my own feelings, hiding behind the façade of perfection."

Christian nodded, his gaze steady. "It's okay to feel that way. We all have our scars, and they don't define us unless we let them. But you have the power to shape your story, just like you shape the clay. Embrace your imperfections; they make you who you are."

His words resonated with her, and for a moment, Kara felt a flicker of hope ignite within her. "I want to be brave like that, to confront my fears rather than shying away from them. I want to embrace my journey, however messy it may be."

With a newfound sense of determination, she continued, "I want to forgive myself for not always living up to expectations—my own and others. I want to celebrate the moments when I take risks, like this trip, instead of worrying about what's next."

Christian smiled, a spark of admiration lighting up his features. "That's the spirit! You're already on the right path, Kara. Just remember that every step counts, no matter how small. And I'm here for you, every step of the way."

Feeling a wave of gratitude, Kara reached for his hand, intertwining their fingers. "Thank you, Christian. For sharing your story and for being so understanding. I didn't expect to have such a deep conversation while making pottery."

He chuckled softly, the tension in the air dissipating as they shared a light moment together. "What can I say? Pottery is a profound experience."

As they continued to mold their creations, the conversation flowed naturally, weaving in and out of laughter and reflection. Kara felt a deeper connection forming between them, one built on mutual understanding and vulnerability.

In that moment, they were able to explore the complexities of love intertwined with their histories. Each shared story, each moment of honesty, brought them closer together, creating a bond that felt both fragile and unbreakable.

After what felt like hours of sculpting, they finally stepped back to admire their work. Kara's bowl was lopsided but charming, a true representation of her journey. Christian's figure, though still a whimsical blob, had a certain character that made Kara burst into laughter.

"Look at that masterpiece!" she teased, playfully nudging him with her elbow. "I think it deserves a name."

Christian feigned offense. "It's a complex figure, Kara! I call it 'The Spirit of Adventure!'"

"More like the spirit of chaos," she countered with a grin. "But I love it. Just like I love that we're finding our own paths, no matter how messy they are."

He beamed at her, and Kara felt a sense of warmth radiating between them. The sun began to set outside the studio, casting a warm glow that filtered through the windows, illuminating the space with a golden hue.

In that cozy pottery studio, surrounded by the remnants of their creativity, Kara realized that they were both learning to embrace the beauty in imperfection. And as they stood together, hands covered in clay, Kara felt a renewed sense of hope—a belief that their pasts did not define them and that together, they could create something beautiful amidst the chaos of life.

CHAPTER 24

Beneath the Stars

As the sun dipped below the horizon, the sky transformed into a canvas of deep purples and fiery oranges, casting a warm glow across the beach. Kara and Christian stepped outside the pottery studio, their hearts still buzzing from the vulnerability they had shared moments before. The air was filled with the scent of salt and the rhythmic sound of waves crashing against the shore, inviting them into a realm where time seemed to stand still.

"Let's go for a walk," Christian suggested, his voice light and carefree as if the weight of the world had been lifted from his shoulders. "There's something magical about the beach at night."

Kara smiled, her heart fluttering at the thought of exploring the moonlit sands with him. "I'm all for magic," she replied, her tone playful. "Lead the way, adventurous artist."

They strolled down the path leading to the beach, the soft sand shifting beneath their feet. The moon hung low in the sky, illuminating their surroundings and casting silvery reflections on the water. Kara felt a sense of freedom wash over her, the worries of her day-to-day life fading into the background as she focused on the moment.

"Do you remember the first time you went to the beach?" Kara asked, her curiosity piqued.

Christian chuckled, his eyes sparkling with mischief. "Oh, I was a wild child. My parents took me to the beach when I was about six. I ran straight into the water, fully clothed, convinced I could swim like a dolphin. Spoiler alert: I couldn't. Ended up soaked and shivering, but it was the best day ever."

Kara laughed, picturing a young Christian splashing around in the waves. "That sounds like you. I can't imagine you ever being still."

"Stillness isn't in my DNA," he admitted, his tone lighthearted. "What about you? Any memorable beach moments?"

She paused, searching her memory for a story that would match his spontaneity. "I remember going to the beach with my family when I was a little girl. My dad and I built the biggest sandcastle you could imagine. We decorated it with seashells and seaweed, and I was convinced it was the grandest palace ever built."

"That sounds amazing," Christian said, genuinely intrigued. "Did it survive the tide?"

Kara smiled wistfully, her gaze drifting to the horizon. "For a little while, but then the waves came in and washed it away. I was devastated at first, but my dad told me it was just like life—beautiful things can be temporary, but the memories we create last forever."

"Your dad sounds like a wise man," Christian replied, his voice filled with warmth. "It's true, though; we have to cherish the moments, even if they don't last."

The wind rustled through the palm trees lining the beach, wrapping around them like a gentle embrace. As they continued to walk, Kara felt a wave of vulnerability wash over her, urging her to share her fears. "You know, sometimes I find it hard to be vulnerable. Sometimes I feel like I need to project an image of perfection, like I have it all together, especially with my family."

Christian turned to her, his expression serious yet compassionate. "That's something I can relate to. It's easy to feel like we need to be perfect, but it's in those moments of vulnerability where we connect the most."

Kara met his gaze, sensing an unspoken understanding between them. "What about you? Have you ever struggled with vulnerability?"

Christian took a deep breath, his demeanor shifting as he prepared to open up. "Yeah, I have. There was a time when I lost someone very close to me. It shook my world and made me question everything. I felt lost and didn't know how to cope. I started seeking adventure, thinking that if I could escape my pain through new experiences, I'd find the answers I was looking for."

Kara felt a pang of empathy for him, recognizing the depth of his struggles. "I'm so sorry to hear that, Christian," she said softly. "It must have been incredibly hard."

"It was," he admitted, his voice steady but tinged with emotion. "But it also taught me that running away doesn't solve anything. I realized that I needed to face my grief head-on to confront the feelings I had tried to bury. It was the scariest and most liberating thing I've ever done."

"Facing our fears can be terrifying," Kara replied, her heart swelling with admiration for him. "But it's also a path to growth. I think that's something we can both work on together."

"Absolutely," Christian said, his eyes gleaming with excitement. "We can embrace the messiness of life, support each other, and create something beautiful out of it."

As they walked, the sound of the waves crashing against the shore echoed their earlier conversation, a reminder of the ebb and flow of life. Kara felt a surge of gratitude for this moment—the shared stories, the laughter, and the unguarded honesty that had brought them closer together.

"Look at the stars," Kara said, her voice filled with wonder as she pointed toward the sky, where countless stars twinkled like diamonds. "They're so beautiful and endless."

"They remind me of our dreams," Christian mused, glancing up at the vast expanse. "Each one is a possibility waiting to be explored."

"Exactly," Kara replied, feeling a sense of hope wash over her. "And just like the stars, we can shine even in the darkest moments."

They paused at the water's edge, the cool waves lapping at their feet. Christian turned to face her, his expression tender and sincere. "Kara, I want you to know that I care about you—more than I can put into words. You've brought light into my life, and I'm grateful for every moment we've shared."

Kara's heart raced at his declaration. "I feel the same way, Christian. You've helped me see things in a new light, and I cherish our connection."

The world around them faded away, leaving only the two of them under the starlit sky. They stepped closer, their hearts beating in sync, and in the stillness of the night, they whispered the words they had both been longing to say, "I love you."

CHAPTER 25

A Canvas of Dreams

As dawn broke over the horizon, the golden rays of sunlight spilled onto the beach, illuminating the world in warm hues of amber and soft pastels. The rhythmic sound of waves lapping against the shore serenaded Kara and Christian as they stirred from their slumber. The air was fresh, filled with the invigorating scent of saltwater mixed with the faint aroma of coffee wafting from the beachside café nearby.

Kara blinked her eyes open, taking a moment to soak in the beauty around her. She turned to find Christian still asleep, his handsome features softened by the morning light, a gentle smile grazing his lips. She felt a rush of warmth at the sight of him, a feeling that lingered in her heart like the remnants of a beautiful dream.

"Good morning, sleepyhead," she said softly, brushing her fingers through his tousled hair.

Christian stirred, his eyes fluttering open as he grinned at her. "Morning! Is it too early to say I love waking up to this view?" He gestured toward the beach, his voice playfully sleepy.

Kara laughed, her heart fluttering. "I don't think it gets any better than this. The beach at sunrise is pretty magical."

As they got ready for the day, the excitement of their newfound connection hung in the air. Breakfast at the quaint café was filled with laughter and lighthearted banter. They settled at a cozy table outside, the ocean breeze tousling their hair as they sipped their coffees.

"What's on the agenda for today?" Christian asked, leaning forward with a glimmer of curiosity in his eyes.

Kara pondered for a moment, her mind swirling with ideas. "I was thinking we could start working on that painting project we talked about last night when we first met on the beach. You know, the one that embodies our journey together?"

Christian's eyes brightened. "I love that idea! There's something so special about creating art that reflects our experiences. It's like each brushstroke tells a part of our story."

"Exactly," Kara said, her passion igniting. "We can gather inspiration from the beach, the colors, the emotions… everything around us can be a part of it."

As they finished their breakfast, their conversation flowed effortlessly from dreams to aspirations. Kara shared her vision of intertwining their artistic styles to create something unique, while Christian excitedly described his adventurous plans for the future, wanting to use his art to inspire others.

"Art has this incredible power," Christian said, his voice filled with conviction. "It can heal, connect, and ignite change. I want our painting to embody that."

Kara nodded, her heart swelling with admiration for him. "I believe that too. Our experiences shape us, and if we can convey that through art, maybe we can help others feel less alone."

With their vision solidified, they wandered down the beach, gathering shells, driftwood, and bits of inspiration. Kara delighted in the way Christian's eyes sparkled with enthusiasm. His adventurous spirit was infectious, and she found herself caught up in his excitement.

"Look at this piece of driftwood!" he exclaimed, lifting a gnarled branch as if it were a treasure. "We could incorporate this into our painting somehow."

"Definitely," Kara agreed, her mind racing with possibilities. "We can use it as a frame or as a texture on the canvas. It adds a raw, organic element."

As they meandered along the shoreline, they began to sketch ideas in the sand, their laughter mingling with the sound of waves crashing. Kara felt alive, her heart dancing in rhythm with the ocean's pulse.

"I can already picture it," she said, drawing in the sand with her finger. "We start with a wave representing the journey we've both been on, and then we can blend in colors that represent our dreams."

Christian watched her with admiration. "You have a beautiful way of visualizing things, Kara. I love how you see the world."

Their playful banter evolved into deeper conversations, exploring their vulnerabilities and the healing power of art. They shared stories of their past, their dreams, and their fears, weaving a tapestry of connection that deepened with every word.

"I've always felt that art is a way to confront our inner struggles," Christian admitted, his tone turning serious. "It's a form of expression that gives voice to what we sometimes can't say out loud."

Kara nodded, her heart resonating with his words. "I agree. It's like therapy for the soul. Through creativity, we can confront what weighs us down and transform it into something beautiful."

As they continued this heartwarming exchange, the sun climbed higher in the sky, bathing them in radiant light. Kara felt a sense of peace enveloping her, a feeling that she was exactly where she was meant to be, with the person she was meant to be with.

Just as they were caught up in the bliss of their conversation, Kara's phone buzzed insistently in her pocket, breaking the enchanting moment. She pulled it out and glanced at the screen, her heart dropping slightly at the sight of her father's name.

"Sorry, I need to take this," she said, trying to mask her unease.

Christian gave her an encouraging nod. "Of course. I'll be right here."

Kara stepped a few paces away, her heart racing as she answered the call. "Dad?"

"Hey, Kara! I hope I'm not interrupting anything important," her father's warm voice came through the line, instantly soothing her nerves.

"No, not at all. I'm just spending some time with Christian on the beach," she replied, glancing back at him, where he was trying to appear unfazed but was clearly listening.

"That's great to hear! But I wanted to talk to you about something important," he said, his tone shifting slightly. "Your mom and I have been discussing the family reunion next month. We'd love for you to come."

Her heart sank at the thought of the reunion—an event that always stirred up a mix of emotions for her. Last year's silence at the dinner table still resonated louder than any argument. "Of course, Dad. I wouldn't miss it. But... you know how it can be, right?"

"I do, honey. I know it can be challenging, especially with everything that's happened—"

"I just don't want to confront my past, Dad. It feels overwhelming," she admitted, her voice tinged with vulnerability.

"I understand," he said gently. "But remember, you're not alone in this. We're your family, and we're here to support you. Sometimes facing those unresolved issues head-on can lead to healing."

Kara took a deep breath, her father's words resonating deeply within her. "I know you're right. It's just... I don't know if I'm ready."

"Take your time, Kara. Just know that we love you, and we want you to be happy. I believe in you."

As the call ended, Kara felt a swirl of emotions. She turned back to Christian, who was watching her with an expression of concern. "Everything okay?" he asked softly.

"Yeah, just family stuff," she replied, forcing a smile, though the weight of her father's words lingered on her heart. "They want me to come to the family reunion next month."

Christian stepped closer, his presence comforting. "Are you okay with that?"

"I don't know," she confessed, looking out at the waves. "It brings up a lot of unresolved feelings. I feel torn between wanting to be there for my family and the fear of facing old wounds."

He nodded thoughtfully, understanding the complexity of family dynamics. "It's okay to feel that way. Just remember, you have the power to decide what's best for you. And if you ever need someone to talk to about it, I'm here."

Kara felt a surge of gratitude for his support. "Thank you, Christian. It means a lot to know you're here for me."

As they stood together, the sun warming their skin and the ocean breeze swirling around them, Kara realized that the journey ahead—whether it involved family reunions or creative projects—would be more manageable with Christian by her side. Together, they would navigate the complexities of life, embracing both the challenges and the beauty that came with it.

CHAPTER 26

A Canvas of Colors

As Kara and Christian continued their leisurely stroll along the beach, the sun hung high in the sky, casting a warm and inviting glow over the sandy shore. The sound of waves crashing against the rocks created a soothing backdrop, while the scent of saltwater mingled with the fragrant notes of blooming flowers from the nearby dunes. Kara felt the weight of her earlier conversation with her father begin to lift, if only slightly, as she immersed herself in the beauty of the day.

They walked hand in hand, their fingers intertwined, sharing stories and laughter that seemed to float on the gentle breeze. Christian's adventurous spirit infused every word he spoke, and Kara found herself inspired by his enthusiasm. It was as if the world around them had transformed into a vibrant canvas, waiting for them to leave their mark.

"Look over there!" Christian exclaimed, pointing toward a cluster of colorful tents and canopies that had sprung up in the distance. "It looks like there's an art festival setting up! Let's check it out!"

Kara's heart raced with excitement at the thought of exploring the festival. She could already envision the eclectic mix of art, music, and culture that awaited them. "Absolutely! I can't wait to see what they have!"

As they approached the festival grounds, the atmosphere shifted, buzzing with energy and creativity. Artists were arranging their displays while musicians tuned their instruments, and the air was alive with laughter and chatter. The vibrant colors of paintings, sculptures, and handmade crafts caught Kara's eye, and she felt a sense of wonder wash over her.

"This is amazing!" she said. "Just look at all the creativity on display!"

Christian nodded, his eyes gleaming with excitement. "It's like a treasure trove of inspiration! We should definitely take our time and explore everything."

They wandered through the festival, stopping to admire the intricate details of various artworks, from abstract paintings to stunning sculptures crafted from recycled materials. Kara felt a spark of inspiration igniting within her as she took in the diverse expressions of creativity around her.

"Hey, look at this booth!" Christian called out, motioning toward a colorful tent adorned with paintings depicting the ocean in all its glory. "These pieces are incredible!"

Kara joined him, her eyes widening at the vibrant blues and greens that seemed to dance on the canvases. "Wow, the colors are so alive! It's like they're capturing the very essence of the sea!"

As they marveled at the artwork, a nearby artist noticed their admiration and approached them with a warm smile. "Thank you! I draw inspiration from the ocean and the beach. It's where I find my peace and creativity."

Kara smiled back, feeling a connection with the artist's passion. "I can see that! The way you've captured the movement of the water is breathtaking."

"Art has a way of speaking to us, doesn't it?" the artist replied. "It allows us to express emotions that words sometimes fail to convey."

Kara exchanged a glance with Christian, who nodded in agreement. "Absolutely. It's almost like a language of its own."

As they continued to explore, they stumbled upon a sign advertising a collaborative painting competition. The booth was bustling with activity, and participants were encouraged to create a piece of art as a team, drawing from their unique perspectives and experiences.

Kara's heart raced at the thought. "Should we sign up?" she asked, her voice tinged with excitement and a hint of nervousness.

Christian's eyes lit up. "Yes! Let's do it! It could be a fantastic way to channel our creativity together."

Taking a deep breath, Kara stepped forward and signed them up, her heart pounding with both anticipation and apprehension. "All right, we're in!"

With their registration complete, they were given a large canvas and a palette of paints. The vibe of the festival fueled their creativity, and Kara felt the weight of her earlier anxieties begin to fade as they set up their workspace.

"Okay, so what do you want to start with?" Christian asked, his voice playful as he dipped his brush into a vibrant blue paint.

Kara thought for a moment, her mind racing with ideas. "How about we start with the ocean? We can blend in some colors that represent our journey and what we've talked about today."

"Sounds perfect!" Christian replied, flashing her a broad grin. "Let's make it a beautiful wave that symbolizes both of us."

As they painted side by side, their chemistry ignited, and laughter filled the air as they playfully splashed paint on each other. Kara felt a sense of freedom wash over her as they worked together, creating a piece that was uniquely theirs. Each brushstroke became a representation of their shared experiences, emotions, and dreams.

But as the vibrant colors began to swirl together on the canvas, Kara's earlier conversation with her father crept back into her mind. The anxiety about the upcoming family reunion resurfaced, and she found herself hesitating with her brush mid-stroke.

"Hey, what's going on?" Christian asked, noticing the shift in her demeanor. "You seem a bit distracted."

Kara sighed, putting down her brush as she turned to face him. "It's just... the family reunion is coming up, and I can't shake this feeling of dread. What if I can't handle it? What if I face everything I've been avoiding?"

Christian stepped closer, his expression softening. "You know, it's okay to feel that way. It's a big step, and it's natural to be anxious about it. But maybe you can use that energy in our painting. Channel those feelings into your art. Let it all out."

She looked at the canvas, the colors swirling together, vibrant yet chaotic. "You think it would help?"

"Absolutely," he encouraged, his tone earnest. "Art is a powerful way to confront what's inside. Let's create something that reflects not just our journey but also the struggles you're facing."

With a deep breath, Kara picked up her brush and began to paint with renewed purpose. She let the colors flow, using bold strokes to represent her fears and softer hues to capture her hopes. As she painted, she felt her emotions pouring out onto the canvas, transforming her anxiety into a visual narrative.

Christian joined her, mirroring her movements, and together, they created layers of color and texture that told a story of resilience and vulnerability. The canvas became a reflection of their connection, woven together through shared experiences and emotional expression.

As they worked, Kara felt a sense of liberation. With every stroke, she released the weight of her fears, transforming them into something beautiful. The colors on the canvas became a representation of her journey, filled with both struggles and triumphs.

"See? You're doing it!" Christian exclaimed, his enthusiasm infectious. "This is incredible! You're pouring your heart into it, and it shows."

Kara looked at the canvas, the vibrant colors blending harmoniously, and for the first time, she felt a flicker of hope. "Maybe

I can face my fears after all," she admitted, her voice filled with newfound determination.

"Of course you can," Christian said, his gaze unwavering. "You're stronger than you realize, Kara. And no matter what happens at the reunion, you'll have your art and your voice to express how you feel."

With a renewed sense of purpose, Kara continued to paint, feeling the support of Christian beside her. Together, they created a piece that was more than just a painting; it was a testament to their journey, a celebration of their connection, and a canvas of colors that captured the essence of their shared experiences.

As the competition drew to a close, Kara stepped back to admire their work. The canvas was alive with energy, a beautiful blend of colors that told their story. And in that moment, she realized that even amidst uncertainty, there was beauty to be found in embracing her emotions and the journey ahead.

CHAPTER 27

The Canvas of Expectation

As Kara and Christian stepped back from their completed painting, the vibrant colors swirled together on the canvas like a beautiful chaos, reflecting not only their shared creativity but also the emotional journey they had embarked upon that day. The festival grounds, now bathed in the golden glow of the setting sun, buzzed with excitement. Kara felt a mixture of pride and apprehension as she gazed at their work, the vibrant blues and greens capturing the essence of the ocean they both loved.

"Wow, Kara, we did it!" Christian exclaimed, running a hand through his tousled hair, his eyes shining with enthusiasm. "Look at this masterpiece! It's a true representation of our adventure today."

Kara smiled, feeling warmth spread through her chest at his infectious excitement. "I can't believe we created this together," she replied, her voice tinged with disbelief. "It's like each stroke of our brush tells a story."

Just as they were basking in the glow of their achievement, a voice amplified across the festival grounds, cutting through the hum of conversation. "Ladies and gentlemen, we have an exciting announcement! We are thrilled to introduce our surprise guest artist who will be judging our painting competition!"

Kara's heart raced at the unexpected news. She turned toward the stage where a crowd had gathered, their attention now focused on the speaker. The name that followed sent a jolt of both thrill and anxiety coursing through her.

"Please welcome the incredibly talented and renowned artist, Sofia Marquez!"

Gasps of excitement rippled through the crowd as Kara's breath caught in her throat. Sofia Marquez was not just any artist; she was a visionary whose work had inspired countless individuals, including Kara herself. The thought of her standing just a few feet away felt surreal, and yet, it brought a wave of insecurity crashing over Kara.

"What if she doesn't like our painting?" Kara whispered, her gaze fixed on the stage, where Sofia was now approaching the judging area with an air of confidence and grace. "What if it doesn't measure up?"

Christian noticed the shift in her demeanor, his playful energy momentarily subdued. "Hey, it's just a competition," he reassured her, stepping closer and gently squeezing her hand. "We created something beautiful together. That's what matters."

"I know, but..." Kara hesitated, her mind racing with self-doubt. "What if she looks at our painting and sees all the flaws? I'm not a real artist like her. I'm just a manager who loves to paint on the side."

"Kara, listen to me," Christian said firmly, his voice steady. "Art isn't about perfection; it's about expression. You poured your heart into this, and that's worth celebrating. No one else can tell your story the way you do."

As she took a deep breath, Kara felt the weight of her insecurities pressing down on her, but Christian's words resonated deeply within her. She knew he was right—art was about sharing a piece of oneself, not just about winning accolades. Yet, the thought of Sofia's discerning eye made her stomach churn.

"Why don't we take a moment to step away from the crowd?" Christian suggested, sensing her unease. "Let's find a quieter spot to gather our thoughts."

Kara nodded, grateful for his understanding. Together, they made their way to a small patch of sand just beyond the bustling festival area. The sound of waves crashing against the shore provided a soothing backdrop as they settled onto a log, the salty breeze tousling Kara's hair.

"Just look at the ocean," Christian said, gesturing toward the horizon where the sun was beginning to dip below the waves. "It's vast and unpredictable, yet it's beautiful in its own way. Like art, it's never perfect, but it's always authentic."

Kara watched the waves, each one unique as they ebbed and flowed. "You're right. The ocean doesn't apologize for its imperfections," she mused, feeling a flicker of inspiration ignite within her. "Maybe I need to embrace that same mindset."

"Exactly! And remember, Sofia Marquez is judging based on her own experiences and perspective. You can't control how she sees your work, but you can control how you feel about it." Christian smiled, his confidence infectious. "So, let's focus on what we created together, not on what someone else might think."

Kara took a deep breath, letting the salty air fill her lungs. "Okay, I'll try," she said, a hint of determination creeping into her voice. "I just want to be proud of what we made."

"You should be! And no matter what happens, this day has been incredible. We've shared our creativity and our emotions, and that's what makes it special," Christian replied, his eyes sparkling with excitement.

As they returned to the festival, Kara felt a renewed sense of purpose. The anxiety still lingered, but Christian's unwavering support fortified her resolve. They rejoined the crowd, where the atmosphere was electric with anticipation. Artists and onlookers alike gathered around the stage, eager to hear Sofia's thoughts on the competition.

Sofia stood at the center, her presence commanding attention. Kara's heart raced as she listened to the renowned artist speak about the importance of creativity and self-expression.

"Art is a journey," Sofia said. "It's about exploring your emotions, pushing boundaries, and being true to yourself."

Kara felt a connection with Sofia's words, the tension in her chest easing as she realized that the very essence of art was being celebrated. She glanced at Christian, whose encouraging smile reminded her of the bond they had forged through their creative process.

As the judging commenced, Kara watched intently as Sofia moved from one canvas to another, offering insights and praise. When it was finally their turn, Kara's heart pounded in her chest. She felt exposed, standing before an artist she admired, holding the story of their day wrapped in color and emotion.

"This piece is striking," Sofia remarked, examining their painting closely. "The colors evoke a sense of movement, almost like the waves of the ocean. I can feel the energy of your collaboration."

Kara's breath caught in her throat. Sofia's words were more than she had hoped for; they were validation that her voice had been heard through the art they created together.

"What inspired you to create this?" Sofia asked, looking directly at Kara and Christian.

Kara exchanged a glance with Christian, feeling a rush of warmth as she spoke. "We wanted to capture our journey together—the beauty of the ocean, the challenges we face, and the emotions that come with it. It's a representation of our connection and the stories we share."

Sofia nodded, a smile crossing her lips. "It's a beautiful expression of your relationship with each other and with the world around you. Thank you for sharing it."

As they stepped away, Kara felt a sense of relief wash over her. She realized that it didn't matter whether they won the competition. What mattered was the experience they had shared and the courage she had found within herself.

Christian turned to her, his eyes sparkling. "See? You did it! You embraced the moment and expressed yourself authentically!"

Kara couldn't help but laugh, the tension from earlier dissipating like the waves on the shore. "Thank you for believing in me, Christian. I couldn't have done it without you."

"Always," he replied, pulling her into a playful side hug. "Now, let's celebrate our creativity, no matter the outcome!"

As they rejoined the crowd, Kara felt lighter than she had in days. The festival around her transformed into a vibrant celebration of art, community, and self-discovery. She had stepped beyond her insecurities and found her voice, and for that, she felt grateful.

In that moment, surrounded by the energy of creativity and the warmth of friendship, Kara realized that the true value of the experience was not in winning or losing but in the journey they had taken together—the vibrant canvas of their shared adventure now etched in her heart.

A Canvas of New Beginnings

As the sun dipped below the horizon, casting a warm orange hue over the festival grounds, Kara and Christian felt a palpable sense of excitement in the air. The buzz of laughter and chatter filled the space around them as families and friends celebrated the culmination of a day filled with creativity and connection. The vibrant colors of the canvases surrounding them glowed in the twilight, and for Kara, they represented not just the artistry but the journey she had begun to embrace.

"Can you believe we did this?" Kara asked, her voice laced with wonder as she gestured to their painting. "Just a few hours ago, I was so nervous about even showing it to anyone."

Christian grinned, his eyes still sparkling from the exhilaration of the day. "You were amazing! I told you that once you let go of the fear, the magic happens. Look at the joy on everyone's faces!" He gestured to a group of children who were animatedly discussing their own artworks with wide-eyed enthusiasm.

Kara chuckled, feeling the warmth of the moment wrap around her. "I guess I needed that push, huh?" Her gaze drifted over to the stage, where Sofia Marquez was still mingling with festival attendees, her presence a magnetic force that drew people in.

Just then, Kara and Christian were approached by Sofia herself. Kara felt her heart leap into her throat, a mix of awe and nerves swirling within her. "Hello, you two!" Sofia greeted them, her smile radiant and genuine. "I wanted to take a moment to personally commend you on your painting. It's full of life and emotion, and I can see the connection you share through your art."

"Thank you so much!" Kara managed to reply, feeling a blush creep into her cheeks. "That means a lot coming from you."

Sofia leaned closer, her expression shifting to one of excitement. "I'm actually hosting a workshop next weekend for aspiring artists, and I'd love for both of you to join. It's a chance to explore new techniques and really dig into your creative processes."

Kara's heart raced with a mixture of thrill and anxiety. A workshop with Sofia Marquez? It was an opportunity she had dreamed of, yet doubt crept in like a shadow. "I don't know, Sofia. I mean, what if I'm not good enough? What if the other participants are much more experienced?"

Christian noticed the flicker of uncertainty in Kara's eyes and gently squeezed her hand. "Kara, this is your chance to grow. Every artist starts somewhere, and you've already taken such huge strides today," he said, his tone encouraging. "You can't let fear hold you back from something that could be amazing."

Sofia nodded in agreement, her gaze unwavering. "Exactly! Art isn't about competition; it's about exploration and connection. I want to see you both thrive."

Kara took a deep breath, feeling the weight of her hesitation. "Okay, I'll do it," she said, finding a spark of courage within her. "Thank you for the invitation."

"Wonderful! I can't wait to see what you create," Sofia replied, a glimmer of excitement in her eyes. With that, she waved goodbye and moved on to speak with another group of artists, leaving Kara and Christian standing together amidst the festival's vibrant energy.

"Wow, I can't believe you're really doing it," Christian said, pride evident in his voice. "I knew you could!"

Kara smiled, the initial excitement mingling with the nerves that still lingered. "I hope I can keep up with everyone else. I feel like I'm still figuring things out."

"Trust me, we all are. It's part of the journey," Christian reassured her. "Just think about how far you've come in such a short time. You're not the same person you were before this festival. You're evolving, and that's what makes you an artist."

As the festival began to wind down, the sounds of laughter and music slowly faded into the background, replaced by the soft whispers of the ocean waves. Kara looked out at the horizon, the beauty of the moment washing over her like the tide. She could feel the possibilities stretching out before her like an endless canvas.

That evening, as they walked back to Christian's car, Kara's mind buzzed with thoughts of the workshop. "I wonder what I'll learn. I hope I can find my voice in all of this," she mused, her eyes shining with anticipation.

"You will," Christian said confidently. "Just let yourself be open to the experience. It'll be an adventure, just like today."

As they drove home, the streets illuminated by streetlights and the fading glow of the sunset, Kara's thoughts drifted to the family reunion scheduled for the following weekend. It was a gathering she always looked forward to, filled with laughter, stories, and, of course, a healthy dose of family shenanigans.

But amidst the excitement of the reunion, another thought crept into Christian's mind. As he glanced at Kara, who was lost in thought, he couldn't help but wonder about taking their relationship to the next level. The idea of proposing to her had been swirling in his heart for some time now, and the thought of doing it at the reunion felt just right. Surrounded by family, the people who loved them most, it could be a moment to remember.

Yet, he knew he wanted to talk to Jodi first. Jodi had always been a voice of reason for him, and he respected her opinion. Plus, she had always been Kara's biggest supporter. Christian felt that if he could get Jodi's blessing, it would mean the world to him.

"Are you okay?" Kara asked, her playful tone snapping him out of his thoughts.

"Yeah, just thinking about how exciting the next few weeks are going to be," he replied, his heart racing at the idea of sharing his plans with Jodi.

Kara smiled, her enthusiasm infectious. "I can't wait for the workshop and then the reunion! So much to look forward to!"

As they pulled into the driveway, Kara's excitement radiated through her. "And who knows? Maybe by the end of the workshop, I'll have something amazing to show at the reunion."

Christian chuckled, his heart swelling with admiration for her determination. "I have no doubt you will. You're going to surprise yourself."

They stepped out of the car, and as they walked toward the front door, Kara turned to Christian with a playful glint in her eyes. "You better be ready for me to blow everyone away."

"Always ready," he said, grinning back at her. "You've got this, Kara. Just remember to have fun."

As they entered the house, the warmth of home enveloped them, and Kara felt a sense of belonging and purpose. The canvas of her life was stretching with new colors, new opportunities, and new friendships. With Christian by her side, she felt emboldened to paint her future with the vibrant strokes of her own voice, ready to embrace whatever came next.

CHAPTER 29

Embracing the Canvas of Self

The days leading up to the workshop felt like a whirlwind for Kara. Each morning, she awoke with a flutter of excitement, only to be followed by a wave of anxiety that crashed over her like an unexpected tide. It was a curious mix of emotions, and she often found herself oscillating between eager anticipation and paralyzing self-doubt.

As the sun rose higher in the sky, Kara could feel the warmth of the day seeping into her bones, yet her mind was a tempest. She was determined to embrace her creativity, but the thought of standing alongside accomplished artists made her heart race with trepidation. What if she didn't belong there? What if her art was deemed inferior?

Christian had been incredibly supportive, encouraging her every step of the way. "Kara, every artist has a unique voice," he would remind her. "It's not about being the best; it's about expressing yourself." His words echoed in her mind as she prepared for her late-night art session, a ritual she had embraced as a way to calm her fears and unleash her creativity.

That evening, Kara set up her easel in the living room, the soft glow of a single lamp illuminating her workspace. The scent of linseed oil and paint filled the air, grounding her in the moment. With a deep breath, she picked up her brush and began to stroke the canvas, letting her emotions guide her hand.

As she painted, the world around her faded away. She lost herself in the rhythm of color and form, each brushstroke a release of pent-up feelings. Memories of the festival, the laughter of children, and the warmth of Christian's support danced in her mind, weaving a tapestry of inspiration. Yet, despite this rush of creativity, an uneasy feeling still lingered at the back of her mind, a whisper that questioned her worth.

It was during the quiet of her artistic endeavor that her phone buzzed unexpectedly. Startled, she glanced at the screen and saw Sofia Marquez's name. Her heart skipped a beat. She hesitated for a moment, a swirl of disbelief and excitement coursing through her. What could Sofia want?

"Hello?" Kara answered.

"Hi, Kara! It's Sofia," came the warm reply, the familiar cadence of the artist's voice wrapping around her like a comforting blanket. "I hope I'm not interrupting anything."

"Not at all! I was just painting," Kara said, a smile spreading across her face. "What's up?"

There was a pause on the other end, then Sofia continued, her tone earnest, "I just wanted to check in on you before the workshop. I know it can be a bit daunting, and I wanted to share something with you. When I first started, I struggled with self-doubt too. I was terrified of being judged and felt like I didn't belong. But then I realized something crucial: art is a personal journey. It's about expressing your truth, not competing with others."

Kara felt a lump form in her throat as she listened. The vulnerability in Sofia's voice resonated deeply with her. "I guess I've been feeling that way," she admitted. "What if I'm just not good enough?"

"Kara, everyone has their own path," Sofia reassured her. "What you create is valid because it comes from you. Embrace your unique perspective. It's what will set you apart and make your art resonate with others."

The words resonated with Kara, igniting a flicker of hope. "Thank you, Sofia. That really means a lot," she said, her voice steadying. "I've been trying to remind myself of that."

"Good! I can't wait to see what you come up with. Remember, it's about enjoying the process. Let your heart guide you, and don't worry about the outcome," Sofia said before they exchanged a few more pleasantries and hung up.

With renewed energy, Kara turned back to her canvas. Inspired by Sofia's wisdom, she picked up her brush once more, this time with a sense of purpose. She began layering colors in a way that reflected her journey—swirls of blues and greens representing the calm ocean waves that had always brought her peace, intermingled with bursts of vibrant reds and yellows that embodied her excitement and passion for life.

As she painted, she poured her anxieties, joys, and dreams onto the canvas. Each stroke became a cathartic release, an affirmation of her identity and creativity. Kara smiled as she worked, losing track of time as the colors danced before her eyes. She finally felt a sense of freedom, as though she were breaking free from the chains of self-doubt that had held her captive for so long.

Meanwhile, while Kara was painting her heart out, Christian sat in his living room, nervously rehearsing what he wanted to say to Jodi. The idea of proposing to Kara had taken root in his mind, and he felt it was time to seek his best friend's advice. Jodi had always been a guiding light in both their lives, and he knew her perspective would be valuable.

He grabbed his phone and dialed her number, anticipation fluttering in his stomach. Jodi answered almost immediately, her voice bright and cheerful. "Hey, Christian! What's up?"

"Hey, Jodi! I was hoping we could meet up. There's something important I want to discuss," he said, trying to keep his tone casual despite the gravity of the moment.

"Of course! I'd love to! How about that little coffee shop we used to visit? I could use a good latte and some of their pastries," she replied, her excitement infectious.

"Sounds perfect. I'll see you in a bit," Christian said, hanging up and feeling a mixture of nerves and excitement.

He grabbed his jacket and headed out, his mind racing with thoughts of Kara and the life he envisioned for them together.

At the coffee shop, the aroma of freshly brewed coffee mingled with the sweet scent of pastries, creating an inviting atmosphere. As Christian walked in, he spotted Jodi at a corner table, her vibrant energy lighting up the room. He waved and made his way over, sliding into the seat across from her.

"Hey! You look a little tense. What's going on?" Jodi asked, her keen eyes noticing the apprehension etched on Christian's face.

Christian took a deep breath, gathering his thoughts. "So, I've been thinking a lot about Kara and our relationship," he began, feeling the weight of his words. "I want to take the next step and propose to her at the family reunion this weekend."

Jodi's eyes widened in surprise and delight. "Oh my gosh, Christian! That's amazing! Have you thought about how you want to do it?"

"Yeah, I have some ideas, but I wanted to get your input. You know her so well, and I really want it to be special," he explained, his heart racing at the thought of making this commitment.

Jodi leaned in, her enthusiasm palpable. "I think it's a fantastic idea! Kara will love the surprise. Maybe you could incorporate something personal into the proposal, like a memory you both share or something related to her art."

Christian nodded, feeling inspired by Jodi's suggestions. "That's a great idea! There's something about the way she expresses herself through art that truly captivates me. I want to honor that in some way."

As they continued to brainstorm, Christian felt a sense of clarity wash over him. He was ready to take this leap, to create a moment that would intertwine their lives forever.

Meanwhile, Kara was lost in her own creative world, her heart full and her spirit soaring. With every stroke on the canvas, she felt more connected to her journey and the possibilities that lay ahead. She was ready to embrace her true self, to let her art reflect her inner voice, and to share that with the world.

CHAPTER 30

The Canvas of Possibility

As dawn broke over the horizon, casting golden rays of sunlight through her bedroom window, Kara felt a peculiar flutter in her stomach. Today was the day of the workshop, the event she had been both eagerly anticipating and dreading. She stared at her reflection in the mirror, taking a moment to appreciate the woman staring back at her. There was a spark of determination in her hazel eyes, a reflection of the countless emotions she had navigated over the past few weeks.

"Okay, Kara," she whispered to herself, "you've got this."

She smoothed down her outfit—a simple yet elegant sundress adorned with soft floral patterns that reminded her of the blooming spring outside. As she gathered her materials—her favorite brushes, a palette of vibrant colors, and her sketchbook—she couldn't shake the feeling of nervous energy coursing through her veins.

Driving to the venue, Kara played her favorite playlist, the upbeat melodies filling her with encouragement. The closer she got, the more she felt the thrill of possibility mingling with self-doubt. Images of accomplished artists flashed through her mind, each one a reminder of her insecurities. What if her art didn't stand up against theirs? What if she couldn't capture the essence of her creativity in front of others?

Taking a deep breath as she parked, Kara stepped out of her car and walked towards the venue. The building was an old warehouse transformed into an art space, its walls covered in murals and the atmosphere buzzing with excitement. As she entered, she was greeted by a kaleidoscope of colors and sounds. Artists mingled, discussing techniques and inspirations, laughter filling the air like an infectious melody.

Kara's heart raced as she navigated through the crowd, her eyes darting from one vibrant piece to another. The walls were adorned with works that spoke of passion, struggle, and the beauty of the human experience. She felt small amidst such talent, and for a brief moment, a wave of despair washed over her. Maybe she didn't belong here.

Just as those thoughts began to spiral, she caught sight of a familiar face across the room. It was Sofia Marquez, her mentor and beloved artist, deep in conversation with another participant. Kara's heart leapt. Sofia's presence was like a lighthouse in a stormy sea, guiding her back to her purpose. She made her way through the crowd, her feet carrying her toward Sofia, who was animatedly discussing color theory.

"Kara!" Sofia exclaimed, her face lighting up as she turned to greet her. "I'm so glad you made it!"

"Thanks, Sofia! I almost didn't," Kara admitted, her voice tinged with a mix of relief and excitement. "I've been feeling a bit overwhelmed."

Sofia placed a reassuring hand on her shoulder. "That's completely normal! Remember, it's all about self-expression. There's no right or wrong here, only your unique perspective. Are you ready to share your work?"

Kara hesitated, her heart pounding. "I don't know... What if it's not good enough?"

Sofia's eyes sparkled with warmth and understanding. "Kara, the only person you should be comparing yourself to is the one you were yesterday. This day is about growth, not competition. Trust in your journey and the beauty of your art. You have a voice that's waiting to be heard. I want you to showcase your work by the end of the day. I believe in you."

The sincerity in Sofia's voice resonated within Kara, igniting that flicker of hope once more. "Okay, I'll think about it," she replied.

The workshop began, and Kara found herself engaged in various activities—painting techniques, discussions on artistic influences, and collaborative projects that sparked creativity. Each session was a delightful blend of learning and sharing, and Kara felt herself starting to relax, the initial tension melting away.

As the hours passed, she immersed herself in the process, her worries fading into the background as she painted alongside other artists. The camaraderie was palpable, and Kara found herself laughing and exchanging ideas, feeling the warmth of creativity envelop her. For the first time in what felt like ages, she was simply enjoying the art of creation, losing herself in the colors and textures.

During a break, Kara stepped outside to take a breath of fresh air. The sun was shining brightly, and she could hear the distant sound of laughter from the courtyard. It was there that she spotted Christian, standing with a group of friends, his athletic build and easy smile drawing people in like a magnet. He looked effortlessly charming, his lighthearted nature shining bright as he animatedly recounted a story. Kara's heart fluttered at the sight of him, a reminder of how he had always been her biggest supporter.

"Hey, beautiful!" Christian called out, catching her eye. He waved her over, and she felt a warm rush of affection as she approached him. "How's it going? Are you having fun?"

"Yeah, I am! It's been amazing," she replied, her heart swelling with joy as they locked eyes. "How about you? What are you up to?"

"I'm just soaking up all this artistic energy," he said, grinning. "And, okay, maybe I'm also plotting how to make the best proposal ever," he added, a teasing glint in his eye.

Kara felt her cheeks flush at his words. "Proposal? Are you serious?"

Christian leaned in closer, his voice lowered conspiratorially. "I am. I've been thinking about it for a while now. I want it to be perfect, something that reflects everything we've built together. But honestly, I'm a bit nervous about it."

"I can't imagine what's going through your mind," Kara said, her heart racing at the thought of their future. "But I know whatever you do will be special, just like you."

"Thanks, Kara. That means a lot," he replied, sincerity in his eyes. "Now, you need to promise me something. At the end of the day, you're going to share your art. Trust me, everyone will love it."

Kara chuckled softly, her heart warmed by his encouragement. "I'll think about it. I just need a little more time to gather my courage."

"Take your time, but don't let that doubt creep in," he said, his tone playful yet firm. "You're an amazing artist, and it's time you show the world what you've got."

With a renewed sense of determination, Kara returned to the workshop, her mind buzzing with possibilities. As the day progressed, the energy in the room heightened. Artists began sharing their work, and their admiration for each other's creations filled the space with warmth and inspiration. Kara watched as her peers showcased their art, their vulnerability and authenticity resonating deeply.

When the time came for her to present, Kara felt a jolt of anxiety shoot through her, but she remembered Sofia's words. Taking a deep breath, she stepped forward, her heart pounding in her chest. With each brushstroke she revealed, she felt the applause and admiration of her peers wash over her like a wave.

Just then, as she connected with the audience, she caught Christian's eye across the room. He smiled at her with such pride that it ignited a fire within her. She poured her heart into explaining the meaning behind her work, sharing her journey and the emotions that had led her to this moment. The applause that followed felt like a warm embrace, and Kara realized she was not just sharing her art; she was sharing a piece of herself.

As the workshop drew to a close and the day came to a breathtaking finish, Kara looked around at the vibrant community of artists who had supported and inspired one another. She felt a profound sense of belonging, a part of something larger than herself.

Meanwhile, as Christian prepared for his moment, his heart raced with anticipation. He knew that his proposal was just around the corner, and as he watched Kara shine in her element, he felt an overwhelming certainty that he was ready to take the leap. Today was a day of creativity, growth, and love—a perfect canvas for what was to come.

CHAPTER 31

Endless Possibilities And Love

As the workshop came to a close, Kara felt a vibrant exhilaration coursing through her veins. The applause still echoed in her ears, and she could barely contain the smile that stretched across her face. Surrounded by fellow artists, she relished the afterglow of sharing her work, a sense of belonging wrapping around her like a warm blanket. Conversations buzzed with excitement as participants exchanged ideas, and Kara found herself swept up in the contagious energy.

"Did you see the way they reacted to your piece?" Sofia approached her, her voice laced with pride. "You captivated them, Kara! That was incredible."

"Thanks, Sofia. I still can't believe I actually did it," Kara replied, her cheeks flushed with a mix of embarrassment and joy. "It felt... liberating."

Kara scanned the room, her heart swelling as she looked at the artwork that surrounded her. Each piece told a story, and she felt a deep admiration for her peers. It was during this moment of reflection that she overheard snippets of conversation from a nearby group. The excitement in their voices piqued her curiosity.

"Did you hear about the upcoming art competition? It's supposed to be a big deal!" one artist exclaimed, her eyes sparkling with enthusiasm. "It could launch your career if you win!"

Kara's heart skipped a beat. The mere mention of an art competition sent a thrill of anticipation through her. She edged closer, eager to gather more information.

"Yeah, I heard the prizes are incredible," another artist chimed in. "Not just cash but also opportunities for gallery exhibitions!"

Kara felt a surge of inspiration wash over her. This could be the chance she had been waiting for, a way to showcase her work on a larger platform. She turned to Sofia, her eyes wide with excitement. "Did you hear that? An art competition! I have to enter!"

Sofia's smile widened. "Absolutely! You've got the talent, and this could be your moment to shine. You should start brainstorming ideas right away."

Determination ignited within Kara as she nodded emphatically. "I will! I just need to figure out what I want to create. It has to represent me, my journey."

"Take your time," Sofia advised, her tone encouraging. "Let your heart guide you. You're ready for this."

Just then, Kara's phone buzzed in her pocket, interrupting the flow of her thoughts. She pulled it out to see a message from Christian. A flutter of excitement danced in her stomach as she read the words: "Can't wait to celebrate your success tonight! Dress up. I have a surprise for you. Love you!"

Kara's heart raced. "Christian's planning something special for tonight! I wonder what it could be," she mused aloud, a grin forming on her lips.

Sofia raised an eyebrow, a teasing glint in her eyes. "Romantic surprise? Sounds like he's got something up his sleeve."

"Knowing Christian, it's probably something adventurous." Kara laughed, her mind drifting to the spontaneity that defined their relationship. "I better get ready. I want to look perfect."

As the workshop concluded, Kara bid farewell to her newfound friends. She headed home, her thoughts a whirlwind of colors and ideas. Once she arrived, she slipped into a playful yet elegant dress, the fabric flowing around her as she twirled in front of the mirror. She applied a touch of makeup, her fingers deftly highlighting her features. Each brushstroke felt like a celebration of her spirit.

As the sun dipped below the horizon, casting a palette of warm hues across the sky, Kara felt a sense of anticipation building. She grabbed her sketchbook, flipping through the pages filled with her thoughts and ideas. The competition loomed in her mind, and she began jotting down concepts that reflected her journey—her struggles, her growth, and the beauty she found in art.

Meanwhile, Christian was busy preparing for their evening. He'd been reflecting on how much Kara had grown, how she had blossomed into an artist who was beginning to find her voice. The proposal weighed heavily on his mind, and he wanted this dinner to be perfect—a moment that would encapsulate everything they had shared.

He set up a cozy picnic on the beach, twinkling fairy lights strung between palm trees, casting a soft glow over the sand. A carefully curated assortment of Kara's favorite foods was laid out, each dish a thoughtful gesture to show how well he knew her. As he added the final touches, he felt a rush of excitement mixed with nerves. Would she love it? Would she say yes?

As Kara arrived at the beach, the golden hues of sunset painted the sky. She spotted Christian in the distance, his silhouette framed by the backdrop of the ocean. The sight sent a rush of warmth through her, and she could feel her heart beating faster. He turned to greet her, his face lighting up with that charming smile that always made her feel at ease.

"Wow, Christian! This is amazing!" she exclaimed, taking in the scene before her. "You went all out!"

"I wanted to celebrate you, your art, and your success today. You deserve it," he replied, his voice filled with genuine admiration. He took her hand, leading her toward the picnic setup.

As they settled down on the blanket, Kara felt a sense of tranquility enveloping her, the rhythmic sounds of the waves creating a soothing ambiance. They shared laughter and stories, the moments flowing effortlessly as they savored the delicious food.

"Today was incredible," Kara said, her eyes sparkling. "I can't believe I finally shared my work. It felt like I was stepping into my own skin."

Christian leaned forward, his gaze steady and filled with warmth. "You were phenomenal, Kara. You've got this incredible talent, and I can see how passionate you are. That competition? You have to enter. You're ready."

Kara smiled, her heart swelling with appreciation for his unwavering support. "I'm going to! I already have some ideas brewing in my mind. But tonight, I want to enjoy this moment with you."

As the sun dipped lower, the sky transformed into a canvas of deep purples and oranges, reflecting the warmth between them. Christian reached for her hand, his thumb brushing gently over her knuckles. There was a moment of stillness, a silence filled with promise and unspoken feelings.

"Kara," he began, his voice serious yet tender. "I've been thinking a lot about us, about our journey together. You inspire me every day, and I can't imagine my life without you."

Kara's heart raced, sensing the weight of his words. "Christian, I feel the same way. You make me feel alive, and I cherish every moment we share."

Taking a deep breath, Christian continued, his voice steady. "I want to take the leap and commit to you completely. You're my partner, my muse, and I want to build a future together."

As the warmth of the moment enveloped them, Kara knew what was coming. She felt an overwhelming rush of emotions as she realized the depth of her love for him. "Christian, I love you. I've loved you for a long time. You make me feel seen and understood."

In that magical moment, under the blanket of stars, they embraced, the world around them fading into the background. Kara felt safe in his arms, the weight of her feelings finally lifting as she let herself be vulnerable.

As they pulled back, Christian looked into her eyes, his expression a mixture of hope and love. "So, what do you think about forever?"

Kara's heart soared. "I think forever sounds perfect. I'm ready for it."

CHAPTER 32

The Colors of Commitment

As dawn broke over the horizon, the soft light shimmered on the ocean's surface, casting a golden hue across the beach where Kara and Christian had shared a night filled with promises and dreams. The waves whispered secrets to the shore, echoing the deep connection that had been nurtured between the two artists. Wrapped in each other's warmth, they had fallen asleep under the stars, their hearts entwined in a way that felt both exhilarating and safe.

Kara stirred awake, the salty breeze tousling her hair as she blinked against the morning light. She turned to Christian, who lay beside her, his face serene and relaxed. His athletic build silhouetted against the soft glow of the sun, and Kara felt a rush of affection. Memories of their heartfelt conversation from the night before flooded her mind, and a smile spread across her lips. This was more than just a romantic moment; it was a promise of forever.

She gently nudged him awake. "Christian, rise and shine! The world is calling, and so is breakfast!"

Christian cracked open one eye, then the other, a playful grin spreading across his face. "I never knew breakfast could be so alluring," he teased, stretching his arms and basking in the early morning light.

Kara chuckled, the sound mingling with the gentle crashing of the waves. "You're quite the charmer, you know that?"

They shared a moment of laughter, savoring the sweetness of the morning. As they packed up the remnants of their picnic from the night before, Kara felt a spark of excitement coursing through her. She was eager to share every detail of their evening with her best friend, Jodi, whom she knew would be thrilled about the depth of Kara's relationship with Christian.

After a quick dip in the ocean to wash off the sand and salt, they headed back home. Kara felt invigorated, her mind already racing with thoughts of the art competition approaching. Yet, there was something deeper brewing within her—an awareness of the upcoming family reunion that loomed just around the corner. Kara had always cherished her family gatherings, but this time felt different. She couldn't shake the feeling of anxiety creeping in, nagging at her confidence about her art and her place within her family.

As they drove towards Kara's workplace, the sun filled the car with a warm glow, and Kara turned to Christian, a spark of mischief in her eyes. "So, what's the plan for today? Are we going to conquer the art world together?"

Christian's expression shifted to one of contemplation. "Actually, I was thinking we could embark on a little artistic journey together. How about a retreat to that artist's haven by the sea? Just you, me, and our creativity flowing like the waves?"

Kara's heart soared at the thought. "That sounds incredible! A weekend of inspiration and collaboration! We could create something beautiful together."

His eyes lit up, and he nodded, his enthusiasm contagious. "Exactly! I want us to paint a mural that symbolizes our shared dreams. Something that captures this moment in our lives."

As they arrived at the doctor's office, Kara's excitement bubbled over. "I can't wait to tell Jodi! She'll be all over this idea!"

After a quick kiss goodbye, Kara rushed into the office, the familiar hum of activity greeting her as she entered. The waiting room was filled with patients, and her colleagues were busy checking in clients. As she settled into her role managing the office, her mind kept drifting back to Christian and their plans for the retreat.

At lunch, she found a moment to call Jodi, her voice surging with excitement. "You won't believe what Christian has planned! We're going to an artist's haven by the sea to work on a mural together!"

"Wow, that sounds amazing! You two are seriously the most adorable couple," Jodi replied, her tone filled with enthusiasm. "But tell me everything! What's the mural going to represent?"

Kara took a deep breath, her heart swelling at the thought. "It's going to symbolize our journey together—our dreams, our love for art, and all the beautiful moments we've shared. I really want it to capture our essence."

Jodi's voice turned serious. "That sounds profound, Kara. But are you ready for it? You know how you can get when you feel pressured about your art."

The reminder of her insecurities washed over Kara like a cold wave. "I know, I know. But I can't let those fears get in the way. I have to push through them, especially with the competition coming up."

"Just remember, you're not alone in this. You have Christian, and you have me. You're going to shine!"

With her friend's words lingering in her mind, Kara finished her shift with a renewed sense of determination. She was ready to embrace her art, ready to dive into the preparations for the competition, and ready to pour her heart into the mural with Christian.

Later that evening, as she arrived home, her heart raced with anticipation. She couldn't wait to see Christian and share her thoughts about their upcoming retreat. Just as she began to settle in, there was a knock at the door.

"Surprise!" Christian exclaimed as she opened the door, holding a bouquet of the brightest sunflowers she had ever seen. "I just wanted to remind you how much you inspire me."

Kara's heart swelled at the thoughtful gesture. "You always know how to make me smile. Thank you!"

They spent the evening brainstorming ideas for their mural, sketching out concepts that reflected their dreams and aspirations. With each stroke of their pencils, Kara felt the weight of her insecurities beginning to lift. Christian's unwavering support and creative energy ignited a passion within her that she hadn't felt in ages.

However, as they dove deeper into their planning, Kara couldn't shake the anxiety about the family reunion. Memories of past gatherings danced in her mind—the expectations, the comparisons, the pressure to succeed. What if they asked about her art? What if they didn't see her as a serious artist?

"Hey, Kara?" Christian's voice broke through her thoughts. "Are you okay? You've gone quiet on me."

She looked up, meeting his concerned gaze. "I'm just...thinking about the reunion this weekend. I feel like I have to prove myself, especially with everything happening in my art career."

Christian's expression softened as he reached out to take her hand. "You don't have to prove anything to anyone. You're an incredible artist, and your journey is yours alone. Just be yourself."

Kara took a deep breath, feeling the warmth of his words settle in her heart. "You're right. I need to focus on my own path instead of worrying about what others think."

As the evening wore on, they continued to sketch, the lines of their mural intertwining like their lives. It was a labor of love, each brushstroke fueling their connection. Kara felt a sense of calm wash over her as she embraced the creativity flowing between them.

In that moment, surrounded by laughter, love, and the vibrant colors of their dreams, Kara began to understand that commitment was not just about the fears that threatened to hold her back; it was also about the courage to step forward, hand in hand with the one who believed in her the most.

CHAPTER 33

Waves of Doubt

The sun hung low in the sky, casting a warm golden light over the coastal artist's haven as Kara and Christian arrived. The air was rich with the scent of salt and blooming wildflowers, and the rhythmic sound of the waves crashing against the shore filled Kara's heart with anticipation. They parked the car and stepped out, the soft sand welcoming their bare feet, sinking slightly with each step. This was the moment they had both been waiting for—a weekend to explore their art and each other, far from the distractions of their everyday lives.

"Look at this place! It's even more beautiful than I imagined," Kara exclaimed, her eyes sparkling with excitement as she took in the vibrant colors of the landscape.

The haven was nestled between lush green hills and the endless expanse of the ocean, a perfect backdrop for inspiration to flow.

Christian grinned, his enthusiasm matching hers. "It's like a painting come to life! I can already feel the creativity pulsing in the air."

He took her hand, and they strolled toward the main building, a charming structure with large windows that overlooked the water.

As they entered, the atmosphere was alive with the chatter of fellow artists, their voices mingling with the sounds of brushes on canvas and the soft strumming of a guitar in the corner. Kara felt a twinge of nervousness as she surveyed the crowd, a mix of seasoned artists and fresh faces. It was easy to get lost in the noise, but she reminded herself that this was a space for growth and collaboration.

"Let's find our studio!" Christian said, his adventurous spirit infectious.

They made their way down a sun-drenched hallway, passing doors adorned with colorful paintings and sketches. Kara felt her own excitement as they approached their designated space—a bright, airy room with large windows that flooded the area with natural light.

"This is perfect!" Kara breathed, stepping inside. The walls were bare, waiting for their creative touch. "I can already envision our mural here."

"Let's set up and dive right in," Christian suggested, his eyes gleaming with enthusiasm. They began unpacking their supplies, laying out paints, brushes, and canvases, each item a promise of the art they would create together.

As they worked, the idyllic surroundings fueled their creativity. Kara lost herself in the colors, her brush dancing across the canvas as she painted scenes inspired by their time together—sunsets on the beach, laughter shared under starlit skies, and the dreams they had discussed so passionately. Christian was equally engrossed, channeling his energy into bold strokes and imaginative forms that seemed to breathe life onto the canvas.

Hours passed, and the sun began to dip lower in the sky, casting long shadows across their studio. Just as Kara felt a sense of accomplishment wash over her, her phone buzzed with a notification. She picked it up, her heart sinking as she read the message.

"Hey, Kara! Can't wait to see you at the reunion. We're staying at the beach house just a few minutes away! Love you!" It was from her mom, and while the love was palpable, the mention of the reunion sent a wave of anxiety crashing over her.

"Everything okay?" Christian asked, noticing the shift in her demeanor.

Kara hesitated, weighing her words. "My family is here too. They're staying at a beach house nearby for the reunion."

Christian's brow furrowed with concern. "Is that a good thing? I mean, I know family reunions can be... complicated."

"I don't know," Kara admitted, her voice shaky. "It's just that... every time we gather, there's this pressure to prove myself, especially with my art. My Aunt Clara can be particularly critical. I just—" She sighed, her brush hovering above the canvas, her thoughts tangling with memories of past reunions filled with comparisons and expectations.

"Hey, you're an incredible artist, Kara. You don't have to prove anything to anyone, especially not to her," Christian said gently, stepping closer. "If she starts asking questions, remember that it's your journey. You get to define what success means for you."

She nodded, though the anxiety lingered. "I know, but it's hard not to feel judged when I'm around them. I've always felt like I'm trying to catch up to their expectations."

"Then let's turn that into inspiration for our mural," Christian suggested, his eyes brightening with an idea. "What if we depict the struggle of rising above judgment? We can incorporate elements that symbolize the weight of expectations and the beauty of breaking free from them."

Kara smiled, feeling a spark of hope. "That's a fantastic idea! It would be a way to channel my feelings into something beautiful."

As they returned to painting, the conversation lingered in the air like a melody, guiding their brushstrokes. Each motion became a cathartic release, and Kara felt the tension start to ebb away.

Later that evening, as the sun dipped below the horizon, casting the sky in hues of pink and orange, they decided to take a break and explore the shoreline. The beach was dotted with colorful seashells, and the sound of the waves provided a soothing backdrop to their conversation.

"Let's go for a walk," Christian suggested, taking her hand. "The ocean always calms my mind."

As they strolled along the water's edge, Kara felt a sense of peace wash over her, momentarily pushing aside her worries. They laughed and shared stories, their feet sinking into the wet sand, but just as Kara began to relax, she spotted a familiar figure up ahead.

"Isn't that Aunt Clara?" she whispered, her heart racing.

Christian turned to look. "It looks like it. Do you want to avoid her?"

Kara hesitated, a mix of apprehension and resolve swirling within her. "No, I can't avoid her forever. Maybe encountering her now is a good thing. I need to face this."

As they approached, Clara turned, her expression shifting from surprise to a critical gaze as she took in Kara's presence. "Kara! What a surprise to see you here. I didn't expect you to be an artist; I thought you were just managing that doctor's office."

Kara felt her stomach twist, but she held her ground. "I'm exploring my art more seriously now. It's something I'm really passionate about."

"Oh?" Clara raised an eyebrow, a hint of skepticism in her tone. "And how's that working out for you?"

Kara's heart raced, but Christian squeezed her hand, a silent reminder of her strength. "It's going well, actually. Christian and I are working on a mural together that represents our journeys."

Clara's expression softened slightly, but the skepticism remained. "Well, that's nice. Just remember, art is a tough business. It's not always easy to make a living, you know."

"I understand that, but for me, it's about more than making a living. It's about expression and connection," Kara replied, her voice steady.

As the conversation flowed, Kara found herself brushing lightly over the surface of her aunt's questions, allowing her to see a glimpse of her passion without revealing all her vulnerabilities. It was a cautious dance, but Christian's presence grounded her, reminding her that she was not alone in this moment.

"Just remember to be practical," Clara said, her tone turning slightly patronizing. "It's wonderful to have dreams, but don't let them cloud your judgment."

"Thanks for the advice, Aunt Clara," Kara said, forcing a smile. "But I believe in chasing my passions. Life is too short not to pursue what makes you happy."

Just then, Christian interjected with a lighthearted tone, "And what makes us happy is creating art that reflects who we are. Isn't that right, Kara?"

The warmth in his voice ignited a spark within her, and Kara nodded, feeling a renewed sense of confidence. "Exactly. Art is about exploring who we are and what we want to say to the world."

Clara looked taken aback for a moment, then offered a curt nod. "Well, I suppose that's one way to look at it. Just don't lose sight of reality."

As they exchanged polite goodbyes, Kara felt a wave of relief wash over her. The encounter hadn't been easy, but she had stood her ground. With Christian by her side, she felt empowered to embrace her journey as an artist, regardless of her aunt's opinions.

"See? You handled that beautifully," Christian said, his voice light and encouraging as they walked away from the shoreline.

Kara smiled, the tension in her shoulders easing. "Thanks for being my anchor. I don't think I could have done that without you."

"Always," he replied, wrapping his arm around her shoulders.

As they continued their walk, the sound of the waves crashing against the shore echoed their shared resolve. Together, they would face whatever challenges lay ahead, fueled by their creativity and the strength of their bond.

The Brunch of Expectations

The first light of dawn crept gently into the studio, casting a warm, golden hue over the walls that Kara and Christian had spent hours painting the previous day. The sun's rays danced across the canvas, illuminating the vibrant colors they had worked so passionately to create. Kara stirred awake, her heart swelling with excitement as she remembered their plans for the day.

"Christian," she whispered, nudging him lightly. He stirred, a sleepy smile spreading across his face as he blinked against the sunlight.

"Good morning, beautiful," he said, his voice still thick with sleep. "Is it too early for a victory dance? Because I'm ready to celebrate our mural!"

Kara chuckled softly, her heart fluttering at his infectious energy. "Not yet! Let's at least have coffee before we start dancing."

Christian grinned and swung his legs over the side of the bed. "You know, I think I might be able to manage that. Coffee first, then a dance-off," he declared, as he made his way to the small kitchenette in the corner of the studio.

As she watched him, Kara felt a surge of gratitude. Christian's spontaneity and adventurous spirit inspired her, but more than that, he made her feel seen. He understood her passion for art in a way that made her heart swell.

After a few moments, Christian returned with two steaming mugs of coffee, the rich aroma filling the air. "Here you go, fuel for our creative fire," he said, handing her a cup.

"Thanks! You're the best," Kara replied, taking a sip and savoring the warmth. It was the perfect start to what she hoped would be a productive day.

As they settled into their morning routine, Kara's phone buzzed on the table, breaking the tranquil silence. She picked it up, her heart sinking as she saw a group text from her family. "Brunch at the beach house! Can't wait to see you, Kara! Love you!"

"Everything okay?" Christian asked, noticing the shift in her expression.

Kara let out a soft sigh. "It's my family. They're having brunch at the beach house... They want me to join them."

"Sounds fun! Are you going?"

She hesitated, torn between her desire to bond with her family and her commitment to the mural. "I don't know. I want to see them, but part of me feels like I should stay here and work on our painting. This mural is important to me."

"Why not do both?" Christian suggested, leaning back against the counter. "You can go to brunch, enjoy some time with your family, and then we can come back here and paint afterward. It's not like the mural is going anywhere."

Kara considered his words, feeling the weight of the decision. "You're right. It's just... I haven't really showcased my art to them before. I worry about their reactions."

"Kara, you're an incredible artist. This is your passion, and it's time you showed them just how talented you are," Christian said, his voice filled with encouragement.

"Do you really think so?"

"Absolutely. Besides, I'll be right there with you. If they say anything, I'll distract them with my stunning good looks."

Kara laughed, a bright smile breaking through her earlier uncertainty. "You are certainly charming, I'll give you that. Okay, let's do this!"

They finished their coffee, and Kara felt a renewed sense of determination. Maybe this brunch could be an opportunity to share her journey, to break through the lingering doubts that had shadowed her family gatherings in the past.

After a quick shower and a change of clothes, Kara and Christian hopped into her car. The drive to the beach house was filled with the sound of waves crashing against the shore and the sweet scent of salt in the air, invigorating their spirits.

As they approached the beach house, Kara's heart raced. It was a charming structure, painted a cheerful shade of blue, surrounded by blooming flowers and lush greenery. Her family's laughter drifted through the open windows, reminding her of the warmth and connection that always brought her back home.

"Ready?" Christian asked, glancing over at her with a playful smirk.

"Ready as I'll ever be," she replied, trying to steady her nerves. They stepped out of the car, and Kara took a deep breath, reminding herself of her purpose.

As they walked toward the entrance, Kara spotted her mom through the window, setting the table with colorful dishes and fresh fruit. She had always been the heart of their family gatherings, her cheerful demeanor lighting up every room she entered.

"Kara! You made it!" her mother exclaimed, rushing to embrace her. "I'm so glad you're here! Everyone has been looking forward to seeing you."

"Hey, Mom!" Kara responded, her heart warming at her mother's enthusiasm.

"Who's this?" her mom asked, eyeing Christian curiously.

"This is my friend Christian. We're working on an art project together," Kara explained, a hint of pride in her voice.

"It's lovely to meet you, Christian! Come in, come in! We have so much food!"

As they stepped inside, Kara was greeted by the familiar faces of her family. Her dad stood by the stove, flipping pancakes with casual ease, while her younger brother, Jake, laughed with their cousins. The air was filled with the tantalizing scent of breakfast and the warmth of familial love.

"Kara!" Jake shouted, running over to give her a quick hug. "You should have seen the last game we played. I totally crushed everyone!"

"Of course you did! You're the reigning champion," Kara teased, ruffling his hair playfully.

"Hey, don't mess up the hair!" he protested, laughing.

As they settled at the table, Kara felt a mix of warmth and apprehension. The conversation flowed easily, filled with jokes and stories, yet there was an undercurrent of pressure. She could sense the well-intentioned scrutiny from her relatives, particularly Aunt Clara, who had a way of asking questions that could pierce through her confidence.

"Kara, dear, how's that job of yours?" Clara asked, her tone polite but inquisitive.

"It's going well, Aunt Clara. I really enjoy managing the office," Kara replied, her voice steady.

"And what about your art? I heard you're still dabbling in that," Clara continued, her eyes bright and focused.

"Yes, I am," Kara said, gathering her courage. "Actually, Christian and I are working on a mural. It's a project that means a lot to me."

"Oh?" Clara raised an eyebrow, feigning interest. "And what's the theme? Hopefully, something that's marketable?"

Kara felt her heart sink for a moment, but she quickly reminded herself of Christian's words. She was not here to seek approval; she was here to share her passion.

"It's about the journey of self-discovery and breaking free from expectations," she explained, her voice gaining strength. "Art is about expressing who we are, not just what sells."

Christian chimed in, his enthusiasm spilling over, "And I'm helping her bring this vision to life! It's going to be incredible."

Kara felt a surge of gratitude for Christian's unwavering support. He had an innate ability to uplift her, even in the face of scrutiny.

"Interesting," Clara replied, the skepticism still lingering in her tone. "Just remember, it's important to have a backup plan."

"Of course," Kara said, forcing a smile. "But I believe in pursuing my passions, even if they don't fit into everyone else's expectations."

The conversation shifted as her dad chimed in, his voice warm and reassuring. "That's the spirit, Kara! Life is too short not to chase what makes you happy. I'm proud of you for following your dreams."

Kara felt a wave of relief wash over her. Her dad's support had always been her anchor, and hearing his words lifted her spirits.

As brunch continued, Kara found herself sharing stories about her art and the mural she and Christian were creating. The more she spoke, the more she felt the weight of her insecurities lifting. Christian's presence beside her was a constant reminder that she was not alone in this journey.

After everyone had finished eating, Kara decided to take a leap of faith. "I actually brought my sketchbook with some ideas for the mural. Would you like to see them?"

Her mom's eyes lit up. "Oh, I'd love to!"

Kara retrieved her sketchbook from her bag, her heart racing as she opened it to reveal her designs. She shared the inspirations behind each piece, her voice growing more animated as she spoke.

As her family gathered around to look, Kara felt a sense of pride wash over her. She was sharing a piece of her heart, and for the first time, she felt their curiosity shift from skepticism to genuine interest.

"Wow, Kara, these are amazing!" Jake exclaimed, his face lit up with admiration.

"Yeah, I can really see the emotion in your work," her cousin added, nodding.

Clara remained quiet, but Kara noticed a slight softening in her expression.

As they discussed the sketches, Kara felt a renewed sense of confidence. Sharing her art with her family had been a challenge, but it was also liberating. With Christian by her side, she was finally able to embrace her passion without fear of judgment.

As the brunch wrapped up, Kara felt a sense of accomplishment. She had faced her fears, and while the journey was far from over, she was beginning to carve her own path in the world of art. With Christian's support, she felt ready to take on whatever challenges awaited her, knowing that she was not just an artist but a storyteller, weaving her narrative through every brushstroke.

CHAPTER 35

Colors of Heritage

The sun hung high in the sky as Kara and Christian returned to the studio, their spirits buoyed by the warmth of family and the celebratory atmosphere of the brunch. Kara's heart felt light, a newfound confidence woven into her artistic fabric after sharing her sketches with her family. She unlocked the door to the studio, and they stepped inside, greeted by the vibrant colors of their mural in progress.

"Alright, let's get this dance-off started!" Christian exclaimed, his eyes sparkling with mischief. He twirled around, mimicking a dance move that was equal parts goofy and charming. Kara couldn't help but laugh, her earlier apprehensions melting away.

"Maybe after we get some real work done, Mr. Dance King," she replied, setting her bag down on the table. "I have some ideas I want to explore."

"Now you've got me intrigued! What's brewing in that brilliant mind of yours?" he asked, leaning against the wall with a playful grin.

Kara took a deep breath, feeling the essence of her family's heritage stirring within her. "I was thinking about incorporating elements from my family's history into the mural. You know, things that reflect where I come from and the stories that shaped me. I never really embraced that part of my identity in my art before."

Christian's expression shifted to one of pure encouragement. "That sounds incredible! Heritage is such a rich source of inspiration. What specific elements are you thinking about?"

Kara glanced at the blank spaces on the wall, the canvas waiting for their next moves. "I've been reflecting on the coastal culture of my grandparents, the way they celebrated life through music, food, and art. I can almost hear the melodies of their old sea shanties, and I remember the vibrant colors of the festivals they hosted. I want to capture that joy and connection."

"Let's brainstorm!" Christian said, his enthusiasm contagious. He made his way to the paint supplies, pulling out a few vibrant hues. "What colors do you associate with those memories?"

Kara closed her eyes for a moment, letting the memories wash over her. "Bright turquoise reminds me of the ocean, and sunny yellows bring to mind the warmth of family gatherings. There's a deep coral that reflects the sunsets we used to watch together. Each color tells a story."

"Perfect! Let's mix those colors and see what we can create. We can use bold strokes to represent the energy of those festivals and softer textures for the more intimate family moments," Christian suggested, grabbing a palette and preparing to mix the colors.

As they began to work, Kara found herself lost in the rhythm of creating. The sounds of brushes against canvas harmonized with the memories flooding her mind, each stroke becoming a tribute to her heritage. Christian moved beside her, his keen eye for detail complementing her broader strokes.

"Kara, this is beautiful! The way you're capturing those memories is so vibrant," he said, stepping back to admire their work. "I can see your passion shining through."

"Thanks, Christian. It feels good to finally embrace this side of myself," she replied, her voice softening. "I've always felt a bit disconnected from my roots, but now I see how they can be a source of strength in my art."

As they continued to paint, Kara felt a surge of inspiration. She began to incorporate symbols that represented her family—waves for her grandparents who had lived by the sea, intertwined motifs to signify the unity of their family, and even small elements that hinted at the stories her parents had shared with her growing up.

Suddenly, the phone on the table buzzed, pulling Kara from her creative trance. She wiped her hands on her apron and picked it up, glancing at the screen. The name on the caller ID sent a jolt through her heart: The Coastal Gallery.

"Uh, Christian?" she said, her voice a mix of excitement and apprehension. "It's the gallery."

"Answer it!" he urged, his tone encouraging.

Taking a deep breath, Kara swiped to answer the call. "Hello?"

"Hi Kara, it's Sarah from The Coastal Gallery. I hope you're doing well! We've had a chance to review your submissions, and I must say, we're quite impressed with your work."

Kara's heart raced. "Thank you! That means a lot to me."

"We'd love to discuss the possibility of featuring your pieces in our upcoming exhibition. Would you be available to meet this week?"

Kara's mind was a whirlwind of emotions. The thought of showcasing her art publicly both thrilled and terrified her. "Uh, yes! I'd love to meet and discuss it," she replied, forcing the words out despite the knot forming in her stomach.

"Great! How does Wednesday sound?" Sarah asked, her voice bright and professional.

"Wednesday works," Kara confirmed, trying to keep her voice steady.

"Excellent. I'll send you the details. Looking forward to meeting you!"

As she hung up the phone, a mixture of excitement and anxiety bubbled within her. "Christian! They want to feature my work in an exhibition!"

"Are you serious? That's amazing!" His face lit up with genuine joy, but Kara could see the flicker of concern in her eyes.

"Yeah, but I'm terrified," she admitted, biting her lip. "What if people don't like it? What if I freeze up in front of everyone?"

"Hey, listen," Christian said, stepping closer. "You've just poured your heart and soul into this mural, and you're embracing your heritage. That's incredibly powerful! People will resonate with your story. You have to believe in yourself."

"But what if they don't?" Kara's voice trembled.

"Then that's their loss, not yours," he reassured her. "Every artist faces critics, but what truly matters is how you feel about your work. You're not just showcasing art; you're sharing a piece of yourself. That's something only you can do."

Kara took a moment to absorb his words. "You're right. I need to focus on the message and the joy I want to convey. It's not about pleasing everyone; it's about being true to myself."

"Exactly! And you've already taken the first step by sharing your story with your family," Christian added. "This exhibition could be another opportunity to do that on a bigger stage."

Feeling a swell of determination rise within her, Kara nodded. "Okay, I'm going to do this. I'll prepare and make sure I'm ready to present my work."

"That's the spirit!" Christian said, his excitement infectious. "Let's finish up this mural, and then we can start working on your presentation for the gallery. You'll crush it!"

With renewed energy, Kara picked up her brush and dove back into the mural, her mind racing with ideas for the exhibition. The fear still lingered, but it was now accompanied by a sense of courage and a willingness to embrace the unknown.

As they painted, the studio filled with laughter and creativity, each stroke forging a deeper connection between Kara and her heritage. She realized that this was not just about art; it was a journey of self-discovery, a celebration of her identity, and an invitation for others to join her in the vibrant tapestry of her life.

Kara knew she was ready to step into the light, to share not only her art but her story, and to embrace the colors of her heritage that had long awaited their turn to shine.

CHAPTER 36

The Brush of Love

The colors danced vibrantly on the mural as Kara and Christian continued their work, each brushstroke a testament to their creative synergy. The studio, alive with the sound of soft music in the background, was a cocoon of inspiration where the outside world faded away. Kara stepped back to catch a glimpse of their progress, her heart swelling with pride. The mural was transforming into something truly special, a reflection of her roots, her family's spirit, and the joy of creation.

"Okay, I think we need a splash of that coral you love right here," Christian suggested, pointing to a blank area that seemed to yearn for warmth.

"Agreed! It'll bring out the richness of the turquoise," Kara replied, mixing the colors on her palette. There was a spark of excitement in her voice, a playful energy that had become a hallmark of their collaboration.

As they painted, their banter flowed effortlessly, a dance of words intertwined with their artistic endeavor. "You know, if we keep this up, we might just become the most famous muralists in the world," Christian joked, his eyes twinkling with mischief.

"Famous? More like infamous! A couple of artists who got carried away with colors and forgot how to paint in the lines," Kara laughed, her smile brightening the room.

"Who needs lines when you have passion?" he countered, throwing a playful wink her way.

Kara felt her cheeks warm at the lighthearted teasing. The chemistry between them was undeniable, a current of unspoken feelings simmering just beneath the surface. But amid the laughter, a shadow of doubt crept into Kara's heart, nudging her to confront the fears she had kept buried.

"Christian," she began, her tone shifting to something more serious. "Can I share something with you?"

"Of course! You know I'm all ears," he said, tilting his head slightly, his expression inviting.

"I'm excited about the exhibition, but I can't shake this feeling of fear. What if no one likes my work? What if I freeze up when it's time to present?" She took a deep breath, feeling the weight of her insecurities spill out into the open.

"Wow, dramatic much?" Christian gave her a crooked grin, nudging her shoulder lightly. "You're acting like we're baring our souls to a firing squad instead of showing some art to a bunch of curious strangers. You'll survive. Probably."

"Really?" Kara asked, surprised. "You make it sound so easy, like you have it all figured out."

"Ha, I definitely don't," he admitted, scratching the back of his head. "But I've had my fair share of rejections. There was a time when I thought I'd never make it as an artist. It's tough to put your heart on the line."

His candor touched Kara deeply, and she felt a connection forming—a bridge built from vulnerability and shared dreams. "It's comforting to know I'm not alone in this," she said softly.

"Absolutely not. We're in this together," he replied, his voice earnest. "Art is more than just talent; it's about sharing your story and connecting with others. The right people will see that in your work."

Kara smiled, her heart swelling with gratitude for Christian's support. "Thank you. It really means a lot to have you by my side. I guess I need to focus on the joy of creating rather than the fear of judgment."

"Exactly! You've already made something beautiful with this mural, and that's just the beginning. Whatever happens at the exhibition, you're already a success in my eyes," he said, his gaze steady and sincere.

Feeling emboldened, Kara stepped back to admire the mural again, the colors blending seamlessly. "I think we've captured the spirit of my family, don't you?" she asked, her voice brightening.

"Definitely! It's alive with energy and warmth," Christian said, his eyes sparkling as he took in the mural's vibrancy. "Let's keep pushing it. I have a few more ideas for the details."

They dove back into their work, their laughter echoing through the studio. As the hours passed, the sun dipped lower in the sky, casting a warm golden glow through the windows. The atmosphere shifted subtly, the playful banter giving way to a deeper, more intimate vibe.

After a long day of painting, they paused, stepping back to take a long look at their work. The mural was almost complete, and an undeniable sense of accomplishment hung in the air. Kara felt a mix of exhilaration and melancholy—exhilaration for the journey they had taken together and melancholy for the day coming to an end.

"Wow, we really did it," Kara said breathlessly, her eyes reflecting the colorful mural.

"Yeah, we make a pretty good team," Christian replied, his voice low and warm.

In that moment, they stood close, the air thick with unspoken words and emotions. Kara's heart raced as she caught Christian's gaze, his eyes holding a depth that made her pulse quicken.

"Christian, I…" she started, unsure of how to articulate the whirlwind of feelings inside her.

Before she could finish, Christian leaned in, closing the distance that had felt electric between them. Their lips met in a gentle kiss, a soft brush that sent a wave of warmth through Kara. Time seemed to stand still as the kiss deepened, both tender and charged with emotion.

When they finally pulled away, Kara's breath hitched in her throat, her heart pounding. "Wow," she whispered, a mixture of surprise and elation flooding her.

"Yeah, wow," Christian echoed, his expression a blend of wonder and vulnerability. "I didn't plan on that, but it felt right."

"It did," Kara admitted, her cheeks flushed. "But what does this mean for us?"

Christian hesitated, his playful demeanor replaced by a seriousness that made Kara's heart skip a beat. "I think it means we need to navigate this together, just like we navigate our art. I don't want to complicate our friendship, but I can't ignore how I feel about you."

"Me too," Kara confessed, her voice steadying. "I've felt something growing between us for a while now, but I didn't know how to say it."

As they stood there, the weight of the moment settled around them. The kiss had awakened something new, a blend of excitement and uncertainty. They were on the brink of a shift where art intertwined with love, and the path ahead felt both exhilarating and daunting.

"Let's take it one day at a time," Christian suggested gently, brushing a strand of hair behind Kara's ear. "We can figure this out as we go."

"Agreed," Kara replied, a smile spreading across her face. "But first, I need to focus on the exhibition. I want to make sure I'm ready."

"Same here. I have my own plans brewing," Christian said, a hint of mischief returning to his eyes.

"What do you mean?" Kara asked, her curiosity piqued.

"I'll tell you later. Right now, let's finish this mural and celebrate the magic we've created," he said, his grin infectious.

As they returned to their work, Kara felt a renewed sense of purpose. The mural had become a canvas not just for her heritage but also for the evolving relationship with Christian. Each brushstroke now felt infused with a new meaning, a testament to their shared journey in art and love.

CHAPTER 37

The Colors of Tomorrow

The sun bathed the studio in a golden hue as Kara and Christian stood before their nearly completed mural, the vibrant colors swirling together in a beautiful tapestry of their shared creativity. With the last brushstrokes applied, a sense of accomplishment washed over them, yet a new wave of excitement loomed just beyond the horizon. Tomorrow marked not just the unveiling of their mural but also Kara's family reunion—a gathering that was both a source of joy and anxiety for her.

"Wow, we really did it," Kara said, stepping back to admire their work one last time. "It feels surreal to see it all come together."

"Absolutely! This is going to make such a statement at the exhibition," Christian replied, his eyes sparkling with enthusiasm. "I can already picture the reactions."

Kara chuckled, a hint of nervousness creeping into her voice. "I hope so! I just want my family to appreciate it. I mean, they don't usually get to see this side of me. Will they understand what I was trying to convey?"

"Of course they will! It's a piece of your heart up there," he reassured her, glancing at the mural with pride. "And besides, they love you. They'll see what you've poured into this."

"Thanks, Christian. You always know how to make me feel better," she said, her heart swelling with gratitude. "I just want everything to go smoothly. Family reunions can be chaotic, and I can't help but worry about the details."

"Hey, what's life without a little chaos?" Christian teased, nudging her playfully. "A little bit of unpredictability keeps things exciting! Besides, you have me to handle any last-minute emergencies."

"Right, because you're the king of organization." Kara laughed, shaking her head. "But seriously, I might need your help with the setup tomorrow. Jodi is coming over in the morning, and I could use an extra pair of hands."

"Count me in! I'll be your right-hand man," he declared with a mock salute. "And who knows? Maybe we'll create a new masterpiece while we're at it."

Kara laughed, imagining the two of them frantically arranging tables and decorations, paint-splattered aprons still on. "I can see it now—'The Great Family Reunion Art Installation.'"

"Exactly! I can already picture the headlines," Christian said, his voice dripping with sarcasm. "Local artists take on a family event, chaos ensues."

Just as their laughter faded, Christian's expression shifted slightly, a thoughtful look crossing his face. He glanced at Kara, who was still lost in thoughts about the reunion.

"Speaking of family, how are you feeling about seeing everyone? You know, your dad, your mom, all of them?"

"I'm excited to see my dad, as always," Kara replied, her tone brightening. "He's been looking forward to this reunion. I cherish every moment I get to spend with him. Mom, on the other hand... well, she has her own ideas about how things should go."

"Ah, the classic mom planning committee," Christian said, rolling his eyes playfully. "What's on her agenda this time?"

"Everything! She has a Pinterest board dedicated to the decorations." Kara groaned, but her smile betrayed her amusement. "And don't get me started on the food. I love her cooking, but she wants to make a three-course meal for thirty people!"

"Sounds like a fun challenge." Christian chuckled. "But you'll make it work. Just remember to breathe. You've got this."

"Thanks! I just hope it goes smoothly," Kara replied. "I want everyone to have a good time and feel connected. Family means everything to me."

Christian nodded, sensing her sincerity. "And it will be great. You're the glue that holds everyone together. Just be yourself, and everything will fall into place."

"Easier said than done," Kara muttered, but the warmth in Christian's eyes brought her comfort. She could always rely on him to lift her spirits.

While they continued discussing the reunion, Christian's thoughts began to drift toward an entirely different matter. He had been planning something special for Kara, a surprise that he hoped would deepen their bond even further. His heart raced at the thought of proposing. He envisioned her face lighting up with joy, the way she always did when she was excited.

But before he could put any of those plans into action, he needed to talk to Jodi. She was not only Kara's best friend but also someone who understood the intricacies of relationships and could help Christian select the perfect ring. He had been thinking about it all week, and now the time felt right.

"Hey, Kara," he began cautiously, trying to gauge her mood. "I was thinking, while you're busy with your family stuff tomorrow, I might swing by and meet with Jodi for a little chat."

"Oh? Just a chat?" Kara raised an eyebrow, her playful suspicion evident. "What are you two scheming?"

"Nothing! Just... you know, guy stuff," he replied, attempting to sound nonchalant. "We're just going to talk about art and life, maybe grab a coffee."

"Right," Kara said, her voice dripping with playful skepticism. "You two are definitely up to something. I can feel it!"

Christian grinned, appreciating her playful instincts. "I promise, it's nothing shady. Just a casual meetup. You know how Jodi and I get when we start talking about ideas."

"Okay, okay! I'll let you go." Kara laughed, shaking her head. "Just don't let her convince you to do anything crazy."

"Me? Crazy? Never!" he declared, raising his hands in mock innocence. "But seriously, we'll keep it low-key. I'll be back before the family mayhem begins. Just focus on what you need to do, and I'll handle my end."

"Deal," Kara said, her heart feeling lighter at the thought of Christian being there for her. "Thanks for being so supportive. I really appreciate it."

"Always," Christian replied. "I've got your back, Kara. We're partners in art and life, right?"

"Right," she echoed, feeling a warmth spread through her as she gazed into his eyes.

The bond they shared had transformed into something beautiful and profound, and she was grateful for every moment they spent together.

As the sun dipped below the horizon, casting a soft twilight glow over the studio, Kara felt a sense of hope and excitement within her. Tomorrow would bring challenges, laughter, and perhaps a few surprises. She was ready to embrace it all, supported by the one person who had become her anchor.

With their plans set and the mural complete, they turned off the lights in the studio, stepping out into the cool evening air. The world outside felt alive with possibilities, and Kara felt a mixture of anticipation and tranquility wash over her. She was surrounded by love, art, and the promise of a bright tomorrow.

Colors of Connection

The morning sun streamed through Kara's window, casting stripes of light across the bedroom floor. The golden rays danced with the dust motes in the air, filling the room with a warm glow that hinted at the promise of a beautiful day ahead. Kara stretched, her mind racing with thoughts of the family reunion and the unveiling of her mural. Today was the day she had been waiting for, yet a flutter of nervous energy twisted in her stomach.

She slipped out of bed, her feet touching the cool hardwood floor, and made her way to the kitchen. The familiar scent of coffee wafted through the air, and she smiled at the sight of her mother bustling about, already busy with the preparations. Kara's mom, with her cheerful demeanor and meticulous planning, was in her element, and it was clear she had been up for hours.

"Good morning, sweetheart!" her mom chimed, turning to greet her with a beaming smile. "I hope you're ready for the big day! I've got so much planned, and you're going to love it!"

"Morning, Mom!" Kara replied, trying to match her mother's enthusiasm. "I'm excited, but I hope it's not too overwhelming."

"Oh, don't worry! I've got everything under control," her mother assured her. "And I made your favorite breakfast!" She gestured to the table, which was laden with a spread of pancakes, fresh fruit, and syrup, the sight of which made Kara's stomach rumble.

Kara sat down, her heart warming at the sight of her mother's efforts. "Thanks, Mom. This looks amazing!"

As they ate, her mother recounted the plans in meticulous detail—everything from the seating arrangement to the menu for the day. Kara listened, nodding along, trying to keep her anxiety at bay. The chaos of family reunions was always a little daunting, but knowing that Christian would be there to help eased her nerves.

"Have you spoken to Christian this morning?" her mom asked, her eyes twinkling with curiosity.

"Not yet, but he said he'd be here early to help with the setup," Kara replied, a smile creeping onto her face at the thought of him. "He's always so supportive."

"I'm glad you found someone like him," her mom said, a hint of nostalgia in her tone. "It's nice to see you so happy. You deserve it, dear."

Kara took a deep breath, appreciating her mother's words. She felt a rush of warmth and gratitude for the love surrounding her. "Thanks, Mom. I really do feel lucky."

As breakfast came to an end, Kara's mom launched into a discussion about the decorations, her voice filled with excitement. "I found some beautiful flower arrangements that I think will complement the mural perfectly! You'll love them!"

"Sounds great!" Kara replied, trying to match her mother's enthusiasm while secretly hoping things wouldn't get too chaotic.

After breakfast, Kara dashed upstairs to get ready. She chose a light, summery dress that flowed with her every movement, feeling a sense of comfort and ease in the fabric. The mirror reflected a mix of excitement and apprehension in her eyes as she applied her makeup, reminding herself to stay grounded amidst the impending whirlwind of family.

Once she was ready, she stepped outside to take a breather in the fresh air. The neighborhood buzzed with the sounds of morning—birds chirping, children laughing, and the distant hum of lawnmowers. Everything felt alive, and she took a moment to soak it all in before the chaos of the reunion began.

Shortly after, Christian arrived, his usual vibrant energy lighting up the space around him. He greeted Kara with a warm hug, and for a moment, all her worries melted away. "Ready to take on the world?" he asked, his playful tone instantly lifting her spirits.

"More like ready to take on my family," Kara chuckled, feeling a flutter of excitement at having him by her side. "But I'm glad you're here to help."

"Always, my dear. Just point me in the direction of the chaos, and I'll tackle it head-on!" he said, flashing her a charming grin.

Together, they moved to the backyard, where her mother had already set up a long table adorned with vibrant tablecloths and an array of decorations. Kara felt a rush of gratitude for Christian's presence as they worked side by side, arranging chairs and setting out the decorations. His lighthearted banter made the task feel like an adventure rather than a chore.

As they worked, Kara noticed her father arriving, his familiar silhouette bringing an overwhelming sense of affection. He stepped into the backyard, his eyes crinkling at the corners as he took in the scene.

"Wow, this looks fantastic!" he exclaimed, moving closer to inspect.

Kara's heart swelled with pride as she watched her father study the artwork she displayed for her upcoming gallery display.

She stepped beside him, feeling a sense of intimacy in sharing this moment. "Thanks, Dad. I really hope everyone enjoys it."

"I'm sure they will," he said, his voice warm and reassuring. "You've poured your heart into this, and it shows. It's beautiful."

Kara caught a flicker of something in his eyes—wistfulness, perhaps? She wondered if he saw more in the artwork than just colors and shapes. Maybe he recognized the stories and memories that swirled within the paint.

"What do you think it means?" she asked, wanting to delve deeper into his thoughts.

Her father paused, his gaze lingering on the paintings as if searching for the right words. "It reminds me of our family," he replied, his voice soft. "The way we come together, the colors representing our different personalities, and how we create something wonderful when we're united."

Kara felt a lump form in her throat, touched by his interpretation. "That's beautiful, Dad. I love that you see it that way."

As the day progressed, the backyard transformed into a lively gathering space. Family members arrived, laughter filled the air, and the aroma of delicious food wafted from the kitchen. Kara's mother orchestrated the event with the precision of a seasoned conductor, her enthusiasm infectious.

Throughout the afternoon, Kara navigated between the chaos of her mother's planning and the joy of reconnecting with her family. She shared stories, exchanged hugs, and felt the warmth of love surrounding her. Yet, amidst the laughter and chatter, she couldn't shake the feeling that her father's glances toward the paintings carried unspoken emotions—something deeper that he hadn't articulated.

Meanwhile, Christian had slipped away to meet with Jodi, who was back at the studio, waiting for him with a mischievous grin. "So, how's the family chaos treating you?" she teased, leaning against the counter.

"Fun, but I came to talk about Kara," he said. "I want to do something special for her today, but I feel like I need to understand her better. Can you help me?"

Jodi's expression shifted to one of genuine interest. "Of course! Kara is an amazing person, but there's a side of her past that I think you should know about."

As Jodi began to share stories about Kara's childhood—her love for art, her early struggles to find her voice, and the dreams she had—Christian listened intently. He learned about the little girl who would spend hours painting on the beach, capturing the colors of the sunset, and how those moments shaped her into the artist she was today.

"She's always had a passion for expressing herself through art," Jodi explained, her voice inspiring. "But she's also faced challenges, especially trying to balance her artistic dreams with her responsibilities. Knowing that will help you understand her even more deeply."

Christian felt a surge of admiration for Kara, realizing just how much she had overcome to get to where she was. "Thank you, Jodi. That means a lot," he said, his heart swelling with affection for Kara. "I want to make today memorable for her, and this insight will help."

As the reunion reached its peak, laughter echoed, and children played in the yard while adults shared stories. Kara caught Christian's eye from across the crowd, and they exchanged a knowing smile. She felt a wave of gratitude for his presence, knowing that he was not just her partner in art but also in life.

The sun began to dip lower in the sky, casting a warm glow over the gathering as Kara's mother called for everyone's attention. "Ladies and gentlemen, it's time to unveil Kara's mural," she announced, her voice brimming with excitement.

Kara felt a sense of anxiety come over her. As they arrived and all headed down the hallway towards the studio, Kara could only imagine what everyone would think.

Kara's heart raced as she stepped forward, Christian at her side, ready to reveal the culmination of their hard work. With a flourish, they pulled away the curtain covering the mural, and gasps of awe filled the air. Family members stepped closer, their expressions a mix of admiration and wonder.

As the crowd began to discuss the mural, Kara's father stood back, a thoughtful expression on his face. Kara caught his gaze once more, and for a brief moment, their eyes locked. There was something unspoken between them, a connection that transcended words.

Amidst the flurry of family excitement, Christian felt the moment was right. He glanced at Jodi, who gave him an encouraging nod. With a deep breath, he stepped closer to Kara, his heart pounding. Today was about her, and he wanted to make it unforgettable. As the laughter and celebration swirled around them, the time for his surprise proposal approached—a moment that would forever change the colors of their connection.

CHAPTER 39

The Brushstrokes Of Patience And Understanding

The sun hung low in the sky, casting a golden hue through the windows of the studio as the unveiling of Kara's mural brought the family together in a swirl of admiration and excitement. The air was thick with laughter and the sound of silence as the anticipation was coming to a climactic close. Kara stood at the center of it all, her heart racing with pride and anticipation as she watched her family explore the mural she had poured her soul into creating.

Christian stood beside her, his eyes sparkling with admiration as he took in the scene. He could feel the warmth radiating from Kara, her joy lighting up the surroundings like the vibrant colors of her artwork. He turned his focus back to her, gathering his courage to seize the moment he had been planning for weeks. Today was not just about the mural; it was about their future together.

As the crowd continued to admire the mural, Kara's father, a gentle yet commanding presence, stood off to the side, watching the interactions with a thoughtful expression. He caught Kara's eye, and she felt a rush of affection for him, sensing that he, too, was moved by the artwork that represented their family.

Just as Christian stepped forward, ready to express his love and intentions, Kara's father cleared his throat, his voice rising above the chatter. "Ladies and gentlemen, if I may have your attention for just a moment!" His tone was calm yet resonant, instantly drawing the crowd's focus.

Kara's heart fluttered with uncertainty as she noticed the sudden shift in the atmosphere. The laughter quieted, and curious eyes turned toward her father. "I want to share a story—one that is deeply connected to this beautiful mural." He gestured toward the artwork, his expression rich with emotion.

Kara felt her stomach tighten, a mix of pride and apprehension swirling within her. She wondered what memory he was about to share. "You see, Kara has always had a gift for capturing the world around her. But what many of you may not know is that her inspiration comes from a very special place—one that has been passed down through generations of our family."

Christian, sensing the shift in the mood, felt his heart race. He glanced at Kara, whose eyes sparkled with curiosity and a hint of trepidation. He realized that the moment he had planned to be solely about their love was evolving into something much deeper and more meaningful.

Kara's father continued, "When I was a young boy, my grandmother had a little studio in our home. It was filled with art supplies—paints, brushes, and canvases. She would often take me there and teach me how to see the world through an artist's eyes." His voice softened, carrying a nostalgic tone. "She instilled in me a love for colors and forms, teaching me not just to paint but to express feelings and stories through art."

Kara leaned closer to her father, captivated by the memory as it unfolded. "One of the things she often said was that art is a connection—a bridge between our hearts and the world. It's about sharing our stories, our truths." He paused, looking at Kara with a mixture of pride and tenderness. "I see that same passion in you, my dear."

A wave of emotions washed over Kara; she felt honored to be linked to her grandmother's legacy. "I didn't know you had such a connection to art, Dad," she whispered, her voice barely audible over the murmurs of the crowd.

Her father smiled, his eyes reflecting the warmth of their shared bond. "Art has always been a silent language in our family. But it wasn't until I saw your mural that I realized just how deeply it runs. The colors, the themes—it all brings back memories of my grandmother and the love she shared with me." He took a deep breath, his voice thick with emotion. "And that love lives on through you."

As Kara absorbed her father's words, she felt a connection deepen between them. This mural was not just an expression of her talent; it was a tapestry woven with the threads of her family history—a representation of their shared love and experiences. The realization struck her powerfully, and she glanced at Christian, who watched her with an understanding gaze.

Kara's father continued, "I remember one particular painting your grandmother created. It was of a sunset over the ocean, much like the one you captured here. She said it reminded her of the hope that comes with each new day." His voice grew softer, filled with reverence. "And today, as I look at your mural, I feel that same hope. It's a reminder of our family's journey—of love, loss, and the beauty that comes from embracing both."

The crowd listened intently, some nodding in agreement while others wiped away tears. Kara felt her heart swell, and in that moment, her fears and anxieties melted away. The mural had become more than just her artwork; it had transformed into a symbol of their family's legacy and the love that bound them.

Christian stood back, his heart pounding in his chest. He had planned to propose to Kara in a moment filled with joy and love, but now he understood that this moment was not just about them. It was about honoring Kara's family and the rich history that shaped her as an artist and a person. He felt a deep sense of respect for her father's story and the emotional weight it carried.

Realizing the proposal could wait, Christian took a step back, allowing Kara and her father to bask in the warmth of their connection. The energy in the air shifted, and he could feel the love and admiration flowing among the family members as they exchanged glances filled with understanding.

Kara turned to Christian, her eyes glistening with gratitude. "Thank you for being here with me today," she said softly, her voice filled with emotion. "I know this day means a lot to my family, and I'm so glad you're part of it."

Christian smiled, his heart swelling with affection. "I wouldn't want to be anywhere else," he replied, his tone light yet sincere. "Your family is amazing, and I'm honored to share this moment with you."

As the crowd began to share their own stories and memories tied to art, Kara felt a sense of belonging wash over her. She embraced her father, holding onto him tightly, feeling the weight of their shared history and the love that had brought them to this moment.

"Dad, I didn't realize how much our family's story influenced my art," Kara admitted, her voice trembling. "Thank you for sharing that with me. I feel so connected to you and Grandma right now."

Her father chuckled softly, brushing a tear from his cheek. "Art has a way of revealing our truths, Kara. Never forget the power it holds, both for you and for those who experience it."

As the sun began to set, casting a warm glow over the gathering, Kara felt a sense of clarity. The day had taken an unexpected turn, but it had deepened her connection to her family and enriched her understanding of her artistic journey. She looked at Christian, who stood beside her with unwavering support, and felt an overwhelming sense of love and appreciation.

The moment was theirs, interwoven with family history and artistic inspiration, a celebration of life's complexities and the bonds that hold them together. Kara knew that their love story was just

"Hey," Christian said softly, breaking the comfortable silence. "How are you feeling?"

Kara's heart swelled at the concern in his voice. "Honestly? I'm still processing everything. I never expected today to be so... emotional. My dad really opened up about our family's history with art, and it made me realize how much it means to me."

He nodded, a knowing smile creeping onto his lips. "Art has a way of bringing us back home, doesn't it? It connects us to our roots. Just like this mural connects you to your family."

Kara smiled, feeling the warmth of his words wrap around her like a cozy blanket. "It really does. But I have to admit, I'm still buzzing from the surprise of it all. And I think my dad's story just made me reflect on how much I want to incorporate our journey into my art moving forward."

"Speaking of journeys..." Christian's tone shifted, a playful glint in his eyes. He stepped closer, leaning against the wall beside her. "I've been thinking about how we can create something together. You know, a piece that symbolizes us—our adventures, our love for art, everything."

Her heart fluttered at the suggestion. "That sounds amazing! I can already envision a vibrant piece filled with colors and textures that tell our story. We should definitely brainstorm ideas."

Before she could continue, Christian took a deep breath and turned to face her fully, his expression shifting from playful to serious. Kara's stomach tensed with anticipation, sensing that he was about to say something significant.

"Kara, there's something I've been wanting to ask you. Something that feels right after everything we've experienced today."

Her breath caught in her throat as she met his gaze, the intensity of his eyes sending electric currents coursing through her. "What is it, Christian?"

He reached into his pocket, pulling out a small velvet box, and Kara's heart raced as she recognized the significance of the moment. "You've opened up your heart through your art, and you've shared your family's legacy with me. I want to build a legacy with you. Kara, will you marry me?"

The world around her seemed to fade as her focus zeroed in on the box in his hand. Her heart raced, emotions swirling in a joyous whirlwind. "Oh my goodness, Christian..." she started, her voice trembling with disbelief and excitement.

"Say yes! Say yes!" she could almost hear Jodi's playful chant echoing in her mind, urging her forward. The thought made her smile, but she was still caught in the moment—caught between the reality of what was unfolding and the dreams she had long held in her heart.

"Christian, I..." Her voice faltered, but her eyes sparkled with unshed tears of joy. "This is so unexpected, but... yes! Yes, I'll marry you!"

Time seemed to stand still as Christian opened the box, revealing a delicate ring that shimmered in the fading light. It was simple yet stunning, a perfect reflection of her style. He slipped it onto her finger, and it felt like the final stroke on a masterpiece, cementing their bond with a flourish.

"I can't believe this is happening," Kara whispered, her heart swelling with happiness. "You have no idea how much this means to me."

"I think I do," he replied, his voice filled with warmth. "You've shown me what it means to embrace life fully—to love without reservation. I want us to create a life together filled with art, adventure, and love."

Kara glanced down at the ring, then back up at Christian, feeling a rush of emotion. "I can't wait to start this journey with you. We'll create together, just like we're meant to."

He grinned, the light in his eyes brighter than ever. "And think of all the places we can explore—snorkeling in tropical waters, painting sunsets, and who knows what else?"

"Adventuring and painting our way through life," Kara echoed, her heart singing at the thought.

As they stood there, wrapped in each other's arms, the world outside continued to celebrate. The laughter of Kara's family echoed through the studio, a reminder of the love surrounding them. The mural, a vibrant testament to Kara's journey, now stood as a backdrop to a new chapter in their lives—one filled with promise, creativity, and boundless love.

"Shall we tell everyone?" Christian asked, breaking the spell of their intimate moment.

"Definitely! I can't imagine keeping this a secret!" Kara replied.

Hand in hand, they stepped out of the alcove and back into the lively atmosphere of the celebration. Kara could feel the warmth of her family's love enveloping her, their joy resonating in the air. As they approached, she could see her dad's proud smile and her mom's gleaming eyes, filled with anticipation.

"Everyone!" Kara called out, her voice ringing clear. The chatter began to fade as family and friends turned their attention to her and Christian. "We have an announcement!"

Christian squeezed her hand, a reassuring gesture that ignited her confidence. "What is it?" Jodi shouted from the crowd, her curiosity evident.

Kara exchanged a quick glance with Christian, then took a deep breath. "We're engaged!"

A cheer erupted from the crowd, filling the studio with an electric energy. Kara's mom rushed forward, tears of joy streaming down her cheeks. "Oh, my baby girl!" she exclaimed, wrapping Kara in a tight embrace. "I'm so happy for you both!"

Kara's dad joined in, pulling Christian into a hearty handshake that quickly turned into a warm hug. "Welcome to the family, son. You've made my daughter so incredibly happy."

As the celebrations resumed, Kara felt a sense of belonging wash over her. Surrounded by the people she loved, she knew they were all embarking on a new journey together. A journey not just of love and commitment but one that intertwined their lives through art, family, and the beautiful chaos of life.

She realized that her mural was just the beginning of a much larger canvas, one that would be painted with the colors of their shared experiences, dreams, and love. And as she looked at Christian, she couldn't wait to see what masterpieces they would create together.

Colors of Commitment

The soft light of Monday morning filtered through the sheer curtains of Kara's bedroom, casting gentle shadows on the walls adorned with sketches and color swatches. The air was filled with a sense of anticipation, the kind that buzzed like the first notes of a beautiful symphony. Today marked the beginning of a new chapter in Kara's life, one that intertwined her passion for art with the thrill of planning her wedding. She could hardly contain her excitement as she thought about sharing her engagement news with her colleagues at the doctor's office.

Kara hopped out of bed, her heart racing with a mixture of joy and nerves. She glanced at the delicate ring on her finger, its reflection shimmering in the morning light like a promise waiting to be fulfilled. It felt surreal to be engaged, to have Christian by her side as they embarked on this journey together. Thoughts of their future danced in her mind, but she couldn't ignore the looming meeting with Sarah at the Coastal Gallery. This would be her first opportunity to showcase her work in a professional setting, and the weight of that responsibility was beginning to settle in.

After a quick shower, Kara dressed in a smart yet comfortable outfit—a vibrant sundress that mirrored her artistic spirit. She added a touch of whimsy with a pair of colorful sandals. As she applied a light layer of makeup, she mentally prepared for her day. Sharing her engagement would be a highlight, but she couldn't forget the importance of that meeting. It was essential to present herself with confidence, especially when it came to discussing her artwork.

Arriving at the doctor's office, Kara was greeted by the familiar hustle and bustle of the waiting room. The scent of antiseptic mixed with the faint aroma of coffee from the break room created a strangely comforting atmosphere. She walked to her desk, her heart fluttering as she spotted Jodi already perched on a chair, her eyes sparkling with mischief.

"Did you survive the engagement party?" Jodi teased, feigning a dramatic gasp. "I heard there was dancing, champagne, and possibly even a cake fight!"

"Oh, it was magical!" Kara replied, unable to suppress her smile. "Christian proposed, and it was everything I dreamed of. I feel like I'm floating on cloud nine."

"Floating is good," Jodi said, raising an eyebrow. "But we need to make sure you don't get lost in the clouds while planning this wedding. We have a lot to do! And I already have a million ideas."

Kara laughed, feeling the warmth of her friend's enthusiasm wash over her. "I can't wait to hear them, but first, I need to share the news with everyone."

As she stood up to gather her colleagues, Kara felt a rush of excitement. The news felt like a burst of color waiting to be splashed onto a canvas. "Everyone!" she called out, her voice ringing through the waiting area. "I have something to share!"

The chatter quieted, and all eyes turned to her. "I'm engaged!" she announced, her heart racing. "Christian proposed, and I said yes!"

Cheers erupted, and her coworkers rushed forward to embrace her. Kara felt a wave of love and support surround her, and she couldn't help but feel grateful for the wonderful people in her life.

Amidst the joyful chaos, she caught sight of her boss, Dr. Acosta, smiling warmly at her.

"I'm so happy for you, Kara," he said, extending a hand for her to shake. "You deserve all the happiness in the world."

"Thank you, Dr. Jacobs. It means a lot," she replied, her voice filled with sincerity.

As the initial excitement settled, Kara found herself returning to her desk, her thoughts drifting toward the upcoming meeting at the Coastal Gallery. She had spent countless hours working on her pieces, pouring her heart into each stroke of paint, and now, the opportunity to showcase them was finally within reach. Yet, with that excitement came a wave of anxiety. Would her work resonate with the gallery owner? Would she be able to articulate her vision clearly?

Before she had time to dwell on her worries, Jodi plopped down in the chair across from her, a mischievous grin plastered across her face. "So, have you thought about what kind of wedding you want? Beach? Rustic? Art-themed?"

Kara chuckled, shaking her head at her friend's eagerness. "I have no idea! Part of me wants something simple and intimate, but another part wants to go all out. I can already see us painting the decorations ourselves!"

"Now that's the spirit!" Jodi exclaimed, her eyes sparkling with excitement. "Imagine a live mural at your wedding—a canvas of your love story that guests can contribute to throughout the night!"

"That sounds incredible," Kara agreed, her mind racing with possibilities. "But what if I'm too busy with everything else? I don't want to feel overwhelmed."

"Don't worry! I'll help you with every step," Jodi promised. "We'll make it fun! Plus, planning can be a great creative outlet, and trust me, it'll give you the perfect distraction before your gallery meeting on Wednesday."

As the day progressed, Kara found herself immersed in both the excitement of wedding planning and the preparation for her meeting with Sarah. After work, she met Christian at a cozy café, and they spent hours discussing their visions for their wedding while sipping lattes and nibbling on pastries.

"I can't stop thinking about how we can incorporate art into everything," Kara said animatedly, her hands gesturing as she spoke. "Maybe we could have a mini art exhibit showcasing our journey together."

"I love that idea!" Christian replied, leaning in closer. "We could have photo displays of our adventures and maybe even invite some of our artist friends to contribute pieces!"

The ideas flowed between them like vibrant colors blending on a palette, each suggestion sparking new inspiration. As they brainstormed, Kara felt the lingering anxiety about her gallery meeting fade, replaced by the warmth of Christian's unwavering support. He understood her passion for art and encouraged her to express herself fully.

That evening, they returned to Kara's studio, where she had set up her works in progress. The mural that had once been a solo endeavor was now a collaborative vision reflecting their shared love for art. Together, they stood before the mural, each color telling a story of their journey, their engagement adding another layer of depth.

"Every brushstroke tells a part of our story," Kara said, her heart swelling with emotion. "And I can't wait to see how our wedding will be another chapter in this beautiful tapestry we're creating together."

As they painted, laughter echoed through the studio, filling the space with joy. Kara realized that this was only the beginning—an exploration of their artistic visions, their love deepening with each shared moment.

But as the excitement of planning their wedding consumed her, the anxiety about the gallery meeting lingered like a shadow. She would have to confront her fears head-on, stepping into the world of professional art as she balanced the delicate dance of being an engaged woman and an aspiring artist. The colors of commitment were vibrant and bright, but they also required careful blending, just like the hues on her canvas.

With the sun setting outside, casting a golden glow through the studio's windows, Kara felt a renewed sense of purpose. She was ready to face the challenges ahead, to embrace the beauty of her journey, both as an artist and as a bride-to-be. Each brushstroke, each decision, and each moment would be a part of the masterpiece that was her life, painted with love, passion, and creativity.

CHAPTER 42

A Canvas of Love

The day of Kara's meeting at the Coastal Gallery dawned bright and clear, a perfect reflection of her swirling emotions. She awoke with the sun streaming through her bedroom window, illuminating the sketches and color swatches that had become her second language. Today was not just about showcasing her artwork; it was about weaving her personal narrative into the fabric of her creations. As she prepared, she felt the weight of her dreams resting on her shoulders, both exhilarating and daunting.

After a quick breakfast, Kara slipped into a tailored blouse and a pair of chic trousers that accentuated her artistic flair. The outfit was both professional and comfortable, a balance she aimed to strike in every aspect of her life. She could hardly believe that this was the day she had been waiting for—a chance to share her art with the world, to introduce her creative vision to Sarah, the gallery owner.

With her portfolio in hand, Kara left her apartment, her heart racing with anticipation. The Coastal Gallery was just a short drive away, but it felt like an eternity as she navigated the bustling streets of their coastal town. Each stoplight seemed to extend the moment, and her mind was a whirlwind of thoughts: Would Sarah appreciate her work? Would she understand the essence of what Kara was trying to convey?

When Kara finally arrived at the gallery, she took a moment to soak in the atmosphere. The exterior was an inviting blend of modern architecture and coastal charm, with large glass windows showcasing the vibrant pieces inside. As she walked through the entrance, the scent of fresh paint and polished wood enveloped her, igniting her passion for art.

"Kara! So glad you could make it," Sarah greeted her with a warm smile, her presence radiating confidence. She was a woman of striking elegance, with an eye for detail that had earned her a respected reputation in the art world. "I've been looking forward to seeing what you've prepared."

"Thank you! I'm excited to share my work with you," Kara replied, her voice steady despite the fluttering in her chest.

She followed Sarah into the main exhibition area, where the walls were adorned with a myriad of artistic expressions—each piece a story waiting to be told.

As they settled down, Kara opened her portfolio, revealing her carefully curated collection of paintings. Each canvas was a snapshot of her journey, filled with colors that represented not just her artistic vision but also her experiences. She began to explain the themes behind her work, her passion evident in every word.

However, as Sarah flipped through the pages, her expression shifted subtly. "Kara, your work is undoubtedly beautiful, but I have some concerns about the direction it's taking. It feels a bit… scattered. I wonder if you've fully defined your artistic voice yet."

Kara's heart sank, the weight of Sarah's words pressing down on her. "I understand. I've been exploring different styles and themes," she admitted, trying to maintain her composure. "But I also feel that my art is a reflection of where I am in my life right now."

Sarah nodded thoughtfully, her gaze lingering on one of Kara's abstract pieces. "That's true, but there needs to be a sense of cohesion.

Have you thought about focusing on a particular narrative or concept? Something that ties your work together?"

Taking a deep breath, Kara considered Sarah's words. She had always believed that her art was an extension of her experiences, yet she hadn't narrowed it down to a singular theme.

Then an idea sparked in her mind—one that was both personal and vibrant. "What if I infused elements of my upcoming wedding into my work? I could create pieces that reflect my journey with Christian, intertwining our love story with my artistic expression."

A glimmer of interest flashed in Sarah's eyes. "That's a fascinating concept. Love is a universal theme, and it could provide the cohesion your work needs. If you portray your wedding preparations and the emotions tied to that journey, it could resonate with a wider audience. It's authentic and relatable."

Encouraged by Sarah's response, Kara felt a renewed sense of purpose. "I have a vision of creating a piece that embodies our love story, blending wedding elements with my artistic style," Kara said. "It would showcase not just the beauty of the day itself but the journey leading up to it—the laughter, the planning, the little moments that make it special."

As they discussed the possibilities, Kara's mind raced with ideas for her new project. She envisioned vibrant colors symbolizing her love for Christian, each hue representing a different facet of their relationship. The textures of the canvas would mimic the feel of their shared experiences, from spontaneous beach trips to quiet evenings spent sketching together. This could be more than just art; it would be a celebration of their love, a canvas of memories waiting to be painted.

After the meeting, Kara felt a sense of liberation. As she drove home, she reflected on how bringing her personal life into her art could not only help her professionally but also deepen her connection with her creative process. She had always found solace in painting, but now it would serve as a bridge between her two worlds—the artist and the bride-to-be.

That evening, Kara found herself in her studio, surrounded by the familiar chaos of paint tubes, brushes, and unfinished canvases. Christian joined her, his energy infectious as he entered the room.

"Hey, beautiful! What's got you buzzing this evening?" he asked, leaning against the doorframe with a playful grin.

"I had my meeting with Sarah, and it went... well, but she had some concerns about my work," Kara confessed, her fingers absently swirling a brush in a palette of colors. "But I think I've found a way to address them by incorporating our wedding into my art!"

Christian's eyes lit up with enthusiasm. "That sounds amazing! Tell me everything!" He moved closer, intrigued by the idea.

"I want to create a piece that captures our love story, blending wedding elements with my artistic vision. It'll showcase our journey together, from the engagement to the planning," she explained, her excitement palpable as she spoke.

"Wow, that's brilliant! You've always been great at translating emotions into art. This will be a whole new level," Christian encouraged, his admiration fueling her passion even more.

As they began to paint together, Kara found herself completely immersed in the creative process. With each brushstroke, she poured her heart onto the canvas, mixing colors that symbolized their shared laughter, their intimate moments, and the anticipation of their future together. She could envision the final piece—a vibrant tapestry of love that intertwined their story and the joy of their upcoming wedding.

"Imagine the details we could incorporate," she mused, her voice animated. "Maybe I could paint elements from our favorite beach or even the colors of the flowers I'm considering for the wedding. It'll be like a living memory!"

"Absolutely! We could even add some of your sketches of the venue," Christian suggested, his eyes sparkling with inspiration. "This piece will be a reflection of you—of us—capturing not just the moment but the journey leading up to it."

As the evening wore on, the studio filled with laughter and the sound of paintbrushes dancing on canvas. Kara realized that blending her personal life with her art was not only essential for her growth as an artist but also a beautiful way to celebrate their love. With Christian by her side, the creative process became a joyous adventure, each stroke on the canvas echoing the laughter and love they shared.

At that moment, Kara felt a profound sense of clarity. The way forward was illuminated, and she knew that her presentation at the gallery would not just be about showcasing paintings; it would be about sharing the story of her heart. Her love for Christian would become the essence of her work, a canvas of memories painted with passion and creativity.

CHAPTER 43

The Art of Vulnerability

Kara awoke the next morning with a sense of determination coursing through her veins. The sun had barely risen, but she was already wide awake, her mind racing with ideas for her new project. The night before, she and Christian had spent hours discussing the concept of their love story woven into her artwork, and now it was time to transform that vision into reality. She could feel the creative energy surging inside her, urging her to pick up her brushes and start painting.

After a quick breakfast, Kara made her way to her studio. The familiar chaos of paint tubes, brushes, and unfinished canvases greeted her like an old friend. Today, however, it felt different. Today was about embracing her vulnerability, allowing her emotions to flow freely onto the canvas. She wanted to create a series of paintings that would capture the essence of her and Christian's journey together, from their first meeting to the whirlwind of wedding planning.

But as she stood before her blank canvas, self-doubt crept in. What if her story wasn't compelling enough? What if her narrative didn't resonate with those who would come to view her work? The fear gnawed at her, but she quickly reminded herself of Sarah's advice: art should be an authentic reflection of oneself. Taking a deep breath, Kara pushed the doubts aside and dipped her brush into vibrant hues of coral and azure, colors that reminded her of sunsets at the beach—their favorite place.

As the brush glided across the canvas, Kara found herself lost in the rhythm of creation. She began with a background of soft waves, the colors blending seamlessly, evoking the serenity she felt every time she and Christian visited the coast. The more she painted, the more she felt her heart opening up. Each stroke became a memory, each color a moment they had shared, from playful beach outings to quiet evenings filled with laughter.

"Hey, you!" Christian's voice pulled her out of her reverie, and she turned to see him leaning against the doorframe, a playful grin on his face. "What's the masterpiece in the making today?"

Kara smiled, her heart swelling at the sight of him. "Just trying to bring our story to life on canvas."

"Can I help?" he asked, stepping inside the studio, his curiosity evident.

"Of course! Grab a brush," she replied.

They spent the day painting together, their laughter mingling with the sound of brushes swishing across the canvas. Christian added his own flair, splashing vibrant yellows and greens reminiscent of sunlit afternoons. As they worked side by side, Kara felt the weight of her self-doubt slowly dissipate. With Christian's presence, she was reminded that art was not just about the final piece; it was about the process, the joy, and the connection they shared.

As the sun dipped below the horizon, casting a warm glow through the studio window, Kara stepped back to admire their work. The canvas was alive with color and emotion, a true testament to their journey together. But she knew this was just the beginning. Inspired by the day's progress, she made a decision—she would host an intimate gathering at the Coastal Gallery to unveil her first piece and share the creative process with a small group of close friends and family.

"Let's do it!" Christian exclaimed when she mentioned the idea, his enthusiasm infectious. "It'll be a great way to celebrate your art and invite people into your world."

"Yeah, but what if they don't connect with my story?" Kara's voice turned pensive. "What if they don't see the depth behind it?"

"Kara," Christian said softly, placing his hand on her shoulder, "you have to remember that vulnerability is a strength. Sharing your journey, your story, is what makes your art powerful. Trust in yourself and your experiences. They're uniquely yours."

His words resonated deeply within her, and she felt a flicker of hope ignite in her chest. "You're right. I can do this. I want them to see our love story, the journey we're on, and how it intertwines with my art."

As they began to plan the gathering, Kara also realized that the wedding was fast approaching. The thought of the event filled her with a mix of excitement and anxiety. Her parents were eager to help, and her mother had already started brainstorming ideas for venues. Kara had always envisioned a seaside ceremony, but the logistics felt daunting.

"Let's sit down with Mom and Dad this weekend," she suggested to Christian one evening. "They're excited to help, and it could ease some of my stress."

"Good plan! Your mom has that knack for making everything special. Plus, it'll be fun to dive into all the wedding details together," Christian said, his eyes sparkling with mischief. "And who knows, maybe we can sneak in some beach time afterward!"

"Absolutely!" Kara laughed, feeling a sense of relief wash over her.

The idea of involving her family in the planning made the overwhelming task seem more manageable.

As the days passed, Kara poured her heart into her paintings while simultaneously preparing for the gathering. She spent hours sketching ideas and refining her first piece, determined to convey the emotional depth behind it. Each brushstroke was a reflection of her love for Christian, the anticipation of their wedding, and the memories they had created together.

On the day of the gathering, Kara felt a whirlwind of emotions—excitement, anxiety, and a hint of fear. As she arrived at the Coastal Gallery, she took a moment to steady her breath. The gallery was elegantly set up, with soft lighting casting a warm glow over her artwork. She had arranged for a small space where her friends and family could gather, offering them a glimpse into her creative process.

When the first guests arrived, a wave of warmth washed over her. Jodi was among the first, her vibrant energy filling the room. "Kara! This place looks incredible! I can't wait to see what you've created!"

"Thanks, Jodi! I'm so glad you're here," Kara replied, her heart swelling with gratitude. As more friends and family arrived, the atmosphere buzzed with excitement and anticipation.

Once everyone had gathered, Kara took a deep breath, her heart racing. It was time to unveil her first piece. As she stood before the canvas, she felt Christian's reassuring presence beside her.

"Today, I want to share not just a piece of art but a piece of my heart," Kara began, her voice steady yet filled with emotion. "This painting represents the love story that Christian and I are building together. It's a reflection of our journey, the laughter, the challenges, and the beauty of being on this path together."

As she spoke, she watched the faces of her friends and family, their expressions shifting from curiosity to understanding. Kara revealed the emotional depth behind the piece, explaining the significance of the colors and the moments they represented. With each word, she felt the weight of her self-doubt lifting, replaced by a sense of connection and validation.

When she finished, there was a moment of silence before the room erupted in applause. Kara's heart soared. Their support and appreciation filled her with a renewed sense of purpose.

"Kara, that's beautiful! The colors speak volumes about your journey," Jodi exclaimed, her eyes shining with admiration. "You've captured something so personal and yet universal."

As conversations flowed and laughter filled the gallery, Kara felt a shift within her. The vulnerability she had feared turned into strength; opening up about her personal journey had allowed others to connect with her in ways she hadn't anticipated.

Amidst the excitement, Kara caught Christian's eye, and a silent conversation passed between them. She suddenly realized that art was not just about the final product but about sharing her truth and creating connections with those around her.

The evening continued with a sense of joy and celebration, and as Kara mingled with her guests, she felt a newfound confidence blossoming within her. She was not just an artist; she was a storyteller, weaving the threads of her life into the fabric of her creations. Each painting would serve as a reminder of her journey, a testament to love, vulnerability, and the beauty of sharing one's truth.

Waves of Opportunity

As the last of her guests drifted away, Kara stood at the Coastal Gallery, taking in the remnants of the evening's celebration. The soft hum of music still lingered in the air, mingling with the scent of fresh paint and the warmth of shared laughter. Her heart swelled with gratitude as she thought about the support she had received from everyone who had come. The applause, the words of encouragement—each one was a reminder that she was on the right path.

With a contented sigh, she began to clean up the space, her mind replaying the moments of the night: Jodi's exuberant compliments, her parents' proud smiles, and Christian's unwavering support. But just as she was about to stack her brushes, her phone buzzed on the table, pulling her attention away from the remnants of the gathering.

Curious, she picked it up, and her breath hitched in her throat as she read the message that had just arrived. It was from Michael Hargrove, a renowned art critic whose reviews were known to propel artists into the limelight. The message was brief but potent: "Dear Kara, I had the pleasure of attending your recent exhibition. Your work is mesmerizing. I would love to discuss a feature on your art in my upcoming column. Please let me know a convenient time for you. Regards, Michael."

A whirlwind of emotions flooded through her. Excitement sparked like fireworks in her chest, but it was quickly followed by a wave of anxiety. This was it—the opportunity she had dreamed of, yet it felt overwhelming. What if she failed to impress him? What if her work was not as compelling as she believed? Doubt crept in like a shadow, but she shook her head, trying to push it away. This was a chance to share her story with a broader audience and to connect with more people through her art.

"Hey, you okay?" Christian's voice broke through her thoughts, and Kara turned to find him leaning against the doorframe, a mischievous smile on his face, clearly having just returned from helping Jodi arrange her car outside.

"Yeah, just... look at this!" Kara exclaimed, her voice a mixture of excitement and nervousness as she handed him her phone.

Christian read the message, and his eyebrows shot up in surprise. "Whoa, Kara! This is incredible! You've got to meet with him! This could be your big break!"

"I know, but what if I freeze up? What if he doesn't see what I see in my work?" Kara bit her lip, anxiety creeping back in.

"Hey," Christian said, stepping closer to her and placing a comforting hand on her shoulder. "You've poured your heart into your art. Remember what you said tonight about vulnerability? This is just another way to share that. Just be yourself. You've got this!"

His encouraging words wrapped around her like a warm blanket, but the weight of the opportunity still loomed. "I guess I need to figure out how to respond," she murmured, her gaze drifting back to the canvas that had sparked the entire evening.

"Why don't we take a break from all this?" Christian suggested, his voice lighthearted. "How about a spontaneous weekend getaway to the beach? Just you and me, celebrating your success and unwinding before the wedding madness kicks in. What do you say?"

Kara's heart skipped a beat at the thought. The beach was their sanctuary, a place where they could connect away from the chaos of everyday life. "That sounds amazing, but is it too last minute? I don't want to leave you scrambling."

"Not at all! Let's pack a bag, grab some snacks, and just go. We can talk through this whole critic thing while soaking up the sun. I promise it'll be fun," he said with a grin that melted away her worries.

With a newfound sense of adventure igniting within her, Kara nodded, her spirits lifting. "Okay, let's do it! I'll grab my things!"

Within the hour, they were on the road, the sun setting in a symphony of oranges and purples as they drove toward the coast. Kara felt the tension of the night begin to fade, replaced by the serene anticipation of the beach. She turned to Christian, who was humming along to the music playing softly in the background, his enthusiasm contagious.

As they arrived at the beach, the sound of the waves crashing against the shore greeted them like an old friend. The salty breeze tousled Kara's hair as they stepped out of the car, and she took a deep breath, letting the ocean air fill her lungs.

"This is exactly what I needed," she said, her voice a mix of relief and joy.

Christian took her hand and led her toward the shore. "Let's find a spot to set up. I brought a cooler with some snacks and drinks." He winked, his eyes sparkling under the moonlight.

They settled on a blanket, the sand warm beneath them as they snacked on fresh fruit and cheese. The atmosphere was perfect—moonlight glimmering on the water, the sound of waves creating a peaceful rhythm, and Kara felt her worries begin to melt away.

After a while, they started to talk about her upcoming meeting with Michael. "What are you thinking about saying to him?" Christian asked, his tone light but curious.

"I guess I'll just share my vision and the story behind my work. I want him to understand the emotions I'm trying to convey," Kara replied, feeling the excitement of sharing her art.

"Exactly! And remember, it's not just about impressing him. It's about sharing who you are and what you love. Your passion will shine through," he encouraged, his gaze steady and confident.

"Thanks for believing in me," Kara said softly, feeling grateful for his support. "Sometimes I just need a little nudge to remind me why I do this."

"Anytime! And hey, once you get through that meeting, we can celebrate even more! We'll have to do something big!"

Kara laughed, the weight of her earlier anxiety lifting fully. "Like what? A beach bonfire?"

"Absolutely! S'mores, music—the whole shebang!" Christian's enthusiasm was infectious, and Kara could see the excitement in his eyes as he spoke.

As the night deepened, they walked along the shoreline, the moon reflecting on the water like a shimmering path leading them into the future. With each step, Kara felt her heart open wider, the worries of the world behind her. She reached down to let the waves lap at her feet, the cool water a refreshing contrast to the warmth of the sand.

"Do you ever think about our future?" she asked suddenly, the question hanging in the air between them.

"Of course! I think about us all the time. I can't wait to start our lives together," Christian replied, stopping to look at her. "What about you?"

"I do too, but sometimes I wonder about all the uncertainties. With the wedding coming up and my art career starting to take off, it feels like everything is changing so fast," she admitted, her voice thoughtful.

"Change can be scary, but it can also be exciting! We're building something amazing together. Just remember, no matter what happens, we've got each other's backs," he said, wrapping an arm around her shoulders as they walked.

Kara leaned into him, feeling the warmth of his body against hers. "You're right. I just need to trust the process and embrace whatever comes our way."

As they continued walking, the conversation flowed effortlessly, weaving in and out of dreams and aspirations, fears and joys. Kara felt a surge of inspiration wash over her, the beauty of the night and the depth of their connection igniting a spark within her.

CHAPTER 45

The Tides Of Love And Sketches

Kara awoke to the gentle lapping of waves outside their beach cottage, the sound like a soothing melody that wrapped around her like a comforting blanket. Sunlight streamed through the window, casting a golden glow across the room and illuminating the playful dust motes dancing in the air. She stretched, her body responding blissfully to the warmth of the morning, and a smile tugged at her lips as she took a moment to appreciate the serenity of the moment.

The scent of salt and fresh air mingled with something sweeter, and curiosity tugged at her. She swung her legs over the edge of the bed, her feet sinking into the cool wooden floor, and made her way to the small kitchen area. She found Christian standing by the counter with a mug in hand, his hair tousled from sleep but still effortlessly handsome. He looked up as she entered, his face lighting up with a grin that made her heart flutter.

"Good morning, sunshine!" he called out cheerfully, gesturing to the spread he had prepared on the table. "I made breakfast! Come and get it while it's fresh!"

Kara chuckled, her heart warming at the sight of him. "What did you whip up this time?" she asked, stepping closer to the table where a delightful assortment of fruits, muffins, and a steaming pot of coffee awaited her.

"Just some beach-style breakfast—fruits, pastries, and, of course, coffee to fuel our creative energy!" Christian replied with a wink, pouring a cup and handing it to her. "I figured we could enjoy our morning with a view."

Kara took a sip, savoring the rich flavor as she settled into a chair. She gazed out at the ocean, the waves glistening like diamonds under the sun. "This is perfect," she said, her voice filled with appreciation. "I can't think of a better way to start the day."

As they ate, their conversation flowed easily, filled with laughter and playful banter. Christian shared stories from his childhood, recounting mischief with his friends at the beach, while Kara shared tales from her own adventures, including the time she had tried to teach herself how to surf, only to end up tumbling into the water more times than she could count. They both laughed, the sound mingling with the rhythmic crashing of the waves.

Once they finished breakfast, Christian pushed back his chair and stood up with a mischievous glint in his eyes. "I have a surprise for you," he said dramatically, his voice filled with excitement.

"A surprise? What is it?" Kara asked, her curiosity piqued.

"Wait right here!" he instructed, dashing off to their bedroom. Moments later, he returned, holding a brand-new sketchbook and a set of pencils. "I thought you might want to capture the beauty around us. You're always talking about how inspiring the ocean is, so why not sketch it?" He handed her the sketchbook, his eyes sparkling with enthusiasm.

Kara's heart swelled with gratitude. "Christian, this is amazing! Thank you!" She flipped through the blank pages, envisioning the possibilities that lay ahead.

"Why don't you find a spot on the beach, and I'll set up our little art station? You can draw whatever inspires you," he suggested, his voice lighthearted and encouraging.

Kara nodded, a rush of excitement coursing through her. She grabbed the sketchbook and made her way toward the shore, the sand warm beneath her feet. Finding a cozy spot near the water's edge, she settled down, the sound of waves crashing providing the perfect soundtrack for her creativity.

As she opened the sketchbook, she felt a flutter of anticipation. The ocean stretched endlessly before her, its vibrant blues and greens calling out to her. She took a deep breath, allowing the salty air to invigorate her senses, and began to sketch, her pencil gliding across the page.

Time slipped away as she lost herself in the rhythm of her strokes, capturing the essence of the waves, the delicate dance of the seagulls above, and the way the sun sparkled on the water. Each line was an expression of her emotions, a way to channel the beauty of her surroundings into something tangible.

"Kara! How's the masterpiece coming along?" Christian's voice broke through her concentration, and she looked up to see him approaching with a smile.

She held up her sketch, a depiction of the waves crashing against the shore, and grinned. "Look! I think I'm finally capturing the essence of it!"

"Wow, this is incredible!" Christian exclaimed, his eyes widening in admiration as he studied her work. "You've really captured the movement of the water. It's like I can hear the waves just by looking at it!"

Kara felt a blush creep onto her cheeks at his praise. "Thanks! I'm just trying to express what I feel when I look at the ocean," she replied.

"Speaking of expressing yourself, I was thinking..." Christian began, the wheels in his mind clearly turning. "There's an art fair happening nearby this afternoon. It's a great place for you to network, see other artists, and gain some confidence before your meeting with Michael. What do you think?"

Her heart quickened at the idea, a mix of eagerness and trepidation swirling within her. "An art fair? I don't know, Christian. What if I'm not ready? What if I don't fit in?"

"Of course you'll fit in! It's a friendly community, and you have so much talent to share. Plus, it'll be a great way for you to gain exposure and build connections," he encouraged, his eyes shining with belief in her abilities.

Kara bit her lip, her mind racing. "You really think it would help?"

"Definitely! And besides, I'll be right there with you. We can explore together, and who knows? You might meet someone who can help you with your art career," he said, his tone light and adventurous. "What do you say?"

Taking a deep breath, Kara weighed her options. The thought of stepping into the art fair was daunting, but the prospect of sharing her work and connecting with others ignited a spark of excitement within her.

"Okay, I'm in! Let's do it!" she said, her voice gaining confidence.

"Awesome! Let's grab our things and head out. I can't wait to see you shine!" Christian replied, his enthusiasm infectious.

As they packed up their beach gear, Kara felt a rush of anticipation surging through her. The day was unfolding in ways she hadn't expected, and the possibilities felt limitless. With each step they took toward the art fair, the ocean behind them seemed to whisper encouragement, reminding her to embrace the moment and trust in her journey.

The sun hung high in the sky as they walked hand in hand, the world around them buzzing with energy and color. Kara couldn't shake the feeling that she was on the brink of something transformative, and with Christian by her side, she felt ready to face whatever lay ahead.

CHAPTER 46

A Canvas Of Poetic Love Of Art

The air was thick with excitement as Kara and Christian approached the bustling art fair, their fingers intertwined. The festival sprawled before them, a riot of colors and sounds that danced through the warm afternoon breeze. Kara felt her heart race, a mixture of exhilaration and trepidation swirling within her. The vibrant atmosphere was intoxicating, yet it made her feel small and uncertain in the face of so much talent.

"Look at all of this!" Christian exclaimed, his eyes wide with wonder as he took in the scene.

Artists were setting up their booths, displaying everything from dazzling paintings to intricate sculptures. The sounds of laughter and chatter filled the air, blending seamlessly with the distant sound of waves crashing against the shore.

"Yeah, it's... a lot," Kara replied, her voice barely above a whisper.

She felt a flutter of anxiety in her stomach as they made their way through the throngs of people. The vibrant displays around her were breathtaking, but they also highlighted her insecurities. What if her sketches weren't good enough? What if she didn't belong here?

"Hey," Christian said, squeezing her hand gently. "You're going to be amazing. Just remember why we're here. This is all about expressing yourself and connecting with others who love art as much as you do."

She took a deep breath, trying to absorb his encouragement. "You're right. I just need to breathe and take it all in."

As they wandered through the rows of booths, Kara's eyes drifted from one display to another. She marveled at the creativity surrounding her—the bold strokes of paint, delicate pottery, and mesmerizing photographs. Each piece told a story, and Kara felt a pang of yearning to be part of that narrative. But the closer they got to the heart of the fair, the more her confidence began to waver.

"Let's check this one out," Christian said, pulling her toward a booth filled with stunning landscapes. A painter sat behind a small table, her hands covered in paint as she carefully arranged her canvases. Kara felt her heart race as she approached, feeling both inspired and intimidated.

"Hi there! These are beautiful!" Christian greeted the artist with a warm smile.

"Thank you! I'm Holly," the painter replied, her voice friendly and inviting. "I'm glad you like them! Do you paint as well?" she asked, turning her attention to Kara.

Kara hesitated, her cheeks flushing. "Well, I've been sketching a bit, but I'm not really... serious about it," she stammered, her voice trailing off.

"Nonsense! Everyone starts somewhere. What do you like to draw?" Holly encouraged, her eyes sparkling with enthusiasm.

Kara glanced at Christian, who nodded encouragingly. "I've been sketching the ocean and its waves," she said, her voice gaining a bit more confidence as she spoke about her passion.

Holly's face lit up. "That's wonderful! There's so much movement and emotion in the ocean. Have you brought any of your sketches with you?"

"I... I have a few in my bag," Kara replied, hesitating for a moment.

She felt a mixture of excitement and fear coursing through her veins. What if Holly didn't like them? What if they weren't good enough?

"Go on, show her!" Christian urged, nudging her gently.

With a deep breath, Kara reached into her bag and pulled out her sketchbook, her hands trembling slightly. She opened it to a page featuring her depiction of the waves crashing against the shore, the lines and shading capturing the fluid movement of the water.

Holly leaned in closer, her eyes narrowing with interest as she examined the sketch. "This is incredible! You've really captured the essence of the waves. The way you've portrayed the light reflecting off the water is stunning!"

Kara's heart soared at Holly's praise, her initial trepidation melting away. "Thank you! I've always loved the ocean, and I try to express that in my work."

"Keep sketching! You have a natural talent. I'd love to see more of your work," Holly said. "You should consider displaying your pieces here next year. You have something special."

The weight of Holly's words hung in the air, filling Kara with a sense of possibility she hadn't felt before. "Really? You think so?" she asked, her heart racing with hope.

"Absolutely! Art is all about sharing your perspective. You have a unique voice, and I think others would resonate with it," Holly replied, her enthusiasm infectious.

As they continued to chat, Kara felt her confidence grow. With each passing moment, the initial anxiety that had gripped her began to dissipate, replaced by a sense of connection and camaraderie. Christian stood by her side, beaming with pride as she engaged with Holly.

After a while, they bid farewell to Holly, Kara feeling lighter and more inspired than she had in a long time.

"That was amazing!" she exclaimed, turning to Christian, her eyes sparkling with excitement. "I can't believe how supportive she was!"

"I knew you'd shine! You just needed a little push," Christian said, wrapping an arm around her shoulders. "See? You belong here just as much as anyone else. Let's keep exploring!"

The rest of the afternoon passed in a whirl of color and creativity. Kara felt invigorated as she spoke with other artists, sharing ideas and stories while absorbing their passion for art. The vibrant atmosphere of the fair, combined with the encouragement of her newfound friends, filled her with a sense of determination she hadn't expected.

As the sun began to set, casting a warm golden glow over the fair, Kara and Christian found a quiet spot to rest for a moment, away from the hustle and bustle. They sat on a bench, watching the sun dip toward the horizon, painting the sky in shades of orange and pink.

"I can't believe how much I've enjoyed today," Kara said, leaning into Christian's side. "Thank you for pushing me to come here."

"Anytime! I always knew you had it in you," he replied, kissing the top of her head. "I can't wait to see what you create next."

The warmth of the moment enveloped them, a reservation of serenity that felt like the world had fallen away. As they sat together, a sense of belonging and purpose began to blossom within Kara. This was more than just an art fair; it was a doorway to new beginnings.

As twilight descended, they decided to take a stroll along the beach, the sound of the waves providing a soothing soundtrack. The moonlight shimmered on the water, creating a magical glow that seemed to illuminate their path. Kara felt alive, a sense of adventure coursing through her veins.

"Do you remember our first date?" Christian asked suddenly, breaking the comfortable silence between them.

Kara chuckled, her mind drifting back to that fateful evening. "Of course! You took me to that little seafood place by the pier. I was so nervous!"

"You were adorable," he teased, his eyes twinkling. "And you ordered the spiciest dish on the menu, which you later regretted."

"I had no idea what I was getting into!" She laughed, shaking her head. "But it was one of the best nights of my life."

As they walked hand in hand, the memories of their shared experiences flooded back—each moment a brushstroke on the canvas of their lives together. From spontaneous road trips to late-night talks under the stars, every memory felt like a piece of art that told their story.

"Kara," Christian said softly, turning to face her. "I know we've only been together for a little while, but I can't imagine my life without you. You inspire me every day."

Her heart swelled at his words, and she found herself searching his eyes for the truth behind them. "You inspire me too, Christian. You've shown me parts of myself I never knew existed."

They paused, the world around them fading as they shared a moment of vulnerability and connection. The moonlight shimmered on the water, casting a spell that felt weightless and infinite.

"Let's make a promise," Christian said, his voice steady. "No matter what happens, we'll always encourage each other to chase our dreams."

Kara smiled, her heart racing at the thought. "I promise. No matter where our paths lead, we'll support each other."

With that promise hanging in the air, they shared a kiss, the ocean breeze swirling around them like a gentle embrace. In that moment, Kara felt a surge of passion, a deep connection that transcended words.

As they pulled away, Christian's eyes sparkled mischievously. "Now, how about we celebrate this amazing day with a little fun?"

Kara raised an eyebrow, curiosity piqued. "What do you have in mind?"

"Let's make our own art right here on the beach," he suggested, a playful glint in his eyes. "We'll draw in the sand and let the waves wash it away. It'll be our temporary masterpiece."

Kara laughed, feeling a rush of excitement at the thought of creating something together. "That sounds perfect!"

They knelt in the sand, using their fingers to draw swirling patterns and designs, laughing and sharing stories as the waves lapped at their feet. With each stroke in the sand, Kara felt a sense of freedom and joy, a reminder that art could be spontaneous and fun.

As the last light of day faded into twilight, Kara and Christian shared a quiet moment on the beach, the stars beginning to twinkle above them like distant dreams. The world felt infinite, and in that serene space, they knew they were embarking on a journey filled with new beginnings, creativity, and love.

CHAPTER 47

A New Dawn

The first light of dawn crept through the curtains, casting a soft glow across the room. Kara stirred, feeling the warmth of Christian's body beside her. The events of the previous day flooded her mind like a wave crashing against the shore: the art fair, the encouragement from Holly, and the spontaneous moments they had shared. But it was the intimate connection with Christian that lingered most vividly, igniting a fire of determination within her.

She turned to look at him, his handsome features relaxed in sleep, the sun illuminating the contours of his face. His athletic build was a testament to the active lifestyle he embraced, a reminder of adventures yet to come. Kara felt a rush of affection as she studied him, a boyish charm that made her heart flutter.

"Christian," she whispered softly, leaning closer to him. "Wake up."

His eyes fluttered open, revealing a sleepy smile that made her heart skip a beat. "Morning, beautiful," he murmured, his voice thick with sleep. "What time is it?"

Kara glanced at the clock on the bedside table. "It's just past six," she replied, a sense of urgency creeping into her voice. "We need to get moving if we're going to meet Michael Hargrove and finalize the wedding plans with my parents."

Christian groaned playfully, rolling onto his back and stretching like a cat. "Can't we just stay here a little longer? I could get used to waking up next to you every day."

Her cheeks flushed at his words, and she felt a shiver of excitement run through her. "As tempting as that sounds, we have a big day ahead of us. Besides, I want to make sure everything goes smoothly for the wedding."

With a resigned sigh, Christian sat up, running a hand through his tousled hair. "Alright, alright. Let's get this show on the road! A wedding isn't going to plan itself."

Kara laughed, feeling a rush of energy as they both swung their legs over the side of the bed. "Exactly! Now, let's make some coffee. I'll shower first, and then we can get ready."

"Deal," he replied, hopping out of bed and heading toward the kitchen.

Kara watched him go, her heart swelling with happiness. The thought of their wedding was both exhilarating and nerve-wracking, but with Christian by her side, she felt a renewed sense of confidence.

After a quick shower, Kara emerged feeling refreshed and ready to tackle the day. The aroma of freshly brewed coffee wafted through the air, and as she entered the kitchen, Christian was already pouring two steaming mugs.

"Here you go," he said with a grin, handing her a cup. "The magic potion to kickstart our day."

"Thanks," she replied, taking a sip and savoring the rich flavor. The warmth of the coffee spread through her, fueling her determination. "I can't believe the wedding is just around the corner. It feels surreal."

Christian leaned against the counter, watching her with an appreciative smile. "It's going to be an amazing day, Kara. Just think about it: family, friends, and us, starting a new chapter together. I wouldn't want to do this with anyone else."

His words resonated deep within her, and she felt a wave of emotion wash over her. "You're right. This is a huge step, but I feel ready. I've never been more sure about anything in my life.

With that, they finished their coffee and got dressed, the atmosphere in the apartment buzzing with excitement and anticipation. Kara opted for a light sundress that flowed around her, while Christian chose a casual button-up shirt and jeans, his trademark style that made her smile.

As they stepped outside, the sun was already climbing higher in the sky, promising a beautiful day ahead. Kara took a moment to breathe in the salty ocean air, feeling grateful for the life she was building with Christian. "Let's go! I want to make sure we have everything squared away with my parents before the big day."

The drive to her parents' house was filled with lighthearted banter and laughter, the radio playing a mix of their favorite songs. Kara felt alive, the thrill of the upcoming wedding combining with the joy of being with Christian. They shared stories, reminiscing about their adventures and daydreaming about the future.

When they arrived at her parents' house, Kara's heart raced with a mix of excitement and nervousness. She loved her parents dearly, and their approval meant the world to her. As they walked up the path to the front door, she felt a wave of nostalgia wash over her, memories of childhood flooding her mind.

"Ready?" Christian asked, sensing her apprehension.

"Yeah, let's do this," Kara replied, taking a deep breath before ringing the doorbell.

Her mom answered almost immediately, her cheerful smile lighting up the entrance. "Kara! Christian! It's so wonderful to see you both!" she exclaimed, stepping aside to let them in. "Come in, come in! Your father is in the living room."

As they entered the house, the familiar scent of her mother's cooking wafted through the air, instantly bringing back memories of family dinners and celebrations. Kara felt a sense of comfort envelop her, knowing that this was the place where her roots were planted.

"Dad!" she called, making her way into the living room. Her father looked up from his newspaper, his face breaking into a wide smile.

"Hey there, kiddo! You made it!" he said, standing to pull her into a warm embrace. "And Christian, good to see you, son!"

"Good to see you too, Mr. Carter," Christian replied, shaking Kara's father's hand firmly.

They settled onto the couch, and Kara's mom joined them, placing a tray of cookies on the coffee table. "I thought we could have some snacks while we go over the wedding details," she said, her voice filled with nostalgia. "It's such an exciting time!"

Kara felt a swell of gratitude as they began discussing the wedding plans. Her parents listened intently, offering advice and sharing their own stories of love and marriage. Christian chimed in with his ideas, his spontaneous nature adding a spark to the conversation.

"There's something special about a wedding," her dad said thoughtfully. "It's a celebration of love, and you two have something truly beautiful. I can see how happy you make each other."

Kara's heart swelled at her father's words. "Thank you, Dad. That means the world to me."

As they went through the details, Kara felt a sense of calm wash over her. The nervous energy that had initially consumed her began to fade, replaced by excitement for the future they were building together. Christian's presence beside her was a constant reminder that they were a team, ready to face whatever came their way.

After a productive meeting, they wrapped things up, and her mom suggested they take a family photo to commemorate the occasion. "Let's capture this moment!" she said, her eyes sparkling with joy.

They gathered together in the living room, striking playful poses and laughing as her mom snapped picture after picture. Kara felt a warmth in her heart, knowing she was surrounded by love and support.

As the day came to a close, Kara and Christian said their goodbyes, promising to keep her parents updated on the wedding preparations.

As they walked back to the car, Kara felt a sense of fulfillment wash over her.

"Today went really well," she said, glancing at Christian as they settled into the car. "I feel like we're one step closer to making this wedding a reality."

"Absolutely! And I love how your parents are so supportive," Christian replied, his eyes shining with excitement. "It's going to be an incredible day, Kara. I can't wait to see you walk down that aisle."

Her heart fluttered at the thought, and she smiled brightly. "Me too. And I know that with you by my side, everything will be perfect."

The Art of Unexpected Turns

The sun was dipping low in the sky, casting a warm golden hue across the landscape as Kara and Christian drove back home. The excitement from their productive meeting with her parents still buzzed in the air, but Kara felt a tinge of nervousness, her mind racing with the details of the wedding preparations. She glanced sideways at Christian, who was humming along to the song playing on the radio, his carefree spirit a soothing balm to her anxious thoughts.

"You know, I can't stop thinking about how great today went," Kara said, her voice light yet thoughtful. "It feels like everything is falling into place."

Christian turned to her, a playful grin spreading across his face. "Well, that's because it is! You're going to be a stunning bride, and I can't wait to see you walk down that aisle. I'll be the one with the goofy grin, trying not to trip over my own feet."

She chuckled at his playful demeanor, feeling the warmth of his words wrap around her like a comforting embrace. "You're right! But let's not get ahead of ourselves. We still have a lot to do before the big day."

As they approached a red light, Kara's phone buzzed in her purse, breaking through her thoughts. She fished it out, her heart skipping a beat as she saw Michael Hargrove's name flashing on the screen. The renowned art critic had reached out to her after the art fair, expressing interest in doing a feature on her work.

"Hang on a sec, Christian. It's Michael," she said, swiping to answer the call. "Hello?"

"Kara! It's Michael Hargrove," came his enthusiastic voice from the other end. "I hope I'm not interrupting anything important. I wanted to see if you'd be available for a quick chat about your art."

"Of course! I'd love to," Kara replied, her heart racing. "When were you thinking?"

"How about we meet at that cozy café near the beach? I have a couple of questions lined up, and I'd like to get your insights before the article goes live tomorrow."

"Sounds perfect! I can be there in about twenty minutes," she said, glancing at the clock. "Christian, do you mind taking me there?"

"Not at all! I'll be your trusty chauffeur," he replied, his eyes sparkling with enthusiasm. "I can't wait to see you in action."

They arrived at the café, a quaint little spot with vibrant outdoor seating. The salty breeze carried the faint scent of coffee and pastries, making Kara's stomach rumble with anticipation. As they stepped inside, she spotted Michael already seated at a corner table, a notepad and pen at the ready.

"Hey there, Kara! Great to see you," Michael greeted her warmly as she approached. "You must be Christian. Thanks for coming along!"

"Nice to meet you," Christian replied, shaking Michael's hand with a firm grip. "Kara's been talking about this article for days. I'm excited to see what you come up with."

They settled into their seats, and Kara felt a rush of adrenaline course through her. Michael's reputation preceded him; he was known for his insightful critiques and ability to elevate artists' profiles.

"So, Kara," he started, his pen poised above the notepad. "I want to dive into your creative process. What inspires your work?"

Kara took a deep breath, feeling the passion for her art bubble to the surface. "Nature has always been a big influence for me. I love the ocean, and I often find myself drawing inspiration from its colors and textures. Each piece I create is a reflection of what I feel in that moment."

Michael nodded, scribbling notes with an attentive look. "That's fascinating! And how do you see your art evolving as you approach this new chapter in your life?"

She paused for a moment, contemplating the question. "I think it's about embracing change. Just like planning a wedding, art is a journey. I want to explore new themes and techniques, pushing myself beyond my comfort zone."

Christian watched her speak, pride swelling in his chest. The way Kara articulated her thoughts with such passion was nothing short of inspiring.

Michael continued to ask her questions, delving deeper into her inspirations and aspirations. Kara felt the conversation flow effortlessly, each answer igniting more ideas and reflections. The café buzzed around them, but in that moment, it felt like they were in their own world, surrounded by the warmth of creativity and possibility.

After what felt like a whirlwind of conversation, Michael leaned back in his chair, a satisfied smile on his face. "That was incredible, Kara. I have all the material I need, and I can't wait to share your story with the world. Your art deserves to be celebrated."

"Thank you so much! That means a lot to me," she replied, feeling a mixture of relief and excitement.

Michael left with a promise to send her a copy of his article, leaving her and Christian alone again.

As they finished their coffees, Kara's phone buzzed again—this time, it was a call from Josie, the wedding planner. With a mix of eagerness and trepidation, she answered, "Hi, Josie! What's up?"

"Kara, I need to discuss something important with you," Josie said, her tone indicating urgency. "Unfortunately, there's been a last-minute venue change due to unforeseen circumstances. The original location is no longer available."

Kara's heart sank. "Oh no! What do we do now?"

"Don't worry! I have a few options for you, and I think I found a beautiful seaside estate that could be perfect for your wedding. But we'll need to act quickly to secure it," Josie explained.

"Okay, let me discuss this with Christian, and I'll get back to you in a few minutes," Kara replied, glancing at Christian, who was watching her with a mix of concern and curiosity.

She relayed the news, and Christian's expression shifted from surprise to determination.

"Let's go check it out," he suggested, his adventurous spirit shining through. "A seaside estate sounds amazing! We can make it even more special than before."

Kara felt a wave of gratitude wash over her. "You're right! Let's do this."

After a few more quick exchanges with Josie, they found themselves back in the car, heading toward the new venue. As they drove, Kara could feel the anxiety slowly giving way to excitement. The idea of a seaside wedding was enchanting, and Christian's unwavering support made her feel like they could take on anything that came their way.

When they arrived at the estate, Kara was immediately struck by its beauty. Nestled on a cliff overlooking the ocean, the property exuded charm with its white-washed walls and lush gardens. The sound of the waves crashing against the rocks below added a magical soundtrack to the scene.

"Wow," Kara breathed, stepping out of the car and taking in the view. "This place is breathtaking."

Christian grinned at her reaction. "See? Sometimes the unexpected turns lead to amazing outcomes."

They wandered through the estate, exploring the gardens and peering into the various rooms. Each space was filled with potential, and Kara could already envision the wedding taking shape.

"This could be perfect," she said, her eyes sparkling with excitement. "Imagine the ceremony here, with the ocean as our backdrop. It's like a dream come true."

Christian joined her, wrapping his arm around her shoulders as they gazed out at the horizon. "And we'll have the best view in the house. You'll look stunning walking down that aisle."

Kara laughed, feeling the weight of anxiety lift from her shoulders. "Thank you for being so positive throughout this. I know it's been a whirlwind, but I'm grateful to share it with you."

With laughter and spontaneous moments peppering their exploration, they realized that love flourishes in the unexpected. Each twist in their journey was weaving a beautiful tapestry, one that was uniquely theirs.

CHAPTER 49

Wedding Day Approaches

The morning sun filtered through the sheer curtains of the seaside estate, casting soft patterns of light across the elegantly decorated room. Kara stood at the large window, her heart fluttering with anticipation as she gazed out at the waves crashing against the cliffs. The ocean shimmered under the bright sun, its rhythm a calming backdrop to the whirlwind of emotions swirling inside her. In just two days, she would marry the love of her life, Christian, but an unexpected storm was brewing on the horizon.

Christian entered the room with two cups of steaming coffee, a bright smile lighting up his handsome face. "Good morning, beautiful! I brought you your favorite," he said, handing her a cup. Kara took a sip, savoring the rich flavor as the warmth spread through her.

"Thanks, love. I needed this," she replied, her voice still a bit groggy. She turned back to the view, her mind racing with the details of the wedding preparations that lay ahead. "Today's the day we finalize everything, right?"

"Absolutely! We're going to nail this," he said, leaning against the doorframe with an air of confidence. "After all, we're a team. Plus, it's going to be a beach wedding, which means good vibes all around."

Kara chuckled at his optimism, but her mind was elsewhere. She was still riding the high from her conversation with Michael Hargrove, which had left her buzzing. She had hardly slept a wink, excitement and anxiety dancing in her chest. The thought of showcasing her artwork at a prestigious gallery opening the same weekend as her wedding was both exhilarating and overwhelming.

"Christian, can we talk about something?" she began, setting her coffee down on the windowsill. She could see the concern in his eyes as he stepped closer.

"Of course! What's on your mind?" he asked, his voice softening.

Kara took a deep breath, her fingers nervously tracing the rim of her cup. "Michael wants to feature my art at the gallery opening. It's happening the same weekend as our wedding. I don't even know how to process that."

Christian's brows furrowed slightly, but his expression remained warm. "Wow, that's huge! But it's also a lot to juggle. How do you feel about it?"

"I'm torn," she admitted, her voice trembling with uncertainty. "This could be a once-in-a-lifetime opportunity. But I don't want to take away from our wedding day. This is supposed to be our moment."

"Hey, listen," Christian said, taking her hands in his. "You're an incredible artist, and this is your moment too. I know how much your art means to you. What if we find a way to make both work?"

Kara looked into his eyes, the sincerity of his words washing over her like a warm wave. "You really think so? I don't want to be a distraction on our wedding day."

"Not at all! We can brainstorm how to intertwine the gallery event with our celebration. It could be a beautiful way to share your passion with everyone," he suggested, his adventurous spirit shining through.

The prospect of combining the two worlds sparked something in Kara. "You're right! I could showcase a few pieces at the reception, maybe invite a few gallery guests to join us. It could be an unforgettable experience."

"Exactly! Let's make it a celebration of love and creativity. We can have the wedding and the gallery event all at once," Christian said, his excitement contagious.

Kara felt a smile breaking through her earlier anxiety, and she nodded, her heart racing with renewed energy. "Okay! Let's do it. We can make this work together."

They spent the morning planning, laughter and creativity filling the air as they bounced ideas off one another. Christian suggested they create a small art corner at the wedding where guests could view her work, and Kara envisioned live painting during the reception, capturing the joyous moments as they unfolded.

As they finalized arrangements, Kara's phone buzzed with notifications, and she glanced at the screen to see a message from Jodi. "Can't wait to see you guys! Let's make some magic happen!"

Picking up on the playful energy in Jodi's text, Kara felt a wave of enthusiasm wash over her. "I think Jodi is going to love the idea of integrating my art into the wedding. She's always been my biggest supporter."

"Of course she will! And I can already picture the look on your dad's face when he sees your artwork displayed at the wedding. He'll be so proud," Christian added, his tone inspiring.

"Let's hope so! Speaking of which, I should probably call my parents and update them on the plan," Kara said.

As she dialed her mom's number, she felt a mix of anticipation and nervousness. When her mother answered, Kara could hear the cheerful tone in her voice. "Kara! How are you, sweetheart?"

"Hi, Mom! I'm good! Just wanted to let you know that we're integrating my art into the wedding," Kara announced, her heart racing as she shared the news. "Michael Hargrove wants to feature me at a gallery opening the same weekend, and Christian and I thought it would be amazing to blend both events."

"Oh, darling, that sounds wonderful! You and Christian are so creative together! I can't wait to see how it all comes together," her mother replied, her voice infused with nostalgia. "Just remember to take a moment to breathe and soak it all in."

"Thanks, Mom. I will," Kara promised, the warmth of her mother's words filling her heart. After they hung up, Kara felt a renewed sense of purpose. She turned to Christian, who was busy jotting down notes. "I think this is really going to work!"

"Absolutely! We're going to make this a celebration of love and art," he said, his enthusiasm infectious.

The next morning dawned bright and clear, and Kara awoke to the sound of the ocean waves calling her name. She grabbed her phone, her heart racing as she opened social media to check for updates on Michael's article. As she scrolled, her breath caught in her throat. The headline read: "Emerging Artist Kara: A Breath of Fresh Air in the Art World."

The article detailed her journey, her inspirations, and the upcoming gallery opening, and it was filled with praise for her unique style. A flood of notifications poured in as viewers reacted and shared their excitement. Kara felt a wave of joy and disbelief wash over her; the response was overwhelmingly positive.

"Christian! Come look at this!" she called out, her voice laced with excitement. He rushed into the room, his hair tousled, and a sleepy smile on his face.

"What's going on?" he asked, squinting at her phone screen.

"Michael's article is live! Look at the comments!" Kara exclaimed, her heart racing as she scrolled through the supportive messages flooding in from fans, fellow artists, and even critics who were eager to see her work.

"Wow! This is incredible!" Christian said, reading through the comments and beaming with pride. "You're officially a star, Kara!"

Amidst the chaos of wedding plans, the uplifting news spurred them on. They spent the day finalizing the last details for the wedding setup, each decision made with laughter and love. The outdoor space was adorned with twinkling lights and floral arrangements with Kara's artwork displayed prominently, creating a beautiful blend of their lives and passions.

As the sun began to dip low in the sky, painting the horizon with hues of orange and pink, Kara and Christian stood hand in hand, looking out at the ocean. The waves crashed rhythmically below, a reminder of the journey they were embarking on together.

"We're really doing this, aren't we?" Kara said, her heart swelling with emotion.

"Absolutely," Christian replied, turning to her with a serious yet playful expression. "And we're going to make it unforgettable."

Kara realized that while their wedding was a celebration of their love, it was also a canvas for their dreams, an opportunity to embrace both their passions and their commitment. And as they stood together, the ocean breeze wrapping around them, they knew they were ready to paint their future together, one brushstroke at a time.

C H A P T E R   5 0

The Wedding Day

The sun rose over the horizon, casting golden rays that danced across the waves of the sea. Kara stood in front of the mirror in her bridal suite, her heart racing as she admired her reflection. The delicate lace of her wedding dress hugged her figure perfectly, and her hair cascaded in soft waves around her shoulders. Today was the day she had dreamed of ever since she was a little girl, and yet, a whirlwind of emotions churned within her.

"Just breathe," she whispered to herself, trying to calm the rapid beating of her heart.

She was excited, anxious, and filled with a sense of impending magic. Today was about love, commitment, and the melding of two beautiful lives into one.

Her best friend, Jodi, burst into the room, her radiant smile lighting up the space. "You look stunning! I can't believe you're getting married! Can you feel the energy in the air?" Jodi's enthusiasm was infectious, and Kara felt a rush of warmth as she turned to her friend.

"Thanks, Jodi! I'm trying to soak it all in, but it's hard not to feel a bit overwhelmed," Kara admitted, placing a hand over her heart. "I just want everything to be perfect."

"Perfect is overrated! Just remember, it's about you and Christian. The rest is just fluff," Jodi said, waving her hand dismissively. "Now, let's get you down that aisle. Your prince is waiting!"

As they made their way to the ceremony site, Kara couldn't help but steal glances at the guests mingling under the shade of swaying palm trees. Family and friends had gathered from near and far to witness this momentous occasion. Kara felt a swell of gratitude for every person who had supported her journey, both in life and in art.

But just as they reached the entrance of the sandy path leading to the altar, a familiar figure caught her eye. It was Michael Hargrove, the art critic whose recent article had catapulted her into the limelight. He stood off to the side, dressed in a tailored suit that fit him impeccably. His presence sent a jolt of excitement through Kara, but she quickly glanced back at Jodi, her heart tightening with apprehension.

"Michael is here?" Kara whispered, her voice barely above a breath.

"Looks like it! Are you happy or nervous?" Jodi asked, her eyes sparkling with mischief.

"A bit of both," Kara admitted. She couldn't shake the thrill of seeing Michael, but she was also acutely aware of Christian's simmering jealousy. The last thing she wanted was to create tension on her wedding day.

As if sensing her turmoil, Jodi squeezed Kara's hand. "Just focus on Christian. He's the one you're marrying today. Michael is just a writer in the audience. Remember that!"

With a deep breath, Kara nodded and continued down the path. The sound of the ocean waves crashing against the cliffs echoed in her ears, creating a soothing rhythm that helped her center herself. As she approached the altar adorned with white flowers and seashells, her gaze locked on Christian, who stood there looking breathtakingly handsome in his tailored suit. His eyes sparkled with anticipation, and the moment their gazes met, a smile spread across his face.

She felt a rush of love wash over her, momentarily drowning out her worries. This was her moment, and nothing else mattered. Kara took her father's arm, feeling the strength and warmth radiating from him. He looked down at her with a proud smile, and she could see the glimmer of tears in his eyes.

"You look beautiful, Kara. Just remember, this is about love. Nothing else matters," he whispered, kissing her forehead gently.

As the music swelled around them, Kara's heart raced. She felt as though she were floating, each step bringing her closer to the love of her life. But as they reached the altar, a flicker of doubt crept in. Michael's presence lingered in her mind, reminding her of the artistic path she had chosen and the commitments that came with it.

The ceremony began, and Kara found herself struggling to focus on the vows being exchanged. She could feel Christian's warmth beside her, but the weight of her dual commitments pressed down heavily. She loved Christian with every fiber of her being, but the artist in her felt an undeniable connection to the world of creativity that Michael represented.

"Kara, do you take Christian to be your lawfully wedded husband?" the officiant asked, bringing her back to the present moment.

"Yes, I do," she replied, her voice steady despite the whirlwind of emotions inside her.

"Christian, do you take Kara to be your lawfully wedded wife?"

Christian's gaze was intense. His eyes locked onto hers as if they were the only two people in the world. "Absolutely, I do," he said, his voice filled with conviction.

As they exchanged rings, Kara felt the warmth of Christian's hand enveloping hers, grounding her. Each word they spoke echoed with intention and love, like brushstrokes on a canvas—each vow building a masterpiece of their shared life.

The ocean waves crashed behind them, a rhythmic reminder of the life they would build together. Kara's heart swelled as she thought about all their adventures, the laughter, the challenges, and the passion that had brought them to this moment.

It was time for the closing vows, a moment that encapsulated their love. Kara took a deep breath, her heart racing. "Christian, you are my anchor and my muse. With you, I have found my true self, and I promise to nurture both our love and my art. Together, we will create a life filled with beauty and joy."

Christian's eyes softened, and he replied, "Kara, you are my adventure and my inspiration. I vow to support your dreams and to cherish you every day of our lives. Together, we will paint a future full of love and creativity."

As they sealed their vows with a kiss, Kara felt as though time had stopped. The world faded away, and all that existed was the warmth of Christian's lips against hers, the crashing waves, and the vibrant colors of their shared dreams. It was a kiss that spoke of promises, of passion, of the art they would create together.

Once the ceremony concluded, cheers erupted from their family and friends, and Kara felt a rush of joy wash over her. But amidst the celebration, she caught sight of Michael standing off to the side, a subtle smile on his face. She felt a pang of uncertainty. Would he be a constant reminder of her dual commitments?

Christian stepped back, a playful glint in his eye. "Let's get this party started, Mrs. Hastings!" he declared, pulling her into a warm embrace.

As they walked down the aisle together, hand in hand, Kara glanced over her shoulder at Michael one last time. She felt a mix of gratitude for his support and an understanding that today was about more than just her art. It was about the love they were forging, the life they would build, and the adventures that awaited them.

With Christian by her side, Kara felt ready to embrace whatever came next. Together, they would navigate the tides of life, painting their story one brushstroke at a time.

C H A P T E R 5 1

A Dance of Dreams
and Desires

The reception was a tapestry of laughter, music, and love woven together by the joy that filled the air. The sun had dipped below the horizon, casting a soft twilight glow over the gathering. Kara and Christian stood together, hands intertwined, their eyes reflecting the warmth of the moment. This was their first dance as a married couple, and Kara felt every beat of her heart resonating with the rhythm of the music.

As they swayed to the gentle melody, Kara couldn't help but smile up at Christian. He looked utterly enchanting under the string lights that twinkled like stars overhead, his dark hair tousled just the way she liked it. She could feel the strength of his arms enveloping her, grounding her in the moment, yet a flutter of unease danced at the edges of her consciousness.

"Can you believe we actually did it?" Christian asked, a playful glint in his eye. He spun her gently, and she laughed, her worries momentarily forgotten.

"Not only did we get married, but we also pulled off the perfect beach wedding!" Kara replied, her voice stirring with excitement. "I'll be dreaming about this day for the rest of my life."

As they continued to twirl on the dance floor, surrounded by family and friends clapping along to the beat, Kara felt an overwhelming sense of gratitude wash over her. Yet, in the midst of the celebration, she spotted him—Michael Hargrove. He stood at the edge of the dance floor, his gaze fixed intently on her, a small, appreciative smile playing on his lips.

Kara's heart skipped a beat. She had managed to push thoughts of him aside during the ceremony, but now, his presence felt like a storm cloud gathering on the horizon. She tried to shake off the unease, focusing instead on Christian's laughter and the joy of their first dance. But Michael's gaze lingered, and as she and Christian spun around, she felt a tug of ambition rise within her, mingling with the love she felt for her husband.

The song ended, and amidst the applause, Kara and Christian stepped apart. Just then, Michael approached with a confident stride in his step. Kara felt a rush of anxiety but steeled herself to greet him.

"Congratulations, Kara! You were breathtaking today," Michael said. "Truly, an unforgettable ceremony. And I'm very much looking forward to seeing your work at the exhibition tomorrow."

"Thank you, Michael," Kara replied, her smile faltering slightly. "It means a lot to me. I'm excited but also a bit nervous."

"Don't be! Your art deserves to be seen. It's been a joy to watch your journey unfold," he said, his gaze unwavering. "You have a unique voice; the world needs to hear it."

Kara's heart raced. His words ignited a familiar thrill within her, one she had felt during her earlier days as an artist when she was driven by passion and the desire to share her creations. But now, standing next to Christian, she felt the weight of her choices. Could she truly balance her love for Christian and her ambition as an artist?

"Thanks, Michael," she managed, forcing a smile as Christian slid his arm around her waist, grounding her once again.

"Hey buddy," Christian said, his playful tone slightly edged with protectiveness. "Kara's an artist now, but she's also my wife, so let's keep the compliments to a minimum, shall we?"

"Of course, Christian," Michael replied, an easy smile on his face. "I just wanted to remind Kara of the beautiful work she creates. It's important to keep pursuing your dreams."

With that, Michael stepped back, leaving Kara in a whirlwind of emotions. Christian turned to her, a thoughtful look on his face. "You okay, babe? You seem a bit distracted."

"I'm fine," Kara replied quickly, but the words felt hollow even to her ears. The excitement of the exhibition, combined with Michael's words, pulled her thoughts in different directions. "Just a lot to take in, I guess."

"Right," Christian said, his tone light but his gaze searching. "Tomorrow's a big day for you. I just don't want you to get lost in everything."

"I won't. I promise," Kara reassured him, her heart squeezing at the thought of him doubting her.

She loved Christian and wanted nothing more than to share her life with him, but the artist inside her was restless, yearning for the world to see her work.

"Let's get some air," Christian suggested, sensing her unease.

He led her away from the crowd, the sounds of the reception fading into the background. They stepped outside onto the sandy terrace, where the cool breeze brushed against their skin, carrying with it the scent of the ocean.

"Okay, now tell me what's really going on," Christian said, turning to face her, his expression serious yet gentle. "I can tell you're not just nervous about the exhibition. It's like there's something else on your mind."

Kara took a deep breath, feeling the weight of his gaze. "I guess I just feel a bit torn," she confessed, her voice barely above a whisper. "I want to be the best wife for you, but I also have this passion for my art that's been a huge part of my life. Seeing Michael today reminded me of that... and I'm afraid I'll lose that part of myself."

Christian furrowed his brow and stepped closer, wrapping his arms around her waist. "You won't lose anything, Kara. You're still you, no matter what. I love you for all of you—the art and the woman who loves the ocean."

"But what if I fail? What if the exhibition doesn't go well?" she asked, vulnerability spilling from her heart. "What if I'm not the wife you deserve because I'm too focused on my dreams?"

Christian's eyes softened. "You're more than capable of achieving your dreams, and I'll be right here cheering you on. But don't ever think you have to choose between your ambitions and our love. They can coexist. We can make it work."

Kara felt a rush of relief wash over her, mixed with profound gratitude for the understanding Christian offered. "You really believe that?"

"Absolutely. I mean, it's a part of who you are. Your art inspires you, and it inspires me too. Just as I have my adventures, you have your creativity. We're a team, remember?" He smiled, the light-hearted energy of his voice reassuring her.

Tears brimmed in Kara's eyes, and she leaned into him, resting her head against his chest. "You're right. Thank you for being so support-ive. I just need to find the balance."

"You will," he assured her, tilting her chin up so she could meet his gaze. "Just promise me that you'll talk to me if you ever feel over-whelmed. I don't want to see you struggling alone."

"I promise," Kara said, a smile breaking through her tears. "And I promise to let my passion shine through, no matter what."

With that, Christian leaned down, capturing her lips with his in a kiss that ignited a fire deep within her. Their connection deepened, a shared understanding binding their hearts together. As they pulled away, Kara felt a renewed sense of purpose.

"Now, let's go back inside and celebrate," Christian suggested, his playful demeanor returning. "We've got a wedding to enjoy!"

As they reentered the reception, Kara felt lighter, the worries of the night fading as she focused on her love for Christian. The music swelled around them, and they danced once more, surrounded by family, friends, and the promise of a beautiful future together.

When the night finally came to a close, they slipped away to their seaside chalet. As they stepped inside, the coolness of the ocean breeze was replaced by the warmth of their intimacy. The moonlight spilled through the windows, casting a soft glow upon them.

Kara felt the passion they shared ignite anew, the weight of the world falling away as they embraced. Their bodies moved together, a dance of love and desire that echoed the union they had celebrated earlier that day. Each touch, each kiss was a promise—a blending of their lives, their dreams, and their hearts.

As they fell into the rhythm of their love, Kara lost herself in the moment, surrendering to the heat and passion that enveloped them. The worries of the exhibition, the thoughts of Michael, all faded into the background as she focused on Christian, the man who held her heart.

The next morning, as sunlight streamed through the open window, Kara woke to the sound of gentle waves crashing against the shore. She turned to see Christian still asleep beside her, a peaceful expression on his face. A sense of warmth enveloped her, and she couldn't help but smile, her heart swelling with love.

But as she lay there, her mind began to wander to the exhibition. Excitement bubbled within her as she thought about sharing her art with the world. Today would be the day she would step into the light, not just as Christian's wife, but as Kara Hastings, the artist.

With a newfound sense of purpose, she leaned over and pressed a soft kiss on Christian's forehead, whispering, "Today is going to be amazing."

She could feel the thrill of ambition reignite within her, blending beautifully with the love she felt for the man beside her.

Today was the day she would show her art, her soul, to the world. And with Christian by her side, she was ready to embrace whatever came next.

CHAPTER 52

Brushstrokes Of Accomplishment

The sun peeked through the curtains, casting a golden hue across the room. Kara stirred awake, feeling the warmth of Christian's presence beside her. The memories of their wedding day flooded back, a beautiful cascade of laughter, joy, and love. Yet, mingling with those thoughts was an undeniable flutter of anxiety. Today was the day of her exhibition, and she could barely contain the mixture of excitement and nerves.

She slipped out of bed, careful not to wake Christian, who lay blissfully asleep. As she padded across the cool wooden floor, she glanced at the clock on the wall. Time was ticking away, and she had so much to do—final preparations to make, pieces to arrange, and, of course, the looming presence of Michael, who would be attending. His words from the night of the wedding replayed in her mind, igniting both her passion and her apprehension.

After a quick shower, Kara stood in front of the mirror, staring at her reflection. She applied light makeup and styled her hair, attempting to project the confident artist she aspired to be. Yet, as she put on her favorite dress—a flowy, vibrant creation that echoed the colors of the ocean—she felt the weight of expectation pressing down on her shoulders. What if she wasn't ready? What if her art didn't connect with anyone? And what if Michael was critical, as he had been in the past?

Just then, she heard a soft knock on the door, followed by Christian's voice. "Hey, sleepyhead! Are you ready for the most amazing day ever?" His lighthearted tone instantly lifted her spirits.

"Almost! Give me a minute!" Kara called out, taking a deep breath to calm her racing heart.

While she finished getting ready, she could hear the sounds of Christian bustling around in the kitchen. His boundless energy was infectious, and she couldn't help but smile as she imagined the little surprises he often concocted. After a few more minutes, she finally stepped out of the room, ready to face whatever the day had in store.

When she entered the kitchen, her breath caught at the sight before her. The kitchen table was set with a lovely picnic spread, complete with fresh fruit, pastries, and steaming cups of coffee. Christian stood by the table, an impish grin on his face that sent warmth coursing through her.

"Surprise!" he exclaimed, gesturing to the picnic. "I thought we could kick off your big day with a little breakfast on the beach. Just the two of us!"

Kara's heart swelled with gratitude. "Christian, this is amazing! You didn't have to do this!"

"Of course I did! You need to fuel up before you unleash your art on the world," he replied playfully. "Plus, I can't let you go into this exhibition without a smile on your face."

They settled on a soft blanket spread out on the sand, the gentle waves lapping at the shore providing a soothing soundtrack. As they dug into the delicious spread, Kara felt the tension beginning to melt away. Christian's laughter was infectious, and for a moment, she allowed herself to forget about the day ahead.

"I can't believe we're actually married," Kara said, her voice light and playful as she took a bite of a buttery croissant. "It feels like a dream."

"Yeah, a dream where you get to be the star of your own art show," Christian replied, winking at her. "And I get to be your biggest fan!"

As they shared stories and laughter, Kara began to open up about her feelings regarding the exhibition. "I'm so excited, but I can't shake this feeling of anxiety. What if no one likes my work? What if I embarrass myself?"

"Kara, listen to me," Christian said, his expression turning serious but still warm. "This is your moment to shine. You've put your heart and soul into your art, and that's what matters. Whether one person or a hundred people connect with it, you should be proud of what you've created. You've always had a unique voice, and today is just the beginning of sharing it with the world."

"I know, but Michael will be there," she admitted, biting her lip. "I can't help but feel like he'll be judging me. His opinion means a lot, and I'm afraid it'll overshadow everything else."

"Forget about Michael for a second," Christian replied, a hint of playfulness returning to his voice. "This day is about you, not him. Think of all the people who will support you—your family, your friends, and me. We're all here to celebrate you and your talent. Embrace it!"

Kara nodded, feeling the warmth of his words seep into her. "You're right. I need to focus on what I love and why I started this journey in the first place."

"Exactly! And remember, you're not just an artist today; you're my wife, too! We're in this together," Christian said, reaching across the blanket to take her hand, intertwining his fingers with hers.

The connection they shared felt electric, and Kara couldn't help but smile at the man who had become her partner in every sense.

"Thank you for believing in me, Christian. I don't know what I'd do without your support."

"Hey, we make a great team," he said, grinning. "Now, let's finish this breakfast and get you ready for the spotlight. I'm counting on you to wow everyone with your art!"

As they packed up their picnic, Kara felt a renewed sense of confidence. Christian's unwavering support and their shared laughter had helped ease her anxieties, and she was ready to face the day.

They drove to the gallery, the ocean breeze ruffling her hair as they shared stories and dreams for the future. Kara felt a surge of excitement as they parked, stepping out into the vibrant world of art and creativity. The gallery loomed before them, its walls waiting to embrace her masterpieces.

"Ready?" Christian asked, his eyes sparkling with encouragement.

"More than ever," Kara replied, straightening her shoulders and taking a deep breath. Together, they walked toward the entrance, and as they stepped inside, she felt the weight of the world lift from her shoulders.

The gallery buzzed with excitement, familiar faces mingling with new ones, all eager to see her work. Kara took a moment to absorb the atmosphere, the vibrant colors and the energy of creativity filling the space. Her heart raced as she spotted her paintings adorning the walls, each piece a reflection of her journey, her passions, and her soul.

As the minutes passed, the room filled with guests, laughter echoing through the gallery. Kara felt a wave of warmth as familiar faces emerged—her parents, Jodi, and even some colleagues from her work. Each person beamed with pride, their support wrapping around her like a comforting embrace.

Then, she spotted him—Michael, standing at the end of the gallery, his expression thoughtful as he examined one of her pieces. A knot tightened in her stomach, but she reminded herself of Christian's words. She was not just there for Michael's approval; she was there to share her art.

Taking a deep breath, Kara steeled herself and moved toward her paintings. As she engaged with guests, sharing the stories behind her work, she felt the anxiety melting away. Each compliment and each smile fueled her passion, and she began to see the beauty in her journey.

Finally, she stood before Michael, who had approached her with a genuine smile. "Kara, your work is incredible," he said, his voice steady and sincere. "You've truly captured something special here."

"Thank you, Michael. That means a lot coming from you," she replied, feeling a mix of pride and relief.

As the evening unfolded, Kara felt an overwhelming sense of fulfillment. The exhibition was not just about showcasing her art; it was a celebration of her journey, her love for Christian, and the support of her family and friends.

As the final guests began to filter out, Kara felt a tap on her shoulder. She turned to see Christian, his eyes sparkling with pride. "You were amazing, Kara! I knew you could do it!"

"Thank you for being there every step of the way. I couldn't have done it without you," she said, beaming.

They embraced, and in that moment, Kara felt a sense of wholeness. She was not just an artist; she was a wife, a friend, and a woman who had embraced her passions. The worries of the past had faded, replaced by the promise of a beautiful future filled with love, laughter, and creativity.

As they left the gallery hand in hand, Kara knew that she was ready to embrace whatever challenges lay ahead. With Christian by her side and her art in her heart, she felt unstoppable as she continued to paint her life's journey from each brushstroke from the heart.